THE
MAN
WITH
MANY
NAMES

THE
MAN
WITH
MANY
NAMES

Richard Oliver Collin

St. Martin's Press • New York

Library of Congress Cataloging-in-Publication Data

Collin, Richard.
  The man with many names / Richard Oliver Collin.
    p. cm.
  ISBN 0-312-11392-7
  1. Intelligence service–United States–Fiction. 2. Americans–Arab countries–Fiction. 3. Orphans–Arab countries–Fiction.
I. Title.
PS3553.O474694M36 1994
813'.54–dc20   94-22227
                                                             CIP

First Edition: February 1995

10 9 8 7 6 5 4 3 2 1

This book is dedicated to my sons,
Oliver Reid Collin
and
Matthew Edward Collin.

Colleagues from the Middle East may discern in these pages shadows of the world we once shared. Oxford friends may even hear echoes from the collision of their lives with mine. But there is no autobiography here. Shadows and echoes are all I sought.

Astute readers will note that in dealing with the late 1970s and early 1980s I have done some violence to history. God knows history has done enough violence to us.

THE
MAN
WITH
MANY
NAMES

Chapter One

MATINS

Like a dying bird, the old Dakota turns atremble on its side and begins to fall out of the sky.

It is a darkish three in the morning, with only the sliver of an Arabian moon. Even at twelve thousand feet a high haze cloaks the stars.

There is a sudden gathering of airspeed. The ailerons seem to scream no, no, no, no. . . .

An American intelligence officer is sprawled in the front row of the Dakota's passenger compartment. Just under six foot in height, bone thin, and forty-one years of age, he works for the Defense Department's Long Range Reconnaissance Group. Even by Cold War standards, the L.R.R.G. is a secretive organization. Pentagon insiders talk about the "Lurg," but hardly anyone knows exactly what it does.

Senior L.R.R.G. officials are called Technical Intelligence Advisers, and this Adviser is sound asleep, suffering from emotional and physical exhaustion. His long legs stretch through the hatchway and into the cockpit, and he is snoring. Slumbering behind him are twenty-one British Army enlisted personnel and a couple of officers.

They are being flown off to a place called Dhofar, a remote, unimportant province of the Sultanate of Oman at the bottom of the Arabian Peninsula. Over the course of the past decade, there has been a communist insurgency in Dhofar. The British have supported the right-wing Omanese government with troops and equipment, while the Russians and Iraqis have backed the insurgents. Outside of Oman, hardly anyone has ever heard of Oman or its bloody little war. The British government prefers it that way.

Like everything else in the Sultanate of Oman, this C-47 Dakota technically belongs to His Highness Sultan Qabus bin Said, but the plane is actually being flown by British contract officers. Until this moment, the voyage has been routine. After an uneventful midnight take-off from Muscat, their British pilot took them smoothly over the Al Hajar Ash Harqi highlands, clearing the RAF air traffic control facility at Al Masirah Island and then turning southwest down the coast.

They are high over Dhofar Province and three minutes away from the British Royal Air Force Base at Salalah. To the west is the People's Democratic Republic of Yemen, a Soviet satellite state. To the North is Saudi Arabia and the great Rub al-Khali, the Empty Quarter. Off to the South lie the Arabian Sea and the Indian Ocean.

The plane is now on its starboard side. It is falling.

"Aihhh, fooking hell! Fooking hell, lads, fooking hell!" Sitting behind the Adviser, a sergeant from Glasgow awakens to cry out against the coming awfulness.

But the American is still profoundly asleep. Drugged by fatigue and the drumming of the Dakota's two big Pratt & Whitney engines, he is dreaming about an English woman named Ellen. Once his Ellen, albeit briefly and spuriously.

As gravity seeps away, his body strains upwards against the seat belt. In the tangle of his subconscious, Ellen is bouncing toward him across a strange foamy trampoline of gauze and soft white. Her body is pale, almost bloodless, and she is naked.

Nothing in my life was ever this beautiful, he dream-thinks as he watches the rhythm of her breasts rising and subsiding. There is no longer weight in their world and with a hotness in his loins, the Adviser strives to soar into her arms.

But a perplexing harness holds him back. In his present psychic environment, there is no longer a precise up or down. In anguish, he begins to suspect that he is dreaming. Yet he can hear her speaking in that hard Liverpool accent she sometimes used to remind everyone how far she had come from where she began.

I'll never have your baby, she says, no trace of love in her voice. *You betrayed us all.*

I didn't mean to, he either says or dreams himself saying. Nobody would hear him in either case because the other passengers are waking up and starting to scream. The soldiers were mostly drunk when they came aboard. Some, like the sergeant from Glasgow, are now spewing gravity-free vomit into the air.

"No! No! No!" There is a flight engineer sitting opposite the Adviser with his back against the gray bulkhead of the flight compartment. He is chanting with horrible fear. His voice has become a girlish wail.

Fighting off a quick rush of terror, the American opens his eyes and begins to analyze available data. L.R.R.G. officers are proud of their ability to function even when pathetically afraid.

Christ, what's . . . what's happening?

The cabin lights are extinguished. It is not clear if this is by accident or design. Inertia is pulling him out of his seat, and it takes him a moment to organize his up-down-sideways perspective since the Dakota is pirouetting on its starboard wing as it plunges earthward. Finally, he locates the flight deck by looking down and to the left, his eyes attracted by a faint glow from the instrument panel.

The squadron leader at the Dakota's controls is a balding older man with wisps of white hair around the fringes of his skull. It is cold in the fuselage but perspiration is flowing down the back of the pilot's neck. He is working hard over his instrument panel, running his fingers over dials and levers and turning many switches.

The copilot is so young he could be the squadron leader's son. He sits quietly on the right, his hands folded in his lap, passive, uninvolved.

The old Dakota is shaking itself to bits. This airplane was designed in the 1930s to fly two hundred miles per hour; the airspeed indicator is now registering three hundred and fifty.

"What's happening?" Fighting his seat belt, the American leans forward to shout at the hysterical flight engineer.

In the RAF, it is considered shameful to show fear in the presence of a non-Englishman, and the flight engineer stops howling.

"A Grail!" he gasps.

Ah! This is depressing news. Unverified reports had suggested that the Dhofar guerrillas might have acquired a supply of Soviet-made SA-7B heat-seeking anti-aircraft missiles.

Code-named "Grail" by NATO intelligence, the SA-7B flies at twice the speed of sound and eight times faster than an elderly propeller-driven aircraft.

A Grail, the Adviser thinks as cold sweat forms on his brow. You spend your life seeking various grails. Then one day, a Grail comes seeking you.

"Are you sure?" National pride is at stake here and the American clenches his teeth and tightens his sphincter. Wetting his pants would be in the worst possible taste although there is a chorus of alarm coming from the soldiers behind him and profound barfing does seem to be the order of the day.

"Dunno. Some kinda heat-seeker!"

We are all seeking heat, the Adviser is thinking when the engines go silent. Dropping like a stone, the Dakota begins to tumble and twist and the American feels his stomach trying to escape through his esophagus. It is hard to breathe.

There is no sound but the violent rush of air. Why? Have the engines failed?

No. Abruptly, he realizes that the pilot must have deliberately killed both motors so the Dakota would present a cooler target for the missile soaring up to meet them.

"Harvey, pop the phos!" the squadron leader suddenly shouts, a hoarse rasp in his voice. It is quieter without the engines. Harvey seems to be the copilot but he gives no sign of hearing. In fact, our lad Harvey is crying silently. His eyes are closed.

Catatonic fugue, the American makes the diagnosis. Our copilot's brain has just bailed out. Is this nature's way of suggesting that we have three minutes to live? How long does it take a C-47 to plunge from twelve thousand feet?

It seems to be taking a long time. A quick air accident could be the perfect quietus, he thinks morbidly. There you are, sipping your gin and tonic and looking at the stewardess's bottom and wondering if the bursar is gay when the tinest of navigational errors takes you smack into a mountain at six hundred knots.

Bango. Instant oblivion would be acceptable. But not this endless falling. A man needs weight!

"Harvey? Harvey, pop the phos!" Clinging to his controls,

the pilot is screaming as the plane spirals downward like water through a plug hole. "For the love of God, Harvey! We're going to die!"

"Come on, Harvey!" the Adviser calls out encouragingly. He grapples with his seat belt, wondering if he himself can crawl to the cockpit in time to find and deploy the decoy canister himself. I can do it! For Harvey, England, and Saint George . . .

Suddenly, the squadron leader lashes out with his right hand, slapping the copilot the way leading men in silly movies smack hysterical actresses.

It is a banal gesture but it works. Moving with leaden slowness, Harvey slides a three-foot aluminum tube out of the Dakota's tiny side window. There is a resonant *phoomff* and the smell of cordite fills the cabin.

The Dakota is spinning now, disorienting them all, but the Adviser squirms to his right, trying to follow the phosphorous decoy as it falls beneath them, searing the air, radiating thermal seduction to the coming Grail. I am the ultimate heat, it whispers across the night sky. Embrace me!

They cannot see the missile as it mounts to the encounter, but there is a sudden universe of light to starboard as the Grail detonates somewhere close. The explosion flips the Dakota onto its back. There is a groaning from the fuselage.

"Are we hit? Are we hit?" the Adviser whimpers in fear. They are falling belly up and he digs his nails into the imitation leather seat that is now above him. A sudden wind lashes through the passenger compartment as freezing air streams in from the outside.

"Oh, god, oh god, oh god, no, no, no, no, oh, fucking hell, oh no!" he screams as they plunge upside down toward the earth. Nothing has ever been this dreadful.

It is suddenly cold. The soldiers are all screaming. It is strange, hearing grown men howling with terminal fear. There is no light now anywhere except in the cockpit where the squadron leader is turning switches and pulling levers, trying frantically to get the Pratt & Whitneys firing again. The airspeed indicator has reached six hundred knots per hour.

The Adviser understands that the situation is hopeless. The

Dakota was built before he was born. Metal fatigue will have taken its toll, the aching weariness of endless, aimless flight. Presently, the wings will come off.

The copilot seems to understand this as well. He is once again sitting perfectly still, staring out into the blackness, outwardly placid, as if he has negotiated some private truce with gravity.

There is chaos in the passenger cabin, moaning and the taking of terrible oaths. A soldier with an Irish accent is praying incoherently. "Oh Father, bless me, Father, take me home, Father, I am heartily sorry for all of my sins, forgive me for all of my . . . Father . . . take me home, Father!"

You've got the words all wrong, the Adviser observes. Although he has not himself bothered to get the words right for decades, not since his days at the seminary. Not being much of a practitioner these days. Bless me, Father, he prays tentatively, trying to see if it can still be made to work. For I have sinned. It was wrong, what I did in Oxford. It seemed the only thing to do at the time. I was trying to do my duty, Father. My rendering unto Caesar.

"Oh, fooking hell, lads!" The Scot behind him seems indisposed to pray. "Oh Christ, oh, goddamn it all to hell, lads, we're goin' to dig a fooking hole in the fooking sand!"

There is a roar as the dogged pilot gets his engines rekindled, but the Adviser can see the lights of RAF Salalah rushing up to greet them. He is sure there is no longer enough altitude to stabilize the tumbling airplane.

For an instant, he achieves a fragile inner calmness. Many years before Ellen, just after he joined the Long Range Reconnaissance Group, he knew a woman psychiatrist who told him that he went on these assignments looking for death. According to her, people who had been raised Catholic were too chickenshit to pop a pill and get it over with.

So, he thinks. Hello, Mr. Death. Been expecting you. The end to the hurting. There will be no pain. I am not afraid.

I am not afraid.

I am terribly afraid, he informs himself soberly. Before the nothingness, there will be that moment of impact when we crash into the earth, and I come apart, my body disintegrating. It will hurt. There will be a fragment of anguish before my ceasing-to-be.

The gravities are piling up and it is difficult to breathe. The flight engineer is screaming again, making a thin keening sound and holding his hands over his eyes. Dying is the ultimate embarrassment. The Technical Intelligence Adviser looks through the cockpit windscreen at the Dhofar shore, wondering irrelevantly whether they will crash on sand or sea.

Mist is gathering over the water. It looks soft and inviting and slightly out of focus, like death in the movies.

The ancients called this the Frankincense Coast, he remembers from a classical Greek text he once read. During the Roman Empire, Dhofar was prosperous because the frankincense tree grows wild here and its sap is made into a spice that Europeans once used for preserving their dead. Dhofar made a fortune out of human mortality until some clever bastard invented formaldehyde.

Oh Ellen, his thoughts tumble in tatters as the earth rushes up to embrace them, Ellen, they are turning off my time. It didn't have to be this way. We could have lived together for many years. Happy in England. Oh, to be in England. And not dead molecules in Oman. Why did you . . .

Why?

Why indeed? The American ponders the question, watching the old squadron leader struggle for dominion over his Dakota. The Pratt & Whitneys do valiant battle with hot desert air but the rage of gravity overcomes him and he slips gratefully into insensibility.

"Ellen!" he whispers. At the very edge of consciousness. "Ellen?"

Chapter Two

LAUDS

"Ellen?"

No one answers, although the world has become quiet. Absurd, he thinks. She's not here. His thoughts come in fragments.

Am I still alive? My head aches. I hurt, therefore I am.

Where am I? Is this Oxford?

No, Oxford is behind me now. This is Oman. I am a long way away. The end of the world. The suburbs of the end of the world.

I don't want to be in Oman. I'll keep my eyes closed for a while. Wait for reality to organize itself. The universe lurks on the other side of my eyelids, but it can stay out there until I feel like dealing with it.

There is motion around him. Other lives are being continued. He hears the metallic *clunk-clunk-clunk* of seat belts being unfastened. The soldiers get to their feet, murmuring, "You okay?" "Yeah!" "Bloody awful, weren't it?" "Think we can get a drink?"

They all seem subdued and ashamed. Nobody was excessively brave.

The foulness of vomit fills the air and the Adviser concentrates on shallow breathing. He is shivering despite the heat, certain that he lacks the strength to stand. His head aches powerfully from the rapid change in air pressure.

"Is he all right?" A British officer is standing over him, speaking in a nasal, bored, upper-class accent.

"He passed out just before we landed," the flight engineer explains. His voice is squeaky from screaming, so he coughs and clears his throat to regain his manly baritone.

"Who the hell is he?"

His eyes closed, the Adviser listens with a flicker of curiosity. On the flight roster, they have listed him as a Canadian agronomist from the University of Manitoba.

It is a pointless precaution, but as a matter of policy, the Long Range Reconnaissance Group never dispatches its officers under their own names. Furthermore, London wants the presence of any American official kept a secret; Her Majesty's Government takes the view that there is no communist insurrection in Oman's Dhofar Province, and hence no need for foreign intelligence experts.

"It's the new TIA," reports the engineer.

You're not supposed to know that, the Adviser thinks resentfully. In its relentless search for original acronyms, the Pentagon has reduced the ten unlovely syllables of "Technical Intelligence Adviser" to a euphonious "TIA." In Spanish, "tia" simply means aunt, except in Madrid, where it is also the slang word for "harlot." Among physicians, TIA is transient ischemic attack or ministroke. In the Pentagon, the TIA stands for something too secret to be shared with half the British Army.

Unimpressed, the officer snorts and moves away down the corridor toward the hatch. "Typical! We win the bloody war and they send us a Yank!"

You haven't won bloody anything yet, the Adviser sighs inwardly, reluctantly opening his eyes. His eyeballs ache and for a frightening moment, his vision is blurred. When he is finally able to focus on the luminous dial of his watch, he sees that it is nearly four in the morning. Back in the seminary, the choir would just now be singing Lauds. Praise for the morning.

But it is still night. The Dakota is motionless and the world is level. The cabin lights are extinguished but a searchlight out on the runway is sending shafts of harsh brightness into their shattered little world.

The flight engineer is still sitting where he was, his back against the flight deck bulkhead. There is a strong odor of urine coming from somewhere close, and the Adviser quickly inspects his own trousers. He is heroically dry. With bleak satisfaction, he observes that the flight engineer has wet himself. Abundantly.

"What happened?" the TIA asks.

The flight engineer stares back angrily, as if this were all his fault. "You were unconscious!"

"That heat-seeker missed us?"

"It beat us up a little, but the phos pulled it off course. The captain managed to get us leveled out at about eight inches."

"What's wrong with the door?"

"Missile fragments, I suppose. I'll see if I can get it open." Walking like an old man, the flight engineer hobbles down the companionway to the hatch, where soldiers are struggling with a badly jammed locking mechanism.

On the flight deck, there is no motion whatsoever. The old squadron leader sits with one arm slung around the shoulders of the copilot, whose flying career has just come to an end. Harvey is sobbing noiselessly, his head against the older man's chest. They look like sad lovers who have just agreed to separate.

There is debris all over the passenger compartment, puddles of vomit and paper cups and torn magazines and scraps of half-chewed sandwiches. The troops are patiently assembling their bags and checking their weapons. In defiance of airport regulations, most of them have already lit up British Army smokes, Woodbines, and Players. For a moment, the Adviser is tempted to bum a cigarette from somebody and get some nicotine into his system. Six months ago in Oxford, Ellen persuaded him to quit, but under the circumstances, abstinence seems pointless.

"There she goes!" someone shouts, and the Dakota's sliding door squeals reluctantly back on its rollers. The cabin fills with hot, moist air as the troops begin jumping onto the wing. They are quiet, intelligent, violent men from the English working classes. They avoid touching one another.

The Adviser battles with his seat belt until it surrenders him, then he staggers to his feet, now feeling too nauseous to contemplate smoking. His legs are numb and rubbery.

Am I getting too old for this? Maybe I should have let them send me back to the Pentagon, he thinks. Right now I could be chasing my secretary around a desk. Slowly.

Where the hell is my briefcase?

He panics briefly. At a cost of several billion dollars a year, the Defense Department produces sophisticated satellite and communications intelligence called TechIntel, which is classified well above the conventional top secret level. A TIA negligent enough to misplace TechIntel risks an extended tour of duty in the federal prison at Fort Leavenworth.

It was under my seat, he remembers, dropping to his hands and knees and crawling down the aisle until he sees the shiny black briefcase with the combination lock lodged three rows back against his duffel bag.

He is starting to feel marginally better, but it is too late now to ask for a cigarette since all the soldiers have disembarked. Suddenly alone, the Adviser goes into the Dakota's tiny bathroom to freshen up.

You're okay, he tells himself. It was just an incident. Have a restorative pee. Never know when the next opportunity will arise.

The bathroom light works. His hands are shaking as he unzips. There is a faint pressure on his bladder but no urine will flow, since a valve somewhere inside of him has clenched. Instead, he washes his face, combs his thinning hair, and brushes his teeth, squeezing paste from a tube of Crest purchased two days earlier at the American Embassy commissary in Muscat. Scrubbing his molars, he studies his image in a faded little mirror over the sink.

I look ninety years old, he thinks, gazing into his bloodshot blue eyes. Around his eyes are the deep wrinkles Ellen used to caress with her gentle fingers.

"In your life, you must have known great suffering," she once said, making him promise someday to tell her everything.

The creases are bolder now because his skin is badly sunburned, the cosmetic consequence of an abrupt reassignment from rainy Oxford to sun-seared Oman. The Adviser's features are regular and unexceptional except for a nose which—by all conventional canons of male beauty—is several centimeters too long.

It is amazing that she loved me, he thinks, turning away from the mirror. Given her exceptional beauty. Everyone in Oxford wanted her. She was my Roxanne. I was her Cyrano.

With a quick mingling of sadness and desire, he remembers how, after they had become lovers, Ellen would sometimes—on a dare—leave off her brassiere when she dressed. She liked her own breasts and often touched them in bed. Then they would go out to a party or a protest meeting and all the while her breasts would quiver subtly beneath her blouse, her nipples erect. The Adviser would watch other men staring at her, furtively, the way Englishmen do, looking and then looking away, afraid to be caught staring. Excited, he and Ellen would leave early to go home and fling themselves into bed. Once, they even stopped under a bridge on the M-40 Motorway to make love in his old Ford Cortina.

Did those Englishmen who looked at her ever wonder who I was? The American with the long nose? Did they guess that she loved me? Or did they assume I was a long-lost cousin from the States?

"Hey, Yank! Your escort is here!" the flight engineer calls from outside the bathroom. The Adviser stuffs the comb and toothbrush back into his duffel bag.

"Coming!" He takes one last minute to organize his apparel. Khaki trousers and shirt are standard attire for civilian officials in a war zone, and he completes the ensemble by attaching a Beretta 32-mm automatic pistol to his belt, pulling his shirt out of his trousers to conceal the worn leather holster.

Like most of his colleagues in the Reconnaissance Group, the Adviser dislikes guns. Carrying a weapon implies willingness to commit the ultimate vulgarity of actually shooting someone. Among professional collectors of pure intelligence, the use of violence is a major lapse in good taste.

L.R.R.G. officers even make a fetish of describing themselves as scientists, invisible men who glide like ghosts through complex operational situations, observing what needs to be observed and then vanishing without altering their environment.

When transporting the Defense Department's precious Tech-Intel, however, even the Group's gunshy intellectuals are required by law to carry a weapon. The Adviser copes by carting around what the admiral always indignantly called a "lady pistol." He has never fired the lady pistol in anger and never engages in target practice. The bang makes his ears ring disagreeably.

Then, just when the night seems to have gone quiet, there is a whistling sound above them, followed by a huge explosion somewhere outside on the runway. The half-wrecked Dakota sways alarmingly.

The bathroom light goes out and the Adviser is unable to find the door handle. Trapped in the pitch dark, he fights off a panic attack.

"Hurry! Hurry!" The flight engineer begins to scream and pound on the toilet door. "Come on!"

"Get out of the way!" Ruthlessly, the Adviser braces himself against the toilet and kicks the bathroom door open with his foot. "What the hell is happening?"

"Somebody's firing at us!" The flight engineer leads him rapidly up the companionway toward the door. A wailing siren makes it hard to hear. The airplane is completely dark. There is glass underfoot from the Dakota's shattered windows. "That was an artillery round from somewhere up on the *jebel!*"

"The *jebel?*" His mind is working like molasses but the Adviser manages to locate the word in his Arabic vocabulary. *Jebel* means massif or mountain. About ten miles inland from the town of Salalah, the Dhofar Mountains ascend precipitously, rising three thousand feet to encounter the desert plateau and the beginning of the Empty Quarter.

"Go!" The flight engineer pushes him from behind. "There could be another in-coming any minute."

Trying to get his bearings, the Adviser stalls in the hatchway of the Dakota. It is still quite dark and very misty but in the distance he can see the menacing outline of the Dhofar Mountain *jebel,* where the Popular Front for the Liberation of Oman held out against the Western world for a decade. Last year, the British declared a victory and Dhofar has been quiet for many months. Until now.

But it's not quite over, the Adviser thinks with bleak satisfaction. I was right. I knew it wasn't finished.

His duffel bag over his shoulder and his briefcase under his arm, he climbs awkwardly onto the wing of the Dakota, feeling slippery metal beneath his feet. The air is hot, well over 90 degrees Fahrenheit. The breeze off the beach whispers a rumor of salt brine and rotting fish.

There is a shout from below. "Sir! Drop us your bag!"

Nervously, the Adviser inches his way down to the back edge of the wing where an aluminum ladder has been placed against the ailerons. He drops his duffel bag into the waiting arms of a tall man in a uniform. Then he makes his way quickly down to the concrete surface of the runway, clinging to the ladder with both hands and using his teeth to hold the handle of the briefcase.

"Hello, I'm Sergeant Major John Woodward. Sorry about all the excitement." When the searchlight splashes past them, the Adviser catches a quick glimpse of his escort. Woodward seems to be an agreeable man in his early fifties, tall, tanned, and extremely fit. His features are strong and craggy with laugh lines around the corners of his eyes. Despite the hour and the emergency, he wears an impeccably starched khaki garrison uniform.

"What's happening?" The Adviser's fragile ego is briefly offended that they have not sent someone more senior to fetch him; then he reminds himself that sergeants major have a way of turning out to be more important than officers. He offers his hand but does not bother to volunteer the name the L.R.R.G. assigned him for Oman; Sergeant Major Woodward does not seem to expect it.

"Let's get off the runway. We've just been hit with an artillery round and there could be another one right behind it," Woodward replies tersely as they run to the Land-Rover where a dark-skinned Omanese soldier sits at the wheel. "This is Sergeant Ali Rashidi."

"Assalam aleikum." Sergeant Rashidi is a short, wiry man whose olive drab uniform is two sizes too large for him. There is an Armalite rifle lying on the seat within his easy reach. "Peace be unto you."

"Hi! Hey, listen, peace be unto you too, Sergeant Rashidi." The Adviser hoists himself up on the roll bar and drops into the backseat with his briefcase on his knees. Woodward climbs in with the duffel bag and the Land-Rover sprints away from the damaged Dakota.

The airfield looks like the world's last day. There are chunks of broken cement and shredded tires everywhere and the smell of cordite haunts the air. Dressed only in their underwear, Omanese troops are running frantically across the darkened tarmac, carrying weapons and looking for someone to shoot. An antique Strikemaster jet breaks the sound barrier a few feet over their heads, shaking them down to the molecules as it blazes off toward the *jebel*. Behind them, a chopper lurches into the air like a startled insect.

"Did you realize our Dakota was shot at?" the Adviser gasps. "They almost brought us down!"

"It was rather too close for comfort," Woodward agrees. "We'll get clear of the runway and then have a bit of a think."

They roar toward the perimeter of RAF Salalah and Sergeant Rashidi steps on the gas as Omanese Army guards wave them frantically through. An elaborate perimeter ring of barbed wire circles the airfield and every hundred feet there are "hedgehogs," ugly giant towers built out of fifty-gallon oil drums filled with sand and stacked on top of one another. On top of each hedgehog is a balustrade of sand-filled canvas bags to protect the airport garrison.

Ali Rashidi pulls the Land-Rover into the protective lee of a hedgehog and stands on the brakes. "What do we do now, Sergeant Major?"

"I don't know." Woodward and the Adviser jump down and peer around the edge of the hedgehog at the airfield, where several fires are now burning. Two more RAF Strikemasters scream down the runway. The ground-support jets lift off successfully but the moment they are airborne, another in-coming pounds into the tarmac and quivers the earth.

"Those are Katyushka 120-mm artillery rounds," Woodward concludes quickly. "The buggers are cratering our runway. Thank God the Strikies got away in time."

"Where can they land?"

"They can't come back here until we've repaired the landing field and secured the area around the airport, so the RAF will divert everything with wings to Al-Masirah Island."

Woodward's voice is a deep baritone, tinged with a warm Yorkshire accent. The Adviser finds himself already liking the man. England is upside down, he thinks. It is the only country in the world where people in the north are nicer than the people in the south.

"For a defeated army, your friends in the Popular Front seem to have munitions to burn," he observes. "The missile they shot at my Dakota was a high-altitude heat-seeker, maybe a Grail."

"It certainly looked like one. Ali Rashidi and I watched it go up and detonate into your phosphorus decoy. From a visual point of view, it was very beautiful."

"Beautiful?"

"Well, you had to see it from down here to get the full aesthetic impact."

The Adviser shakes his head impatiently. "Is this the beginning of a ground attack?"

"The war was supposed to be over." Woodward seems perplexed. "We've already had the victory parade. The Prime Minister came down and gave everybody a medal."

"Maybe the celebration was premature. This is September. Isn't this the traditional month for a Popular Front attack?"

"In the past, yes. The *adoo*—that's what the locals call the Popular Front guerrillas—the *adoo* were always very active during September because they could move about underneath the monsoon mists without being seen from the air. But our intel people say all the significant *adoo* units have retreated over the border into South Yemen. There was a small-unit firefight in August and we thought it would be positively the last engagement of the war."

"Look, I've only been in Oman a few days, but it seems to me that there could be another Popular Front offensive," the Adviser tells him urgently. "Everybody in Muscat told me I was crazy, but late last night some intelligence came over the wire that made me think I should brief your commanding officer."

Woodward frowns. "Then we'd better get you to our headquarters."

Sergeant Ali Rashidi puts the Land-Rover into gear, and they race east down a surfaced road. It is still quite dark, but in the faint reflected light from the sky, the Adviser can see the silhouettes of huts and orchards. Ali Rashidi drives very fast until the pavement ends, then he abruptly reduces speed to a crawl, taking care to avoid the tracks made by previous vehicles.

"What's he worried about?" the Adviser whispers.

"When they were active around Salalah, the *adoo* used to dig up a wheel track and bury a land mine," Woodward explains.

"Then they'd use an abandoned tire to re-create the impression of a wheel mark. We haven't lost a vehicle in a long time, but if the *adoo* are back in business we want to stay out of preexisting ruts in the road."

"Then this road isn't secure?" Having had quite enough adventure for one night, the Adviser watches with dismay as the sergeant major extracts an ancient Sterling submachine gun from a box in the back of the Land-Rover and slips a magazine into place.

"Until just now, we thought Salalah airport was secure. Are you armed, sir?"

Oh, Christ. Suddenly, the Land-Rover feels vulnerable, especially with its canvas top rolled down for better visibility. The Adviser extracts his lady pistol and switches off the safety catch. "Yes, I'm armed," he says.

Woodward studies the tiny weapon with a courteous smile. "That will dismay the enemy, sir," he says thoughtfully. Then they all go silent, scrutinizing the shadows around them as the Land-Rover prowls through the night.

They reach their destination safely at twenty minutes after four. The sky is still deathly dark, but British Army Headquarters in Dhofar is bathed in the harsh, assertive brightness of huge perimeter spotlights. In the distance, the Adviser can hear diesel generators grumbling irritably.

"Home sweet home!" Woodward speaks lightly, but there is a hint of serious relief in his voice. He puts the Sterling back into its box.

"Where are we? Is this your headquarters?"

"We've always called the place by its Arab name, Um al Gwarif." The sergeant major shades his eyes against the bright lights around the checkpoint. "There's no room for us with the RAF at the airfield and there would always be too many eyes watching in Salalah itself. So we've been camped out here at Um al Gwarif for years now. This is my third tour in Dhofar."

"It must be lonely."

"Everywhere is lonely," mutters Woodward. It seems a curious thing to say.

As they approach, the Adviser can see a wall of barbed wire

stretching between a row of wooden observation towers. Behind the concertina, there are machine-gun emplacements, foxholes, and trenches buttressed with sand-filled canvas bags.

"What is your position here?"

"Mine? I'm Brigade Sergeant Major. I work for the Commander of the Dhofar Brigade, Colonel Nigel Fine."

"And the English military personnel in general? To whom do you report?"

"That's one of those awkward questions we never ask out loud." Woodward chuckles. "Whilst serving in Oman, we're considered members of the SAF or Sultan's Armed Forces. But our salaries are paid by the British Exchequer and we're all British Army regulars who have been seconded from our home regiments. Colonel Fine and I both come from the Yorkshire Fusiliers."

"And your Omanese troops?"

Almost imperceptibly, Woodward nods toward Sergeant Ali Rashidi, indicating that courtesy precludes a totally honest answer. "We have regular Sultan's Armed Forces personnel from master sergeant on down, plus a couple of trainee officers. They all speak a little English and we all speak some Arabic, so we muddle through reasonably well. Unfortunately, most of our troops are from the Muscat area and don't know Dhofar very well."

"This is a different country for us, sir!" Ali Rashidi swings around in the driver's seat and favors the Adviser with an expansive grin. "These Dhofar chaps are not speaking good Arabic and they are always forgetting to pray."

At the gate, an English sergeant is on duty, supervising a trio of Oman Army guards who raise a wooden barrier to allow them through. Once past the gate, Sergeant Major Woodward jumps down and goes into the guardhouse for a short telephone conversation. He is frowning when he climbs back into the jeep.

"The situation at the airfield seems to have stabilized just after we left. The Strikies are all safely at Al Masirah and we didn't take any casualties from the shelling."

"Ground force activity? Nothing from the Popular Front?" The Adviser is incredulous.

"As far as we can tell, Dhofar Province is as quiet as the grave.

Captain Fenwich is our intelligence officer, and he's calling it local terrorism for the moment. At any rate, he says there's no danger of a real attack. Take us to the Hilton, Ali."

The Hilton? The Adviser is puzzled. Surely there are officers' quarters available for visiting firemen like him. A moment later, they pass the headquarters building, an ancient two-story fortress built of mud brick and coated with whitewash. There is a huge radio tower and a collection of square white wooden office buildings with painted aluminum roofs. There are brutal electric lights everywhere and teams of Omanese soldiers are patrolling the streets, watching for infiltrators.

Instead of stopping, however, Ali Rashidi roars past the old headquarters fort and around the periphery of the encampment to the south, rolling by row after row of camouflaged two-man tents.

They halt near a helicopter landing pad with a huge red cross painted directly onto hard-packed mud. There is a garage on the other side of the road with barrels of oil and pulleys and lifts and bits of dismembered trucks and jeeps on the ground. The building has a peaked wood roof bearing the words "Vehicle Maintenance Shed" in large black letters. Behind it is a field of shattered cars and trailers and the remnants of what was once a light tank.

Next door is a ramshackle wooden building, its unvarnished boards seared white by the sun and the letters "WC" painted on the door. Mounted on the outside wall is a row of open showers.

"Where are we?"

Woodward points to the nearest tent as he swings his long legs out of the Land-Rover. "We call that the Um al Gwarif Hilton! Sorry we have nothing more elegant but since we're listing you as an agronomist from the University of Manitoba, we thought this was nicely discreet."

"It's discreet as hell. When am I going to see Colonel Fine?"

"When I talked to him on the phone, Captain Fenwich decided that the situation didn't warrant waking the colonel in the middle of the night." Woodward is clearly uncomfortable with the decision. "It's still the wrong side of five and he's put you on the colonel's schedule for seven, right after chapel."

"This is an emergency! I can't go into details but you could get some enemy activity today!"

Woodward is sympathetic, but orders are orders. "I'll go back to our headquarters and look at the situation board but Captain Fenwich's the duty officer tonight and this is his call."

"It's your war!" The Adviser retorts irritably. He climbs down from the Land-Rover's uncomfortable backseat, realizing that insistence is pointless. If the British Army wishes to snooze on a Sunday morning while Marxist insurgents bombard their airport, this is their Britannic prerogative. In his predecessor's reports, there had been complaints about the English unwillingness to take Defense Department TechIntel very seriously.

So they probably aren't going to believe me anyway, he thinks. Screw it!

He feels stiff and dirty, and the idea of a little sleep appeals to him enormously. Since Ellen, he thinks, things have begun to matter less to me. Am I getting old? I used to care so desperately about everything.

"Get your head down for a bit and I'll be back in a while with some coffee," Woodward proposes. "After you've had your chat with the colonel, we'll give you a proper British Army breakfast."

"Wait a minute. Tell me about the weather here. Isn't it normally cooler this time of year?"

John Woodward nods. "Dhofar has a backwards climate. It's warm in the winter because of the latitude, but cools off in the summer because the monsoons bring in a cloud cover that blocks the sun. The monsoon hasn't cleared yet, so we've still got the cloud cover, but it's unseasonably hot."

"Do one favor for me. You maintain a small observation post right on the top of the *jebel,* don't you? Get them on the radio and find out what the ambient temperature of the soil is up on the mountain. I'll need to know before I see Colonel Fine."

"The soil temperature?" The sergeant major looks perplexed as he climbs into the Land-Rover. "I'm going to feel terribly foolish if you do actually turn out to be an agronomist from Manitoba."

Woodward is not cleared for TechIntel, so it is impossible to explain why the temperature of the soil is an authentically crucial piece of intelligence information. The Adviser merely smiles and waves as the Land-Rover departs.

Once alone, he feels abruptly sad. The sky is lighter, and he wishes it were already dawn. Things always seem better when the sun comes up.

Um al Gwarif looks like every other military encampment in the world. There is no one around, although an electric light burns in the bathroom across the street. In one of the tents nearby, a radio is murmuring an anonymous rock-and-roll song on the shortwaves. Sitting in front of the maintenance shed is an ancient 1000 cc Morris Minor Traveller, a miniature station wagon. Painted the standard British Army olive drab, the Morris is in mint condition with gleaming black tires and smooth, lacquered wood paneling.

The Adviser is too fatigued to spend much time pondering the presence of this collector's item in an army base on the south coast of the Arabian Peninsula. Get some rest, he orders himself, turning away from the Morris with exhaustion sweeping over him. You've only had three or four hours sleep a night for ten days now. Ever since the business with the helicopter.

He stumbles into his darkened domain, groping in the shadows until he discovers a wooden folding table and a battery-operated lamp. The tent is eight feet long by six across. For his comfort and convenience, someone has left a jug of water, a wash bowl, and two canvas-backed chairs. There is a cot with frayed sheets, a lumpy pillow, and two brown wool blankets. A moist, moldy smell comes from the canvas and there is sand on the plastic floor mat. Beneath the table lies a well-thumbed girlie magazine, thoughtfully left behind by some previous tenant.

The Um al Gwarif Hilton, he thinks. Glad the British didn't bankrupt the Exchequer on a place for me to stay. Even the rotten old Pakistani Army always found me a room in a real building, and the Sudanese gave me a servant. The Adviser takes off his shoes and loosens his belt, stretching out on the mattress and closing his eyes.

Was it a mistake, he wonders, to have taken this assignment? Yes. Of course it was a mistake, but was there ever really any choice? No, but . . . no, don't rummage through it all again, he pleads with his tired brain. You keep replaying that scene in your mind like a late-night TV commercial. Forget it! Let it go. Sleep.

But his memory no longer responds to orders, and the parting encounter with the admiral unwinds in his consciousness like a home movie. In your mind, he thinks, the colors are always a little off, but the dialogue is inexorably the same. There is the Atlantic Regional Headquarters of the Long Range Reconnaissance Group on the second floor of the London Embassy Annex. The windows overlook Grosvenor Square.

How long has it been since then? Ten days since the riot at Greenham Common? Nine since he left Oxford. Seven days since the conference with the admiral.

A week. It was just a week ago when the admiral sat him down on a plush leather couch and went through the ritual of brewing coffee.

"You took an awful chance," the old man said bluntly. "And you broke some major rules. Fortunately, the situation repaired itself and I kept the woman thing out of your file, so the operation is still officially a success. But don't let a sexual element arise again, understand?"

"I'm sorry about the way it ended."

"An operation like that is always a cruise in uncharted waters. You sailed in, did more or less what you were supposed to do, and limped back out with your cargo, even though you were holed below the waterline. That's what we pay you for. And you prevented a serious incident at Greenham Common, so relax. Back in the Pentagon, you're the flavor of the month!"

"I don't deserve to be."

There was a moment of silence. From the couch, the Adviser saw the admiral looking at an eight-by-ten glossy photograph of Ellen Huntington. Then he closed that manila folder and opened another one.

"Well, let's get you reassigned," he said. "They could use you back in Belfast, y'know, but I want you out of the United Kingdom for a while. You're not really burned here, but this emotional business left you a little . . . well, singed. Do you want a job in Washington?"

This emotional business. Singed, but not burned. The Commanding Officer of the Atlantic Region of the Long Range Reconnaissance Group controlled assignments from Iceland to the Himalayas, and there were a lot of unpleasant places to send a man who had merely blotted his copybook. But a posting back to the United States was an end-of-career assignment.

"Anything's better than D.C.," the Adviser said quickly, knowing that the admiral would already have made up his mind.

"Back to the Middle East then," the admiral decreed, as if the idea were just then occurring to him. "You've got the Arabic and there's a ticklish situation out in the Sultanate of Oman. We need someone to run TechIntel out to the Brits in Dhofar Province. One of the younger guys could handle the basic TIA function easily enough, but you, y'know, maybe you could bring us a little nuance on the situation. Every time the damn Brits tell us they've won the war, the Popular Front launches one more offensive. Are your legs still up to it?"

Yes, his legs were still up to it. There was no discussion of options or alternatives. They talked about operational details for a while, and the admiral walked him to the door, a comforting hand on his shoulder.

"I realize this Oxford thing had some personal sadness for you," the old man muttered as they shook hands good-bye. "Hey, don't beat yourself up too much! Even spooks fall in love. And deserts are a good place to heal."

So here I am, thinks the Adviser. Back in the lousy Middle East. Lying on my back in a tent in Dhofar. Am I healing or being punished? Trying for redemption? Or trying to get myself killed?

Just do the job, he rebukes himself. We redeem ourselves by doing well what we do best, and there is a job here that badly needs doing. The British are good people and I like them. They are about to be surprised with an attack that I have the means to foresee and they do not. It is my function here to alert them. If they accept my warning and ward off the enemy, they will be grateful. The Long Range Reconnaissance Group will reward me for my skill and forget what happened in Oxford. It is a question of reading maps, and I have always been good with maps. People are complicated, but cartography is simple.

Above him, there is a spider crawling upside down along the peaked roof of the tent, and the Adviser wonders how they manage it, the walking upside down business. If the Reconnaissance Group ever adopts a mascot, he decides, it should be a spider. Nobody knows how we manage it either.

Sleep is coming over him as he flips through the girlie magazine. The Adviser is not immune to the attractions of tasteful middle-class pornography, but this is English working-class smut, a tiresome succession of ugly, naked girls with bad skin. They all seem to hate the photographer. Mostly, they are sticking their fingers into their bodies, staring at the camera with undisguised hostility.

It makes him sad, and he throws the magazine under the cot. Were there girls who really did those things in bed? The nuns always said the body was a temple for the Virgin Mary.

Of course, there were moments when Ellen could be surprisingly coarse, particularly if they drank gin first. After all, she had grown up in a Liverpool dockyard slum and the words were inside her waiting to come out. Sometimes when they were together in the bedroom of their north Oxford flat, she would flow toward her orgasm with a sputter of obscenities, groaning, "Oh fuck me, fuck me, fuck me!" getting louder and louder until she climaxed with a frank scream.

"You make me so crazy," she would confess in the morning, awakening for a day of teaching sixth-form English literature in a school for young ladies. Encountering their neighbors on the stairwell, they would get hostile stares from the old man and woman who lived in the adjoining flat. The English of a certain generation could pretend not to have heard almost anything, but their communal walls were paper thin. Ellen would cringe in humiliation, but the Adviser would feel a certain embarrassed pride.

Last night, this beautiful woman came to my bed, he sometimes wanted to say. You must have heard how I made her cry out. Over and over again, she said that she loved me, calling my name.

One of my names.

Now all that is over, he thinks as sleepiness preys upon him. With yet another name I am in Oman doing penance, lying in a tent and watching a spider walk upside down. Bless me, Father. For I have sinned. Today, I dropped out of the sky to save an

English colonel who will not give me an appointment until later.

I go on living. I am not sure why. There needs to be more meaning than this.

Wishing it well, the Adviser watches the spider move with great precision toward some unimaginable destiny on the far side of the canvas. Then he falls asleep and the spider ventures on alone.

Chapter Three

PRIME

"Napalm."

His eyes remain resolutely closed but sound tugs the Adviser toward consciousness. Speaking in a blandly conversational voice, someone has just uttered the word *napalm*. With a pommey British accent and a lingering on the second syllable. Naypawwwmmm.

Or was it a fragment from some forgotten dream? The American tries to go back to sleep. For the past week, he has been finding reality and dreaming difficult to distinguish. Napalm? Who's talking about napalm?

Of course, in real life and real wars, the stuff could give you nightmares: the barrels tumbling down from the sky, the dark, acrid smell, the yellow flames flaring out when it exploded—enough of it could drive a man mad.

"Napalm?" This time, the word is nuanced with a knowing chuckle, the tone of a sophisticated Englishman offering a particularly good champagne to a woman of discernment.

Disoriented, searching for clues, unsure whether he has slept at all, the Adviser half-opens one eye to see a gray, uncertain light outside the Um al Gwarif Hilton. Has time really passed? Yes, it must have. There is now an urgent pressure on his bladder.

His wristwatch confirms that he has slept for an hour. It is six-twenty in Oman, Greenwich mean time plus four hours. In Saudi Arabia to the north and Yemen to the west, it is still only five-twenty, but across the Persian Gulf in Iran, the clocks are all set thirty minutes faster. It isn't just politics, he thinks. Out here even the time zones are crazy.

The Adviser's body is leaden because his personal biological clock is still synchronized with Greenwich and the prime meridian. In England, it is still the middle of the night. Two weeks ago at this hour he was sleeping, lying on his right side with Ellen tucked into him like a spoon, her back against his chest and her bottom against his thighs. And really sleeping! Two healthy people in love can, with some experimentation, normally achieve satisfactory sex, but afterward, actually getting unconscious together . . . ah, there's the rub. It's finding ways to organize arms and legs and pillows and feel safe and doze off happily while still touching, a hand against a thigh, a cheek against a breast. It was amazing how quickly they mastered even that side of it, as if they had been calibrated for one another at the factory.

Today is Sunday, he remembers. In Oxford, the church bells went wild on Sunday. We always tried to sleep late on Sunday, and every Sunday the damn bells woke us up.

The Technical Intelligence Adviser rubs his eyes, realizing that sleep is now impossible. The Um al Gwarif Hilton has become a sauna, and he needs to pee. He gets to a sitting position like a man who suspects he might have a hangover, moving each limb with great deliberation. Everything seems to work, although there is an obscure pain in his right thigh and a general stiffness in his back and shoulders.

He burrows in his duffel bag for soap and shaving things before staggering outside. The sky is still overcast but it is already hot despite the cloud cover. The humidity is brutal. He pauses, thinking about Big Bird and trying to gauge the temperature. When human beings are the target, 98.6 degrees Fahrenheit is the point at which thermal infrared imagery blurs. For the garrison at Um al Gwarif, this will be the moment of maximum danger and it must be close to that now.

Like a regularly scheduled guardian angel, Big Bird will soar over them again the day after tomorrow, and every three and one half days until eternity. The Adviser gazes skyward, realizing that Big Bird will see nothing unless the weather changes. And three and a half days after that will certainly be too late. If it is going to happen at all, it will have happened by then.

Only three miles away, on the horizon to the south, is the Arabian Sea, a shimmer of amazingly blue water. Looking north, he can just detect the outline of the Dhofar Mountain massif, the *jebel,* jutting up three thousand feet into the mist. It looks menacing and bleak and incredibly rough.

Thank god I don't have to go up there, he thinks. Down here on the coastal plain, it could be pleasant . . . if it weren't so hot.

Thanks to the monsoon rains, Dhofar is greener than he expected. Just beyond the barbed-wire perimeter there is a field of what might be alfalfa, ready for harvesting; off in the distance, he can see an orchard where oranges are nearly ripe.

Inside the barbed-wire fence, however, their soldier's world is drab. The tents are all olive green, old and patched with thick gray duct tape. There are piles of sand everywhere. Where the soil is visible, it is a dark reddish clay that feels moist and slippery. This part of Um al Gwarif seems reserved for British troops. Across the road, men in unpressed brown army fatigues are trudging into the latrine and then coming out again buttoning their flies.

The English do everything the hard way, thinks the Adviser. Even the Marxist-Leninist *adoo* must have Russian-made zippers on their trousers by now.

Beneath one of the latrines' outside showers, a naked man is methodically washing under his arms. His body is a stark, unhealthy white, except for his face and forearms and legs below the knees, where the sun has bronzed his flesh.

With his towel around his neck, the Adviser trudges across the dirt road and into the latrine, where the smells of urine and disinfectant combine to produce an odor so savage that it stings the inside of his nose. There is a row of open toilets along one wall and English tabloid newspapers—the *Sun* and *The News of the World*—strewn about on the cracked linoleum floor. The Adviser is glad to find that the latrine is momentarily empty; it is embarrassing to look at other people defecating and impossible to concentrate on shaving while soldiers fill the room with farts.

On another wall, there is a huge galvanized steel trough that serves as a urinal. The Adviser contributes to the yellow stream at the bottom and then does a quick morning shave and body wash before escaping back into the open air.

The soldiers have all disappeared now except for one man kneeling, as if in prayer, in front of the Morris Minor Traveller. He is a hugely muscled Caucasian in his forties with white, wild, disorderly hair that does not seem to have been brushed in years. His beard is also white and sticks out from his chin at an awkward angle. The man is stripped to the waist, and his British Army fatigue trousers are held up by what seems to be a regimental tie. His unpolished combat boots are unlaced and worn without socks.

"Hey, nice looking car!" The Adviser is hungry for human contact. No one should be this lonely the first thing in the morning, he thinks. "How big's the engine?"

With a clean white rag in one hand and a can of Brasso in the other, the wild man is carefully polishing one of the Morris's chrome headlight rims. He looks up with a cordial smile and the face of an intelligent, sensitive man. He winks, as if there were an enormously subtle joke in play here that only the two of them were clever enough to appreciate. "Napalm," he says in a resonate, self-confident baritone.

"I beg your pardon?"

"Napalm." Pointing to a tiny patch of tarnish on the chrome, he applies a drop of Brasso to the cotton and begins rubbing.

"What's your name?"

"Napalm."

"Well, napalm to you too, kid." The world is demented, he thinks. It's not just me. There is a fundamental irrationality behind the cosmos. The Adviser smiles politely and retreats into the Um al Gwarif Hilton.

Where it is hotter than ever. While trying to change his trousers, he skins one elbow against a post and then discovers a great livid bruise on his right thigh, apparently acquired while he was unconscious during that wild landing at RAF Salalah. He dons fresh socks, but there is sand everywhere, and half the desert infiltrates each sock before he gets it on.

With despair threatening, he flops back on the cot and closes his eyes. God, this is an uncomfortable life, he thinks. The meaninglessness of it all would be easier to endure if it could only be a comfortable meaninglessness. Ulster and Morocco and Sudan and Iran and the Baltic Sea and the Hindu Kush . . . why can't the Defense Department have a crisis somewhere with air-conditioning?

The only comfortable assignment I ever had was Oxford, he

thinks, his mind racing back to the big, three-story Victorian town house on Walton Street where Peter and Ellen lived when he first invaded their lives.

Don't think about Ellen, he orders himself. Think, if you must, about the house. Remember that wonderful sprawling chamber on the ground floor with books and phonograph records and newspapers and bottles of wine. Or my room on the second floor with a view of the Radcliffe Infirmary. And from Peter's study and the master bedroom on the top floor, you could see those famous dreaming spires.

It was the only place I've ever been where I didn't feel out of place, where people actually seemed to like me. Unconditionally. They swallowed the fable about my life as a draft dodger from the Vietnam War. Peter introduced me to all his neo-Marxist friends and invited me to join the Oxford chapter of the Committee for Nuclear Disarmament, his precious CND.

Ellen called me their "pet American" and presented me to all her sisters in the Women's Peace Movement. Like a trophy. Whenever I talked about moving away from Walton Street, they always pressed me to stay. They were at that point in their relationship when they needed a kind of interface. Peter liked having a disciple around to take messages and fix leaky faucets and entertain Ellen when he was in London having his bit on the side. I was their buffer.

And at first Ellen just needed someone to talk to. She was lonely, despite everything. Funny how alone a beautiful woman can be! Everyone saw her as Professor Reston's piece of fluff, the pretty schoolteacher who lived with the great radical scholar and peace activist. Everyone wanted to sleep with her. Nobody ever quite focused on her. Except me. I can see that now.

Perhaps this is why she fell in love with me. Because I was someone she could talk to. Funny how it worked out. Normally, if you become really good friends with a woman, you never do go to bed with her. It seems, after a certain point, like incest.

And Sundays were such peaceful, wonderful days. There is an art to Sundays. Crazy Peter, ordering three newspapers, the *Times* and the *Observer* and even the *Telegraph,* so there would always be enough color supplements and editorial pages to go around.

Lurching around the kitchen in pajamas and that huge, flapping bathrobe, reading articles out loud and explaining why the capitalist press was always wrong. And Ellen cooking us breakfast. Making grits for me because she thought all Americans liked grits.

I hate grits, but for her I said I liked them. If only the lying could have stopped there.

And on Sunday mornings, in the kitchen, standing by the stove, cooking kippers and grits, she always wore that faded pink housecoat over her night dress. When she passed between me and the window, I could see the silhouette of her breasts through the white cotton and sometimes even the dark between her thighs.

Ellen seemed unconscious of this. Was she?

Later, when I could have, I never asked. Not wishing to provoke an exchange of secrets. But I wanted her even then, even in those first few weeks. I thought it would always be impossible, partly because it would create an insane operational situation, but mostly because she seemed so in love with Peter.

Sunday afternoons were wonderful too. Before dinner, Peter would go upstairs to work in his study, ruthlessly deconstructing some defenseless Arabic text while listening to *Parsifal* on BBC Radio Three and simultaneously watching Liverpool United play soccer on television. Wagnerian opera was his idea of light musical entertainment. It always drove me downstairs to the kitchen.

With Ellen. I would spread my book and dictionary out on the kitchen table and decipher my assignment from the *Quran*. While she made us cups of cappuccino and manufactured our Sunday dinner.

"You don't seem to have a companion," she once commented. Out of the blue.

"There is no one particularly important to me at the moment," I told her cautiously. Except for you, I thought. And I can't have you.

"But . . . you like women, don't you?"

"You're asking me if I'm a homosexual?" I laughed, thinking how much intelligence officers and closet homosexuals have in common. Rites and forbidden rituals. Secret signs and safe houses. We are the International Brotherhood of Anonymous Fuckers.

"No, I can tell you're not gay."

"How can you tell?"

"Because you often look at my breasts," she blushed and turned away. "But there are straight men who only like women in bed. And even then not very much."

Was she talking about Peter?

"I'm sorry about staring at your breasts. I didn't realize . . ."

"It's alright." She turned back to me, her arms crossed over her chest. "How about you? Will you ever settle down and marry someone?"

"I love women," I confessed, experiencing a frightening urge to say something true about myself. "I'm just not very competent with them."

"Have you had a lot of women?"

"No. A couple of women have had me."

"That isn't the same thing," she said. "Not the same thing at all."

A few minutes before seven, they come for him in the same battered Land-Rover. Ali Rashidi is still at the wheel, looking sleepy and disheveled, but John Woodward has shaved and changed into fresh, inflexibly starched olive drab fatigues. His short brown hair is just beginning to gray, and he wears it swept rigorously back off his forehead.

"It's gone quiet. There has been no more *adoo* activity since we last talked." Woodward swings his long legs out of the Land-Rover and proffers a one-pint plastic thermos. "Colonel Fine feels that the incident was a die-hard effort to persuade Popular Front supporters in Salalah that the war isn't really over. Here, we brought you some coffee."

"Thanks." Grateful, the Adviser pours himself a cup of dark, sweet coffee and feels the caffeine frolic through his veins. "Any news on the soil temperature?"

"It's funny weather! Up on the *jebel,* the ground temperature was ninety-four at sunrise. Is that good?"

"That's bad," says the Adviser. "We need to see Colonel Fine right now."

"Chapel should be finished in a minute. Since our chaplain became indisposed, the Colonel does the service himself and he does it very quickly. Nigel's heavenly father is a businesslike diety who likes brisk adoration."

The Adviser pours himself another cupful of coffee. "Somehow it doesn't feel much like Sunday."

"I know. We usually take some time off on Friday when the Moslems have their day of worship," Woodward explains. "So our work week actually starts on Saturday, which has the psychological impact of a Monday. In emotional terms, Sunday is actually a Tuesday and I always feel vaguely depressed on Tuesdays."

"Me too." the Adviser is agreeing when they are interrupted by the muscular bare-chested man who has been polishing the Morris Minor.

"Napalm?" With his right hand, he mimes the insertion of a key into an automobile ignition.

With a sympathetic smile, Woodward shakes his head. "Not now, Napalm. If I have time later, we'll go for a ride."

"Napalm . . ." The wild man sighs with disappointment and wanders back toward his Morris.

"What did he want?" Draining his coffee, the adviser climbs into the back seat of the Land-Rover.

"Ah . . . Napalm sometimes wanders off in that Morris of his and forgets to come home. I've had to confiscate his car keys. For his own protection."

"Where did that car come from?"

"The Traveller? The British Army used them as staff cars back in the sixties. Wonderful vehicle with a brilliant little four cylinder engine that would take you anywhere. That one was junked years ago. After his breakdown, Napalm restored it to mint condition. We thought it might be therapy for him, but . . . well, nothing seems to work."

Ali Rashidi is taking them slowly across the encampment now. There is a mess hall to the right and a soccer field to the left where a unit of Sultan's Armed Forces troops are standing in formation and being inspected by a British officer.

"And he can drive?"

"That's the oddity of it all," Woodward remarks. "He does

most things brilliantly, including driving, and he knows Dhofar like the back of his hand. It's just that he does everything precisely on his own terms and says 'napalm' all the time. It's a little upsetting."

"He's clearly suffering from a major mental illness. Shouldn't he be hospitalized until he gets better?"

"He isn't going to get better." Woodward seems a little defensive. "We've had him looked at and the quacks all say it's hopeless. The problem is that at home he has a wife, two elderly parents, and five children to support. The military authorities in London would bang him into an asylum and give his family a tiny disability allowance on which they could never survive. There would be questions asked in awkward places. Out here with us he seems happy. He finds ways to make himself useful, and his family gets his full salary. It has all been arranged."

"I should think your officers would take better care of an enlisted man suffering from battle-induced trauma . . ."

Sergeant Major Woodward begins to look uncomfortable. "Well, this is family business," he says, firmly terminating the discussion. "As it happens, Napalm is an officer. Although rank distinctions no longer interest him very much."

Ali Rashidi turns in the driver's seat as they park in front of the Headquarters Building. "Napalm is touched by God," he declares fervently. "God loves Mr. Napalm very much."

The adobe walls of the old fort are thick, and it is significantly cooler inside, although the air smells faintly of mildew and sweat. The floor beneath their feet is ancient buff brick, uneven and dusty, and the inside walls are modern plywood painted white.

With a nod to the duty NCO, Sergeant Major John Woodward escorts the Adviser past the reception desk, and they plunge down a short corridor into a huge open office in the very center of the building. In the Um al Gwarif operations center there are a dozen officers and NCOs working at desks. An Arab corporal distributes tea from a trolley. One alcove houses a communications center with telephones and VHF gear.

As they pass the wireless operator, the Adviser hears the characteristic crackle of a shortwave radio and the calm, confident voice of a woman speaking from Bush House in London.

"This is the BBC," she says. "At the sound of the tone, it will be three hours, Greenwich mean time."

Then come the comforting chimes of Big Ben. The announcer begins reading the news. There have been more anti-American demonstrations at Greenham Common organized by the Committee For Nuclear Disarmament. As vice-chairman of CND, Professor Peter Reston has announced that the campaign against atomic weapons will be extended to U.S. nuclear strike forces at Upper Heyford, Lakenheath, and Mildenhall. The British Ministry of Defence pronounces itself concerned. The Committee for Nuclear Disarmament proclaims its determination to rid Britain of weapons of mass destruction.

The announcer moves on to other news but the Adviser knows from experience that the Sultanate of Oman will never be mentioned by the British Broadcasting Corporation. Nor by anybody else.

This is the best kept secret in the world, he marvels privately. There isn't a single journalist in the entire country. Nobody gets in without the personal approval of the Sultan. For a decade and a half, the United Kingdom has fought a major war here with armies and casualties and heavy weapons and battles.

And the British government has simply decided that no one will ever know about it. The English adore secrecy. None of this would be possible with Americans in charge. The first time we won a battle, the Pentagon would call a press conference. The President would come over and tell us to win their hearts and minds.

"This is our headquarters." Woodward delivers the geography lesson. "Down that corridor we have a field surgical team run by Dick Barnet, who's a bloody good doctor even if his uncle is a duke. At the rear of the building is Captain Fenwich's intelligence and prisoner interrogation facility. Up that way is the mess, where you'll have a real British Army breakfast with all the trimmings after your chat with the Colonel. Here's his office."

The words "Commander, Dhofar Brigade" have been printed with magic marker on a piece of yellow paper and taped to the door. It all looks vaguely provisional. The sergeant major administers a perfunctory knock and pushes open the door.

"Our visitor from the American Embassy, sir," he announces and then withdraws.

Colonel Nigel Fine is a balding man in his sixties with a white mustache and violently assertive freckles. His fatigues are disgracefully unpressed and his half-frame spectacles give him an owlish, scholarly air.

Reading a dispatch, the colonel nods but neither rises nor offers to shake hands as his guest enters. Regular infantry soldiers seldom have much use for intelligence officers. The Adviser knows that he suffers from the twin social stigmas of being a spy and a non-Englishman.

On the other hand, most British officers are more courteous than this; Colonel Fine seems intent upon setting some new Empire and Commonwealth record for Rudeness to a Contemptible Foreign Spook.

"What have you got for me?" Without raising his head, Fine gazes coldly over the top of his glasses. His enunciation of vowels suggests an education at one of those posh secondary schools that the British call "public" and everybody else calls "private."

Irritated, the Adviser places his briefcase on a conference table and takes out his maps and documents before reciting the sacred formula. "This is American Defense Department TechIntel material. If you wish to integrate it into your operational plans, then you must accept my help in disguising its source. You are cleared for limited operational access to TechIntel, but no one else in Dhofar is, so you may not discuss our sources and methods with your subordinates."

Nigel Fine glares at him, irritated at the implication that his subordinates might be untrustworthy. Americans are only granted TechIntel clearances after a thorough background investigation and a polygraph examination. The British will clear anyone who went to Eton or Harrow or Winchester.

"This is my corner of the desert!" he snaps. "And your predecessor never brought me anything sufficiently remarkable to bother my subordinates with. What do you have?"

"First, I have some Communications Intelligence product from the past two weeks." The Adviser produces a thick folder with the words "TOP SECRET COMINT CHANNELS ONLY" printed in emphatic red letters across the top and bottom. COMINT is a foreign radio transmission that has been intercepted, deciphered, and translated, and there are many such reports here. Colonel Fine gazes at the thick packet of papers without visible enthusiasm.

Is there something in all that wad that should interest me?"

"Well, yes. There's a lot here relating to Dhofar."

"How exactly did you acquire it? Do your people have a presence here that I don't know about?"

There is an awkward pause. COMINT is collected for the Department of Defense by the National Security Agency. To fish the oceans of the world for radio waves, NSA has a fleet of Advanced Range Instrumentation Ships, the so-called ARIS class. In fact, there is a 600-foot ARIS vessel floating in the Arabian Sea, a hundred miles off the coast of Dhofar, and its technicians are listening around the clock for—among other things—radio transmissions from the Popular Front for the Liberation of Oman.

Unfortunately Colonel Fine is cleared for none of this. "You would have to address that question to your own U.K. COMINT authority at GCHQ Cheltenham," the Adviser replies with a certain malicious pleasure.

"The buggers wouldn't tell me the time of day," snaps the colonel. "Right, perhaps you could summarize your findings?"

"Certainly. Most of the smaller Popular Front units have gone silent over the course of the past month. The material in front of you is all from the headquarters of the Nine June Regiment. I'm not sure what the name means."

"It celebrates the anniversary of Nine June in nineteen sixty-five when the *adoo* first launched their rebellion. And the Nine June Regiment is the main Popular Front strike unit. We beat them up pretty badly in May, and after a skirmish in mid-August, they retreated over the border into a town called Hauf in Yemen. Where do your boffins think they are?"

"Their transmitter is still generating signals from Hauf over in the People's Democratic Republic of Yemen, but . . ."

"Good! Well, that's that, then," Colonel Fine begins to study other documents on his desk. "As long as they stay on their side of the border and we stay on ours . . ."

The Adviser is exasperated. A great deal of effort has gone

into the collection of this material, but no one has actually thought about it very much. The original signals were intercepted by the ARIS crew, who triangulated the *adoo* emitter with the help of an antenna array on the island of Diego Garcia in the Indian Ocean. Once the broadcast source was identified, the Popular Front emissions were double-enciphered for dispatch to the National Security Agency headquarters at Fort George Meade in Maryland, where the primitive Popular Front encoding system was broken by computer.

Translated into English, the resulting document was then sent over to the Defense Intelligence Agency in the Pentagon, where somebody looked at it just long enough to realize that it needed to be retransmitted to Oman. Milliseconds later, the text was zapped around the world via the SPINTCOM network to the American Embassy in Muscat, where a communications-center clerk surrendered it to the Adviser to take to Colonel Fine.

Who isn't actually going to look at it.

"I think we need to think about this material."

"This is a particularly busy day." The colonel flips casually through the seventy-five page packet of intercept material and then tries to hand it back to the adviser. "The Nine June Regiment can stay in Yemen and the British Army will stay in Um al Gwarif and all will be well with the world. We've told the Sultan's government and our people in London that the war is now effectively over."

"We know that the Nine June headquarters transmitter is over in Yemen, but COMINT won't tell us where the regiment itself is. If you go back through the files, you find that the character of their transmissions has changed radically from those of a few weeks ago. They have completely stopped broadcasting normal logistics and tactical information. Instead, what you have in front of you is several chapters from Lenin's *State and Revolution*. You can find it in any library in the world and it's not secret. So why are they enciphering it? To whom are they broadcasting? And what for?"

Irritably, Fine tosses the COMINT report back on the table. "You tell me!"

"Maybe the Nine June radio isn't broadcasting operational material because the regiment is nowhere near the transmitter.

We've located them with elementary triangulation, but this technique isn't unknown. The Russians would have warned the *adoo* that we can find and identify their radio. If they don't realize that we're also reading their codes, they could be staying on the air to convince you the regiment is still safely over the border in Yemen."

A little less bored now, Nigel Fine shakes his head. "Good thinking, but your interpretation doesn't fit certain known facts. Look, you're new here, but the *adoo* have suffered one shattering defeat after another. Their transmitter is probably broadcasting gibberish to conceal the fact that the regiment is falling apart. If Nine June were coming this way, my intelligence people would pick it up and so would your absurdly named Big Bird."

"Big Bird" is a Lockheed Talent Keyhole-9 reconnaissance satellite, launched by a Titan III-D rocket into a complicated polar orbit that takes it over Dhofar once every eighty-four hours. Big Bird has powerful optical cameras, but for South Arabia they produce little direct visual information between May and the end of September because of the Dhofar monsoon cloud cover.

But Big Bird's scanners also collect several bands of electromagnetic radiation below the spectrum of visible light. With multispectral scanners, the technicians at the Defense Department's National Reconnaissance Office can use computer-enhancement techniques to look through the monsoon mist for changes in ground temperature.

On a cool day, even one enemy soldier generates enough heat to be detected from space, allowing Big Bird to spot enemy troops right through the cloud cover.

"Maybe yes, maybe no. Okay, let's go over to infrared and look at the latest Big Bird chart!" The Adviser spreads his thermal maps of Dhofar Province out on the table, wondering if he should try to explain how it all works, even though Colonel Fine is not cleared for the details.

"I don't need help reading a map!" Irritated, Colonel Fine circles his desk and bends over the latest Talent Keyhole-9 master overlay. "How old is this information?"

"About nine hours. Big Bird passed overhead a few minutes after ten last night."

"How did you get it here this fast?" Nigel Fine is studying the chart intently.

"We work very quickly, sir," the Adviser evades the question, not wishing to distract the British officer with a complicated technical discussion. After Big Bird's ten o'clock pass, thermal radiation from Dhofar Province was compartmentalized by an on-board computer into pixels that were each assigned a numerical value. The Talent Keyhole-9 then beamed these values down to the U.S. Air Force base in Adana, Turkey, where they were retransmitted to the National Reconnaissance Office in Washington. With photo interpretation and computer-enhancement techniques, the NRO created a heat map of Dhofar Province and sent it over the SPINTCOM net to a super-secret graphics plotter in the Defense Attaché's Office in Muscat.

The new Dhofar Province map emerged from the Muscat Embassy printer at eleven-fifteen in the evening. The Adviser took one look at it and knew he needed to catch the midnight C-47 shuttle for his first trip to Salalah.

"Well, there is clearly nothing on my side of the border to worry about."

The Adviser shakes his head. On the second floor of the Pentagon, photo-interpretation analysts looked quickly at this same imagery, saw what Colonel Fine is now seeing, and jumped to the same conclusion. Very dark, irregularly shaped markings indicate a heat source of some kind, a running motor or a camp fire. A village with a moderate population surrounded by live vegetation prints out as a diffuse patch of magenta red. There are a few dozen very hot spots over on the Communist-controlled side of the Yemen-Oman border, but the Defense Department analysts found nothing alarming anywhere near Salalah.

"To detect the presence of enemy troops, there needs to be a measurable difference between body temperature and the surrounding thermal environment," the Adviser explains. "As I understand it, Dhofar usually cools off in the summer because of the monsoon winds and the cloud cover."

"It can be pleasant," Colonel Fine allows. "We've had balmy weather in the low eighties most of the summer."

"Good, but for the past two weeks, there's been freakishly hot weather on the *jebel,* hasn't there? You've still got the cloud cover, so Big Bird's optical sensors aren't helping, but the temperature has been up in the mid-nineties, almost as warm as a human body. The whole Russian Army could be hiding up there, and Big Bird might pick up almost nothing."

"But vehicle motors would surely show up!"

"Unless the *adoo* are riding camels, or donkeys, or walking."

"Their radio generates heat."

"It sure does and there it is on the map, generating heat back in Hauf. They came over the border without it."

"In the past, they've lit camp fires in the evening."

The Adviser shakes his head and begins to organize his charts in chronological order, since the Talent Keyhole-9 passes overhead every three and a half days. "Our enemy commander now understands that the British can somehow see in the dark!" The TIA begins to place one map after another before the puzzled colonel. "Look what's happened over the past two weeks! Twelve days ago when it was still relatively cool, we detected a huge concentration of heat sources near the border, maybe a thousand or more people. For three consecutive Big Bird passes, there was furious activity right on the border."

The colonel's finger stabs at the next map. "I know! Your predecessor was hysterical about it! But then everything went back to normal and my intelligence officer tells me that the *jebel* is quiet."

"What do you think was going on?"

"I don't know. Maybe it was a feint, or a regimental picnic, or maybe the *adoo* troops mutinied, but wherever they were going, it wasn't Salalah, because they've disappeared! Why should they attack now? If they want to continue the war, they'll need the winter over in Yemen to rebuild."

"They haven't got time to rebuild! Look, the Chinese have gone home and Dhofar was always a sideshow for the Soviet Union. The Russians and the Iraqis will cut their losses and get out if it looks like a humiliating defeat for them. The Popular Front has fought doggedly for more than a decade and the leadership needs a historic battle or they will lose foreign support."

"I'm a soldier, not a political scientist."

"Then think like a soldier and put yourself in your opponent's shoes. Under the circumstances, why would your opposite number in the Popular Front round up his best regiment, march it around in circles for a week, and then send everybody home?"

"I told you: I don't know and I don't care!"

"You need to care! That Popular Front commander has come to understand that we can see him in the dark and beneath camouflage netting. We can see him when he lights a fire or turns on a radio or runs a motor."

"About bloody time!"

"And now he's realized that his forces become almost invisible when he refrains from generating heat and when the weather is both hot and misty. Have you been outside recently? It's hot and misty."

Colonel Fine is growing red in the face. He is about to reply, when the phone rings. He picks up the receiver and listens briefly, running his fingers through his gray, thinning hair with obvious irritation. "Look, keep trying! The relay transmitter at Mirbat must be up the spout. Can't you get through to Muscat or Al Masirah? Right, get back to me when you've discovered what the problem is."

Colonel Fine puts down the phone, breathing heavily.

"I know what the problem is!" The Adviser reminds himself that while he is in Dhofar, Fine is technically his commanding officer. But he is feeling abrasive and careless. If any of us are still alive in three days' time, he predicts sardonically, Colonel Fine will call the American Ambassador in Muscat to complain that the latest TIA was rude. The Ambassador will call the admiral and the Long Range Reconnaissance Group will send me back to Upper Volta. Upper Volta if I'm lucky. Otherwise, it's the Pentagon.

"What?" The colonel looks up, thinking about the problem with the telephone. For a moment he seems unable to place the Adviser. "Ah yes, well, thanks awfully for coming down to visit us, and I expect we'll be seeing you again. John Woodward will see that you get a good British Army breakfast."

"The *adoo* just blew up Mirbat transmitter, Colonel." The Adviser packs up his maps and intercept reports and closes his briefcase. It's not your war, he tries to tell himself, but he is getting angry. John Woodward and Ali Rashidi are decent men; why should their lives be put at risk because this fatuous colonel refuses to face facts?

"The situation . . ." the colonel begins, but the Adviser rolls right over him.

"Last night the Popular Front closed your airport with a Katyushka, and you can't use your helicopters because you haven't neutralized that Grail team yet. Your Strikemaster wing is at Al Masirah Island which is forty-five minutes away but you can't call for ground support because the Popular Front has just cut off your communications. How am I doing so far?"

"Get out!"

"Maybe we should all get out, Colonel!" the Adviser shouts back. "There could be a thousand heavily armed men descending on this position, determined to conquer you or die in the process. You don't know where they are. Or when they are going to attack!"

"Out!"

"Did somebody mention a British Army breakfast?" The Adviser turns and opens the door. Sergeant Major John Woodward, who has clearly been standing in the corridor listening, jumps back in alarm. "Have a real nice day, Colonel," says the Adviser and he slams the door.

Disconsolate, the Technical Intelligence Adviser sits in the Dhofar Brigade Headquarters' mess.

It is a large, rectangular, windowless room. The walls are white-washed plaster, bare except for strips of flypaper hanging in the corners. A lethargic fan dangles from the ceiling, reorganizing the hot and humid air. There are eight huge wooden tables banged together with iron nails and rough-hewn pine planks. The Adviser sits on a rusty, steel folding chair, watching an Indian cook manufacture his promised British Army breakfast.

The Adviser is alone. Looking worried, Sergeant Major John Woodward has disappeared on some urgent, unspecified errand. The other officers and NCOs of the Dhofar Brigade have long since eaten their Sunday morning meal and gone to work.

In due course and with a polite smile, the Indian cook delivers an enormous mug of milky, heavily sugared China tea and a tray of greasy scrambled eggs with strips of Canadian bacon and roasted tomatoes and mushrooms and some fairly decent fried potatoes, and even slices of fresh bread fried in bacon fat. On a separate plate is a kippered herring, simmered and seasoned and sliced down the middle.

The Adviser is hungry, and his mouth waters at the sight and scent of it. There is enough cholesterol here to occlude a dozen arteries, and with a burst of nostalgia he remembers how he and Peter once fled from Ellen's vigorous regimen of high-fiber-low-fat organic health food to a student beanery in Oxford's covered market where they "pigged out"—Peter's favorite Americanism—on a thousand calories apiece.

Yes, that was the meal when Peter—with a mixture of pride and embarrassment—confessed about his other woman, the lady in London with whom he spent nights after CND meetings.

"And in the morning, she cooks me breakfasts like this," he commented. "It's not so much the sex as the chance to be deliciously unhealthy. There are days when I cannot face another macrobiotic quiche."

To be with a woman like Ellen I would stay home every night of my life, the Adviser thought immediately. And eat every revoltingly healthy thing she put in front of me.

"I only mention it because another woman in London who does reasonably good breakfasts has been making inquiries about your availability. Unless you actually prefer a life of scholarly celibacy, you might come along some weekend and deploy that rustic colonial charm of yours."

"Sure," he said, but he found Peter's faithlessness irritating. What makes him think that I am automatically on his side? Hasn't he noticed that Ellen and I are already unacknowledged best friends?

Am I falling in love with her? I wondered. I mustn't.

I shouldn't have. Instead, I should have gone with him for those weekends in London, the Adviser sighs. I could have found someone safe to love. Someone who wouldn't serve me grits in the morning. There were always women around, and the draft-dodger saga did work wonders with lady peaceniks.

But I didn't go to London because—when Peter was away—I had Ellen all to myself. We took turns cooking dinner or went out to one of those Indian restaurants on the Cowley Road and ate vegetarian curry and poppadums and drank Tiger beer. We saw modern dance at the Oxford Playhouse and watched steamy Italian flicks at the Penultimate Picture Palace. Or we stayed home so that she could correct themes from her sixth-form composition class while I hit the books, an Arabic-English dictionary and a mug of China tea by my side.

That China tea was our first little rebellion against the authority of the great professor. When he was home, Peter always insisted upon Indian tea even though Ellen preferred Chinese and I couldn't tell the difference. Whenever he was out of the house, we covertly switched to Chinese.

It was inevitable that there would come a day when it would be impossible to go on pretending to be just good friends. It was a Sunday in late November, toward the end of Michaelmas term. Peter was off in search of sex and cholesterol. Ellen and I walked up the Cherwell River to the Victoria Arms Pub for lunch. The sky was dark and threatening, but over a couple of pints of Yorkshire Brown Ale we began the ritual exchange of autobiographies.

Mine, of course, was phony, worked out at Reconnaissance Group headquarters. But I liked it so well that I wished it were true. I had a family out of *Good Housekeeping* with a home in upstate New York. My father was a high school geography teacher who coached the basketball team. My dedicated mom sang in the choir and did the ironing and packed lunches with cheese and bologna sandwiches and always made her apple pies from scratch.

I bought a fourth-hand Ford for five hundred bucks in my freshman year of college. Dad helped me replace the engine rings when it started to burn oil. I had all of Joan Baez's records. I rented a tuxedo for the senior prom and bought a yellow corsage for my girlfriend. What was her name? Melanie. Her name was Melanie, and I heard later that she married a dentist.

I had just graduated from our local college when the draft notice arrived and my father assumed that I would do my duty to God and my country, but I thought the war was morally wrong and I went over the border one night into Canada with a friend and we found jobs working construction in Ontario. All my bridges burned. Warrants and the Federal Bureau of Investigation coming to the house. My mother in tears. My patriotic father saddened and puzzled by his subversive son. Disgraced. Can't ever go home. Won't ever go home. Not now.

And then, oh Christ, oh, the memory floods back over him, the first time I presented the fable—sitting in the dining room of the Victoria Arms Pub over fried plaice and mushy peas and chips—was the first time she touched me. She reached across the table and stroked my cheek with her fingers.

"If only there were some way of making it right for you because you have suffered so much for what we believe in and it makes me cry," she murmured. She said that. Touching my face. With tears in her eyes.

He is eating scrambled eggs and fried bread and thinking about Ellen when the door opens and Colonel Nigel Fine walks slowly up to his table. The Adviser is startled and nearly spills his China tea.

Leave Oxford, he pleads with his mind. Stay in Oman. You have work here.

The Indian cook has disappeared and the mess is empty except for the colonel. John Woodward is standing guard at the door, and he shoots a quick, conspiratorial glance across the room, but the Adviser cannot decipher its meaning.

The colonel now looks old and ill. He makes a helpless, supplicatory gesture with one hand as if asking permission to join the Adviser at his table.

"Sir?" The American half-rises, dropping his fork, and Colonel Fine slumps into a chair opposite him.

There is a long moment's silence and when he speaks, his voice is choked and unsteady. "Look, sorry about being irritable. There are days since Teddy . . . Did anyone tell you about my son?"

Stunned, the Advisor shakes his head. Colonel Fine seems to be talking to himself, staring down at the wooden surface of the table.

"Well, of course, it's family business, but I thought John Woodward might have mentioned it. Teddy, uh, that's my son, Teddy and I were both up at Winchester and then Sandhurst, my only child, y'know, and I hoped he'd follow me into the British Army, but the blighter insisted upon the Royal Marines. Wanted to prove he was tougher than his old man, I suppose. Actually, his mother—women are wiser than we—his mother wanted him to stay out of the military altogether. She would never say so, but in her heart she must . . . certainly . . . ah, blame me."

The Adviser feels his hands and feet going cold as if something were wrong with his circulatory system. There is a pile of unused silverware on the table, and the colonel is collecting all the spoons within reach and carefully stacking them one on top of the other. He achieves an unstable stack five spoons high before it collapses with a clatter.

"What happened to Teddy, sir?"

The colonel's eyes are red and watery. "Our intelligence people sent him to Belfast on some foolish undercover assignment. Never much fancied our intelligence chaps, really, foolish things they get up to . . . I mean, Teddy never had the training for that sort of thing. The boy was as English as Yorkshire pudding! How could he pretend to be something he wasn't? Anyway, six months ago the Provisional IRA put an American-made explosive device under his car and blew him up. The bomber fled to Boston where he was arrested, but last week a Massachusetts judge denied extradition on the grounds that murdering my son was a political crime. Made me into a proper anti-American fanatic. Wanted to apologize for being rude to you, but it all seems so . . . so bloody unfair."

"I'm sorry. I never made the connection between you and . . . your late son." The Adviser murmurs the obvious and looks away, embarrassed. Of course, the British press has been full of furious stories about the martyred young Royal Marine and the American judiciary's refusal to extradict the culprit.

"It's all right. Since Teddy's death, I've just wanted this damned war to be over so I could take my poor wife home to England and comfort her as well as I can. So when you bounced in with the news that we were about to be attacked again, I . . . desperately wanted you to be wrong."

"Maybe I am wrong, sir." The Adviser finds himself liking the colonel, despite everything. "I've only been here a week and I've spent that time up in Muscat being briefed by our embassy people and looking at charts and intelligence reports. I know the Middle East fairly well, but I've never been in Oman before and everybody else does think the war is over. Ah, what did happen to your relay station in Mirbat?"

"As you said, somebody blew it up." With a visible effort, Nigel Fine pulls himself together and coughs several times to clear the phlegm from his throat. "When we couldn't get our calls through, I sent a technical team up in a chopper. They found our antenna array lying on its side. We can replace it in a few hours, but for the time being Dhofar is cut off."

"That means . . ."

"That something wicked this way comes." There is more energy in the colonel's voice now, and the Adviser senses that the aristocratic old thug has one more good scrap in him. "Any ideas about a probable target?"

"They might try something along the lines of a Tet Offensive." The Adviser remembers Saigon in 1969. "They could shoot for the headlines by hitting soft, civilian targets."

Colonel Fine nods. "Perhaps. I'm thinking a series of spoiling attacks to throw them off-balance before they get to Salalah. But I'm worried about the lack of air support. Our dirty little secret here is that, on a man-to-man basis, our Omanese troops never were a match for the *adoo*. We'll need fighter cover to defeat them."

"We'll have to find them first." The Adviser gets his briefcase open and spreads the latest TechIntel chart on the table. He runs his finger along Dhofar's only access route, a road running north from the town of Salalah and climbing up the center of the *jebel*. Three thousand feet above sea level at a town called Thamrait, it turns right into the open desert and meanders a thousand kilometers across the Arabian Empty Quarter toward Muscat and Abu Dhabi and the Persian Gulf. "Now, this road here . . ."

"It's called the Midway Road," Nigel Fine informs him. "For political reasons, it's crucial to keep the Midway open so the *jebeli* people can drive their goats and cattle down to the Salalah market."

"I think your enemy force is deployed in small units on either side of this road."

"How do you know? You said he was invisible."

"I said he was almost invisible. Everybody else has been looking for gross heat changes indicating a large number of men," the Adviser explains, running his pencil about halfway up the *jebel*. "If our enemy commander understands how Big Bird works, then he is going to avoid creating much of a thermal presence. So we're looking for subtle changes and some of the villages to the west of the Midway Road have fluctuated very slightly over the past two Big Bird runs. It's hard to see on these charts, and the Pentagon did not see the fluctuation as exceeding the standard variation for a pixel-based printout, but . . ."

"Oh God, speak the Queen's English!" Nigel Fine pleads.

"In English, sir, it means that the weather has been too hot recently for a reasonable infrared reading, so maybe this is just a meaningless technical anomaly. But some of these villages appear to have gone cold, while others are suspiciously warm, indicating population shifts."

Abruptly, the colonel taps a location on the map with his finger. "Two days ago, the Scout Platoon took a prisoner right here, just outside of one of your warmish villages."

"This one?" The Adviser scrutinizes the chart. "Bait al Muktar?"

"That's the one. The prisoner is a young well-dressed man, and my intelligence people think he might be a political officer. But we haven't got much out of him."

"Would you like me to talk to him?"

"I can use all the help I can get."

"I'll do what I can, sir," the Adviser volunteers, wondering what Ellen would have wished him to do under these circumstances. She hated violence, but there is no way of preventing more fighting in Dhofar; it is now merely a question of deciding whose violence would prevail.

"We might need a Yank on our side today. We seem to have a battle ahead of us."

"We'll win it for Teddy Fine, sir." That's corny, he thinks. But it felt good to say it.

Too powerfully moved to speak, Nigel Fine squeezes the Adviser's hand in gratitude and rushes from the room.

No more of the mixed emotions and divided loyalties I felt in

Oxford, the Adviser resolves. Here the issues are a little clearer. I am on this side. The other side is the other side.

"It's not precisely torture, but I have always been uncomfortable with the SEP process," John Woodward confesses carefully as he leads the Adviser through a labyrinth of narrow, winding corridors to the Dhofar Brigade's Interrogation and Intelligence Center. "It would be different if they were hardened soldiers or professional Marxist agitators, but most of our SEPs are just simple peasants and it seems . . ."

"What's an SEP?"

"A Surrendered Enemy Personnel. Everybody else calls them POWs, but we are obliged to say SEP because the Sultan takes the position that every *adoo* in custody has undergone a change of heart and surrendered rather than been captured. Here we are."

They halt before a barrier of steel bars. On the other side, there is an English master sergeant, a big, brutal-looking man with bad skin and hollow, angry eyes. The Adviser remembers something from Oscar Wilde about being responsible—after a certain age—for your own face. Has being an interrogator made this sergeant ugly? Or does he hurt people for a living because he was born hard to look at?

I am on this side, he reminds himself. The other side is the other side.

"How many have we got today?" Woodward speaks stiffly. The two NCOs do not exchange greetings.

"Just the one." The master sergeant admits them to his sinister precinct and gestures toward a closed cell with a solid steel door and a sliding peephole. "Captain Fenwich interrogated him yesterday. The bastard will debate world politics with you, but he's keeping his mouth shut about the Popular Front."

"Captain Fenwich has a very forceful way of asking questions," Woodward mutters as the Adviser pushes back the slide and looks into the cell. It measures eight feet on each side, and the walls are old, stained cement. A vague smell of excrement mingles with disinfectant. A garden hose lies coiled in a bucket. Mounted high in one corner, there is an old-fashioned loudspeaker.

Beneath a bare light bulb in the center of the cell stands a slender young man, entirely naked. His head and face are covered with a canvas hood that is loosely tied around his neck. The prisoner is extremely thin, almost emaciated, and he has scarcely any body hair. As is customary with South Arabian natives, he has been radically circumcised; nearly all the external skin from his thin, shriveled penis has been removed. His arms are handcuffed behind his back, and the cuffs are attached to a length of chain that runs to a hook in the ceiling, so that the SEP cannot sit or kneel.

"What's been done to him?" The Adviser tries valiantly not to identify with the prisoner. He fails. This could have been me, he reflects. A half-dozen times when I was lucky instead of unlucky. How long would I have kept my silence?

"He has not been tortured," Woodward insists quickly. "Our interrogation specialists are all trained at the English Intelligence Centre in Maresfield in Sussex where they learn the famous 'Five Techniques' approach the British Army developed in Kenya and Aden and Cyprus."

"What five techniques?"

"Well, first is sensory deprivation, which we accomplish with that hood over his head. Second, we periodically disorient him with high-pitched white noise from that speaker. The third step is to make him stand for long periods of time, which undermines his physical resistance without specifically hurting him. Technique four involves denying him food, and the fifth is keeping him awake for several days."

"Why is he naked?"

"To maximize his sense of vulnerability. Look, I've got to help Nigel. Do you need a translator?"

The Adviser shakes his head and enters the cell. The prisoner tenses as he reacts to the Gothic squeak of the opening door, but he makes no sound.

"Assalam aleikum." The Adviser slips gingerly into the Arabic he learned in Peter Reston's Oxford classes as he murmurs the standard Arabic greeting. "Peace be with you." It seems a strange salutation under the circumstances.

How would Peter feel if he knew that I was a career intelligence officer who used the language of the Prophet for prisoner interrogations? Could he hate me any more than he already does?

"Wa aleikum assalam." The prisoner replies courteously in classical Arabic, his voice muffled by the mask. It is a young voice, speaking with the same accent that Peter's Iraqi friends used. "And peace be with you."

"I came only to talk. I will not hurt you or ask you for secrets."

"Please, I am very tired. Can you let me sit down?"

"I have no authority here," the Adviser admits. "I am just a visitor."

"I am frightened."

"I know. What is happening to you must be terribly upsetting. Are you from Baghdad? You sound like an Iraqi friend I once had."

"No, I am from a village in the mountains here in Dhofar. I studied at the University of Baghdad and learned proper Arabic there. My people are the al-Qara and our dialect is called Shheri. You would find it a hard tongue to understand."

"What is your village called?" From the intelligence reports he read in Muscat, the Adviser knows that the al-Qara are the dominant tribe on the *jebel* and the backbone of the Popular Front. They are tough mountain people who have always despised Oman's ruling dynasty.

"Bait al Muktar," the prisoner explains. "It is a small place of no importance."

"You were captured near your own village? What were you doing when they captured you?"

"I was going to see my mother."

"Have you been away from home a long time?"

"It has been a year."

"You are a member of the Popular Front for the Liberation of Oman?"

The *adoo* simply shrugs and the Adviser decides to begin probing gently. Omanese political life is complicated, but according to the U.S. Embassy briefing staff, the former sultan had been a man named Taimur bin Said, a caricature of an oriental despot who kept his kingdom locked in the Middle Ages. Under Taimur, the Omanese had no political parties, no legislatures, no universities or high schools, no roads, no radio, no television, and no hospitals. When Taimur had finally slipped into terminal looniness, the British had orchestrated a palace coup to replace him with his son, Sultan Qabus.

"They tell me that the old sultan was wicked, but his son seems a good man. Why have the al-Qara taken up arms against him?"

"Do you have sultans in America?"

"We do not have sultans in Canada." The Advisor winces, wondering if real Canadians have this problem. How irritating it would be for an authentic agronomist from Manitoba to live under the constant accusation of being an American spy. "Why do you imagine that I am American?"

"We always wondered how long it would be before America turned its attention on us. You have been sent here to find out why your British puppets are taking so long to restore order among their Omanese puppets."

"That is not it at all. I am just a friend, visiting friends."

"Well, friend, will you tell me what time it is?"

I'm getting nowhere, the Adviser thinks as he glances at his watch. It is nine fifteen. "It's still early morning."

The *adoo* sighs with disappointment. He's been waiting for the attack to begin, the Adviser speculates. He wants to hear the sound of his own cannon, and he is now digesting the news that it is twelve hours until sundown. Does the attack come at sundown?

"I only ask these questions to understand. Why have the al-Qara people rebelled against your sultan?"

"He is not our sultan. We al-Qara are a different folk. While the English sat by and watched, the old sultan starved us and whipped us and thrust us in prison. My father was executed by the old sultan's men. Are we supposed to believe that everything has changed because a snarling old tyrant is gone, and a smiling young tyrant has taken his place?"

"Are your people communists?"

The *adoo*'s shoulders rise and fall in an eloquent shrug. There is desperation in his voice, and the Adviser wonders if this conversation is depleting his last reservoirs of strength. "Some of the others have convinced themselves that they are real Marxists.

Most of us just say the words in order to get the weapons we need."

"From the Russians?"

"Who else would give us guns? The Russians will not support us unless we talk to them about Lenin. But when this war is over, all the foreigners must go away and leave us in peace. Even the Russians."

"Dhofar is a very beautiful country."

"Dhofar is a very poor country," the prisoner points out. "I have never understood why the British and Americans are so interested in us. We have nothing here for you imperialists to steal. Once we sold frankincense, but no one needs it today. So we feed our cattle on dried sardines and raise a few vegetables. Do you want our dried sardines?"

This is not easy to explain in any language and the Adviser is not sure why he bothers to try. "The other end of Oman juts out into the Persian Gulf. Whoever controls that peninsula can control access to most of the world's oil reserves. It doesn't have much to do with Dhofar's dried sardines."

There is a long silence. "The Persian Gulf is twelve hundred kilometers from Dhofar and there is a great empty desert between us and this other world. Must we remain the subjects of a foreign tyrant because one end of a country to which we do not wish to belong is near your oil?"

"The British and American governments are dedicated to free enterprise and they worry about the possibility of Marxist control over your movement. Even though you say you are not a Marxist yourself."

The Adviser wonders if he has translated all the words properly, but the *adoo* snaps back immediately.

"You need to go up on the *jebel* to see how we live. We raise goats and eat them. Whether you call us communists or capitalists, we are still just poor people living on the side of a mountain eating goats."

"If you lay down your arms, the sultan will let you eat all the goats you want."

"The sultans are foreigners who have imposed their government on us. We are Dhofari people, not Omanese. We have never been allowed to vote. I thought Americans believed in freedom!"

The Adviser sighs audibly, unable to think of a response. Ellen's friends in the Greenham Common Women's Peace Movement always said the same thing, demanding to know why the United States insisted upon sponsoring right-wing dictatorships all over the world. "These are things I do not understand," he says finally. "I am a simple man."

"You seem like a good man," the prisoner comments suddenly.

"I am not a particularly good man."

"You will have to do. Can you help me?"

"I have no authority here."

"I have been standing too long, and I cannot endure it any longer. I was trained to be a schoolmaster, not a soldier. I have not the strength of a soldier."

"Then tell me something that I could tell them," The Adviser quickly puts his hands on the prisoner's shoulder and feels his body trembling with fear. "They already know that the Nine June Regiment is somewhere on the *jebel* and will strike soon. They need to know where it is, and what it intends to attack. You could tell me that."

"My own people would kill me if I talked to you."

"I would see that you were protected."

"How can you protect me if you have no authority?"

"What is your name, *adoo?*"

"I am Mahmoud."

"Mahmoud, I am the only friend you have here in Um al Gwarif. If the Popular Front attacks today and you keep silent and many English people die, they will hold you responsible."

"What will they do to me?"

"I don't know. But no one knows you are here and no one knows your name. If you died in this room, no one would ever know what happened to you."

"Then I will die. It is all right. . . ." A bold declaration, but there is a shudder in Mahmoud's voice and the Adviser understands that he would prefer not to die, unless it is absolutely necessary.

"When the war is over, the al-Qara people will need school-teachers." He tries to give him an honorable way to choose life. "If you can tell me just a little, I will ask the English to bring you food and let you sit down."

"I will be cursed by God!" Mahmoud begins to sob.

We will all be cursed by God, the Adviser thinks, but he puts amateur theology aside and begins to take notes as Mahmoud tells him about the 9 June Regiment.

"How did you break him?" There is admiration in Nigel Fine's voice.

"I didn't." The Adviser decides not to take too much credit. "I just happened to be standing there when he ran out of gas."

"Does he know where Nine June is deployed?" John Woodward asks quietly. They are standing at the door to Nigel Fine's office. Around them in the operations center, the sleepy Sunday-morning atmosphere has shifted smoothly into the quietly frantic activity that the British do so well. With a burst of memory, the Adviser recalls how Peter and Ellen and their CND colleagues planned their war on Cruise missiles with the same subdued fixity of purpose. In the Pentagon, he thinks, we would have shouting and hysterics.

"No," he confesses. "Nine days ago, our SEP left Hauf in the People's Democratic Republic of Yemen. He had orders to prepare the clandestine al-Qara irregulars on the *jebel* for one last uprising. He came alone, but he assumes that the Nine June Regiment has since followed him over the border, since that was the plan."

"That was the plan," Colonel Fine repeats slowly. "So he admits that an offensive is coming?"

"Yes, but he's not sure when."

"And what's their target? Did he confirm your theory about a Tet Offensive-style assault on Salalah?"

"No, the model is Dien Bien Phu," the Adviser asserts. "Their intention is to lay siege to the British garrison."

"What?"

"You. Us. Headquarters, Dhofar brigade. Um al Gwarif."

"Um al Gwarif?" Nigel Fine is incredulous. "They wouldn't

dare! This is the most heavily fortified position in South Arabia."

"If they launch a concentrated attack on you here, can you fight your way out and defeat them?"

Nigel Fine strides into his office with John Woodward and the Adviser following him like acolytes. The colonel glares out the window and studies the overcast sky.

"How many troops are we talking about?"

"Count on a thousand men."

"We still have too much cloud cover for effective air support," Fine admits. "Even if we could call it in. So if the Popular Front has a thousand men out there and they don't mind dying in large numbers, they could put us in some difficulty. It could be three or four days before we could get help."

"That will be long enough to give them the headlines they need. London won't be able to keep it out of the newspapers if a British garrison is cut off."

"But even if they did overrun us here in Um al Gwarif, they must know we will strike back with reinforcements. Winning here doesn't mean winning everywhere."

"At this stage in the conflict, they just need to avoid losing," the Adviser asserts. "If you're pinned down here, you won't be able to defend Salalah. They can hold out there long enough to execute the provincial governor and shoot up the city center, and it will be a long time before the people of Dhofar trust the British Army again."

There is a silence. The Adviser watches as Nigel Fine circles his desk and looks again at the chart. On the wall is a framed picture of a young Royal Marine lieutenant in dress blues and sword. The colonel gazes at the photograph as if seeking advice from his dead son. Then he stands up, his voice clear and decisive.

"I'll be damned if I'll let them bottle me up here!" Nigel Fine sweeps his left hand across the map. There is a sudden smile on his face as if he has just remembered how much he enjoys a brawl. "We'll sweep westward with the First Regiment to shield Salalah and the airport. We'll move the Second Regiment into a phased defensive position north of here to protect Um al Gwarif and the road to Mirbat. And Bernie Fenwich will take his Scout

Platoon right up the Midway Road until somebody shoots at him. Once we know where the buggers are hiding, we'll deal with them. What do you think?"

"It sounds good to me, sir. On the basis of my TechIntel, I could give your Captain Fenwich some suggestions on where to look."

"Splendid! Look, you'd better leave the rest of your classified stuff here in my safe and just take the most recent map with you." Nonchalantly, Colonel Fine picks up the Adviser's brief-case and stuffs it into the bottom of a three-drawer steel cabinet.

Oh, Christ. Feeling slightly faint, the Adviser realizes that Fine wants him go up on the *jebel* to help the Scout Platoon locate the Popular Front. It is not at all clear that the colonel has the neces-sary authority. The Adviser is generally under British command here in Dhofar, but no one can send him out on an operational assignment without permission from the deputy commander of the Long Range Reconnaissance Group—who, like the rest of the world, cannot at the moment be contacted.

The colonel turns to his brigade sergeant major. "Listen John, this is asking a lot, but could you go along and keep Bernie out of trouble? We'll say that our Technical Intelligence Adviser needs an escort."

"Of course, sir," John Woodward promptly agrees. "We can't have a Yank wandering around the *jebel* without somebody to make sure he has Pepsi-Cola and chewing gum, can we?"

"Excellent!" Nigel Fine shepherds the two of them toward the door, one hand on each of their shoulders.

The Adviser's mind is working furiously. This is my last chance to stay out of this, he thinks. This is the moment where I absorb a little embarrassment . . . rather a lot of embarrassment, actually, but here I turn and firmly make my excuses. Sorry guys, but there are a lot of secrets in my head and an executive order forbids me to go into a combat zone where I am in danger of capture and interrogation by forces hostile to the United States of America. Furthermore, I would be more useful here in this heavily defended and air-conditioned fortress interrogating any prisoners your Captain Fenwich produces.

Ready to make his excuses, the Adviser turns at the door of the colonel's office. Suddenly, Nigel Fine throws an arm around his shoulders, hugs him roughly, and then holds him at arm's length, looking him straight in the eyes. The trembly old man seems to have become a decade younger and a few inches taller.

"Y'know, my old dad once told me about the American volunteers who fought in the Battle of Britain. Maybe that Boston judge made me forget that those Yanks who helped save England in nineteen forty represented the real America. And so do you, lad! God bless you and good luck!"

"Ah . . . yes sir," says the Adviser numbly. Brilliant, he thinks.

"John, take good care of him! Both of you keep your heads down!"

"We'll be okay, Nigel." The two Englishmen are shaking hands now.

Great. The Adviser clears his throat to explain that he would not have enjoyed the Battle of Britain and fervently does not wish to go trooping around the *jebel,* but Fine is already moving into high gear. With a vigorous bellow, he shouts for his senior staff, and majors and lieutenant colonels crowd into his office to be briefed on the forthcoming defensive operation.

A moment later, the command center is nearly empty. John Woodward leads the Adviser up the corridor toward the front of the Um al Gwarif headquarters.

"Whenever we English want something from an American, we mention the Battle of Britain." He laughs. "But you don't have to come with us today if you don't want to. This isn't your war, and Nigel gets the knighthood if we win."

"I need the exercise." The Adviser shrugs hopelessly. "Besides, the colonel's a hard man to refuse."

"Tell me about it! I worked for Nigel thirty years ago when he was only a captain, and we've been friends ever since. This spring I was home in York on terminal leave, planting rose bushes in my garden and getting ready to retire. Then he turned up and insisted I come back out here with him for one more tour. My wife, Jenny, said she'd divorce me if I went."

"Did she?"

"It's in the works, I guess. She certainly moved out and filed the papers!"

"Why did you let Fine talk you into coming back here?"

"We've always had a father-son relationship," Woodward

says uncomfortably. "My own dad was something of a bastard and Nigel became my substitute father. When Teddy died I guess I became his substitute son, although I'm a little old for the part. Anyway, when he turned up looking shattered and said that he needed me, I found it impossible to say no."

"Real fathers are always problems. I suppose substitute fathers can be just as bad."

"Did you have a good relationship with your father?"

"I never knew my parents." The Adviser is a little stunned that he and Woodward should start trading intimate truths this early in the day. "A few hours after I was born, my mother apparently abandoned me, and I was raised by Roman Catholic nuns in a series of orphanages."

At first he thinks that it will feel good to have made this preliminary stab at self-revelation, but then, almost immediately, a sense of shame sweeps over him. I was never able to tell Ellen, he reminds himself angrily. This central fact about myself that I am now presenting to a stranger, I could never share with the only woman I ever loved!

"That's sad," Woodward comments tersely. He pauses at the door to the headquarters building. "Do you hate them?"

"The nuns?" It was hard to remember individual nuns, much less to hate them. They all wore the same black habit and seldom touched him.

"No, your mother and father."

"I never knew who they were or what they looked like." For a moment, the Adviser tries to imagine a frightened adolescent girl, impregnated by some casual stranger, thrusting her bundle of illegitimate disgrace into the hands of a nun and disappearing into the night. Leaving me without a name to my name.

My first pseudonym was the name on my birth certificate, he reflects. The nuns made it up.

"Are you very curious about who they were? Some orphans consume their lives searching for lost mums and dads."

The Adviser shakes his head, having come, for the moment, to the end of this transitory fit of honesty. In fact, after his first year of intelligence training, he had taken a month's leave to begin working his way backwards in time, going through diocesan records to identify the first in the long series of bleak orphanages where he had lived as a child. In his memory they all blurred into one, with bricks on the outside and white plaster walls on the inside. The bathrooms were always cold in the morning.

"No, there is no way of tracing my parents and no way for them to trace me." He remembers the day he tracked himself back to his very first orphanage. The building was empty and awaiting demolition. One elderly sister in a nearby convent meandered through her fading memory and thought she remembered him as a newborn infant. But she wasn't sure. There had been so many children, most of them just infants when they came in. Sometimes the mothers didn't even give their real names. The records from his era had long since disappeared. By fire or flood or thrown out with the trash. No one remembered.

Woodward nods and there is a moment of silence. When they arrive at the front door of the Um al Gwarif headquarters building, Woodward detours into an arms room to pick up a NATO 7.62-mm machine gun.

"We call this a 'jimpy,' " he explains, as he signs his name to a register. "A General Purpose Machine Gun. Useful for shooting people. Do you want one?"

"No, I have my lady pistol." The Adviser shakes his head and follows John Woodward out into the midmorning heat.

Off into battle, he thinks. Once more, dear friends. Into the breach. For flag and fatherland. For dear old Dad and all the baseball games we never saw together.

For dear old Mom.

And all the apple pies she never baked.

Chapter Four

TIERCE

It is the third hour after sunrise.

Across the road from the headquarters fort there is a petroleum depot where Captain Fenwich's Scout Platoon is being supplied with diesel fuel. The movement of heavy vehicles sweeps great columns of dust into the air. Everybody is coughing. The heat is intolerable.

As he follows Sergeant Major Woodward into the barbed-wire enclosure, the Adviser is depressed, realizing that he has deftly maneuvered himself into a no-win situation.

I have exceeded my instructions in persuading the British to launch this crusade, he thinks. Thousands of heavily armed men will soon swarm across the face of Dhofar. If they find nothing, the Brigade Command will create a royal Britannic fuss and the Reconnaissance Group will recall me in disgrace.

Conversely, if I am right and the 9 June Regiment is out there somewhere, we are about to have an epic brawl. Smack in the middle of which will be peace-loving little me.

"Watch out! Here's our Saladin." Solicitously, John Woodward tugs on his elbow, pulling him out of harm's way as an enormous armored vehicle rumbles into the refueling compound. Slightly less than a tank but substantially more than a truck, the Saladin has three huge rubber wheels on either side to give it off-the-road capability. On top of the steel fuselage, there is a massive revolving turret supporting a heavy 76-mm field gun and a 50-caliber Browning automatic rifle.

"Isn't that our friend Napalm?" Shielding his eyes against the glare, the Adviser peers through the swirling dust at a barrel-chested figure lounging against the Saladin's turret. Napalm is wearing only his fatigue trousers, combat boots without socks, and an Arab *kafiyah* head scarf. He looks extremely cheerful, handling his jimpy as if it were a plastic toy.

"It must seem strange, but the scouts always take Napalm on patrol. By himself, he forgets to come home, but if you go with him and tell him where you want to go, he'll never get you lost."

"But he's insane!"

Woodward shrugs. "So is the Middle East. Out here there are moments so demented that a normal man gets paralyzed. But Napalm is already crazy, so he keeps on functioning, no matter what."

"You must be the only senior NCO in the British Army who sees combat as an exercise in existential absurdity," comments the Adviser. "None of my business, John, but you seem too much of an intellectual to be a traditional sergeant major."

Woodward looks vaguely pleased. "When I was a lad, the Sunday papers had a cartoon character named Sergeant Dauntless who stomped around shouting vulgarities at terrified enlisted men while bullets bounced off his chest. My father was precisely that kind of sergeant major and always encouraged me to follow in his footsteps. I guess I never quite managed it. Just as well. One of him was enough."

The petroleum depot is filling up with men and vehicles now, and a pair of canvas-covered, four-ton Bedford British Army troop trucks rumble in for fuel. The Bedfords are painted olive drab; the heat inside must be stifling because the passengers immediately drop the tailgates and jump down to mill around the diesel pumps. The din is terrific; everybody is shouting orders and no one is listening. There is fuel everywhere, but the men all light cigarettes.

"Are these ours?" The Adviser is dismayed. The Arab troops are short, unathletic-looking men in their thirties and early forties—elderly for combat troops. Many of them are distinctly overweight. They are all wearing the basic Sultan's Armed Forces dark green uniform, but they have substituted Arabic head scarves for the usual steel combat helmets.

"Yes, this is Captain Fenwich's Scout Platoon. I should explain that Colonel Fine inherited Fenwich from the previous Dhofar Brigade commander. We'd have replaced him had we realized the game was going into extra time."

The scouts are carrying a bewildering variety of weapons. A few have the light plastic 5.56-mm Armalite automatic rifle so favored by the Irish Republican Army. A couple have shotguns or ancient U.S. Army M-79 grenade launchers. To the Adviser's surprise, however, most seem to be toting AK-47s, the famous Russian-made Kalashnikov assault rifle.

"Where do all the Soviet weapons come from?"

"From the enemy. Our friends here will fight very vigorously if they have a chance to kill an *adoo* and take his Kalashnikov," Woodward explains. "They can sell them for a small fortune or carry them to prove how ferocious they are in battle."

"Do they get ferocious in battle?"

Woodward nods, pointing to a short fat man, bustling around giving orders. "Sergeant Mustafa Said is their natural leader and he's getting better every day. Each of the three squads is led by a competent lance corporal. There have been some problems about discipline in the field but they're better combat soldiers than they seem."

"They'd better be. They don't seem massively enthusiastic about this patrol."

"The *jebel* spooks them a little. The Omanese don't mind fighting the *adoo* down here on the coastal plain, but that mountain scares everybody."

"What's scary about a mountain?"

Woodward shrugs. "You'll see." He leads the Adviser toward a long wheel-based Land-Rover that has just entered the fuel compound. A somber Sergeant Ali Rashidi sits on the right behind the steering wheel while his vehicle is supplied with petrol. Mounted in front of the forward passenger seat is a Browning automatic rifle of a vintage normally only encountered in military museums. There are jerrycans with water and extra gasoline strapped to the fenders fore and aft, and a long whip antenna juts skyward from what the British call the "bonnet." As the Adviser climbs into the back with John Woodward, he discovers that there are sand bags beneath the seats to absorb the blast should they roll over a land mine.

"Right, I suppose this is Captain America?" A deep, harsh voice suddenly assails his ears.

The Adviser startles. In all the confusion, he has missed the approach of a broad-shouldered Englishman with closely cropped black hair. The officer is dressed in the same khaki field uniform that Woodward wears, but three circular pips on each epaulet identify him as a captain. He has binoculars strung around his neck and a NATO-issue automatic pistol on his hip. The man is big enough to play American football and looks tough enough to eat tenpenny nails for breakfast.

Ignoring the Adviser's proffered hand, he circles the Land-Rover with brisk, angry strides and jumps into the front passenger seat.

"Ah, yes, sir, may I introduce Captain Bernard Fenwich," Woodward tries to compensate for the officer's abruptness. "Captain, this is our new Technical Intelligence Adviser from the American Embassy in Muscat."

"I thought you were supposed to be an agronomist."

"That was a misunderstanding, sir," Woodward explains, but Fenwich rolls over him.

"Are you military or civilian?" The captain has a tarted-up working class accent from somewhere in southern England. Bracing himself on the machine gun, he pivots into his seat, glaring at the Adviser with open hostility.

"I'm a civilian employee of the Long Range Reconnaissance Group."

"What the hell is that?"

"We're part of the U.S. Defense Department. Down here in Dhofar, I'm under Colonel Fine's orders."

"What's your protocol rank?"

The Adviser hunches his shoulders helplessly. As a GS-14, he is considered the equivalent of a full colonel, but like most of his L.R.R.G. colleagues, he thinks that people who want rank and titles should take Holy Orders. "I don't think I'm important enough to warrant a protocol grade," he says evasively, not wishing to inform Captain Fenwich that he outranks him by a light year. "Why do you ask?"

"Because it needs to be totally clear that you are not in charge of anything today, no matter what happens. This is our war!"

"I have no desire to be in charge of anything!" the Adviser snaps. "I'm only here to offer advice."

Mortified, Sergeant Woodward is looking away, but Captain

Fenwich digs the communal grave a little deeper. "Thanks to your advice, mate, we're launching an operation costing tens of thousands of pounds, and it's going to be an utter waste of time. You know, after the way the Vietnamese kicked your arses out of Southeast Asia, I'm amazed that anyone actually wants military advice from an American!"

"It was your prisoner, who . . ."

"My prisoner, whom you had no bloody business interrogating, was taking the piss out of you! Right now he's probably laughing himself silly!"

The Adviser pictures the frail *adoo* schoolmaster hanging nakedly on the end of his chain. For Mahmoud's sake, he suppresses his anger. "That SEP should be given food and rest while we confirm his statement."

"He was lying and we'll keep him hungry and on his feet until he starts telling the truth." Captain Fenwich rotates in his seat and pokes Ali Rashidi roughly in the shoulder. "Come on, Rashi, let's get this over with."

"Captains outrank sergeants major," John Woodward mutters quietly to the Adviser, his voice covered by the roaring of the motor. "Let it go for now."

There is a barking of Klaxons and screaming of orders as the platoon prepares to depart. Herded by Sergeant Said, the scouts climb two-by-two into the back of their Bedford troop transport lorries. Taking its place protectively at the head of the four-vehicle column, the Saladin steams out of the fuel compound with oily black smoke gushing from its exhaust pipe. Still lounging on the Saladin's turret, Napalm waves merrily as they pass. The command Land-Rover is second in the column and after Ali Rashidi swings into line, the two ancient Bedfords bring up the rear, backfiring as the drivers race their engines to keep them going.

The racket is incredible. "We aren't exactly going to sneak up on anybody," complains the Adviser, but Woodward just shakes his head helplessly. The captain is shouting instructions into a hand-held microphone as they clear the Um al Gwarif perimeter checkpoint.

"There's no danger!" proclaims Captain Fenwich.

"There is." The Adviser lowers his voice so that only Sergeant Major Woodward can hear. "Something is up there on the *jebel*, waiting for us."

"You didn't have to come," Woodward whispers back.

"Yes, I did. I took the seventh vow."

"What is the seventh vow?"

"It's something we talk about in the L.R.R.G.," the Adviser murmurs. "It means you have to go wherever they send you even if you're afraid."

"What are the first six vows?"

"They don't exist. They just provide cover for the seventh," he says glumly. Here we go, he thinks.

Hi-diddle-diddle.

Right up the middle.

A few minutes before ten, they reach the Midway Road and the outskirts of the city of Salalah. The coastal plain looks so calm and pleasant that it seems difficult to imagine that there is any danger of enemy activity. Harvest time is near; on either side of the dirt track, men and donkeys are laboring in cultivated fields.

"What are they growing?" the Adviser inquires.

"Alfalfa," says John Woodward.

"You must be the only agronomist in the world who can't identify alfalfa!" Bernard Fenwich extracts a pack of king-sized Rothman cigarettes from his breast pocket. He lights one with a wooden sulphur match, cupping his hands against the wind.

"Sergeant Woodward has explained that I'm not actually an agronomist," the Adviser protests mildly. Mingling with the exhaust from the Saladin, the tobacco smoke infiltrates his nostrils, and he suddenly realizes that he craves a cigarette. Badly.

How long has it been? Nine months since Christmas, when Ellen had convinced him to kick the habit, just after they had fled from Peter and the house on Walton Street and gone to live together in a tiny flat on the Woodstock Road.

"You're ten years older than I am." She broached the subject with a precise actuarial observation. "And I want to love you as long as I live. So you have to cooperate by living as long as possible, which means giving up those filthy fags. Whenever you want to smoke, eat a pot of my homemade Bulgarian yogurt instead. Bulgarians live forever.

67

The hell with immortal Bulgarians, he thinks. I want a cigarette. He leans forward, ready to ask Bernard Fenwich for a cigarette, but then draws back, recalling the man's rudeness. I'll be damned if I'll ask him for anything, he thinks resentfully. When we stop I'll bum a smoke from one of the men.

The cloud cover is lingering at about a thousand feet. There is mist blowing in off the water but they can see the menacing hugeness of the *jebel,* not far to the North. At this point the Salalah plain seems only a few miles deep. According to Mahmoud, the 9 June Regiment intended to exploit this fact by moving down the mountain under cover of darkness, debouching onto the plain in several places in order to prevent the British from shifting reinforcements up and down the coast.

Balancing his compass on one knee and smoothing the map out on the other, the Adviser orients himself as they approach the Midway Road, an ancient macadam strip with more potholes than paving. A normal compass does not work well in a vehicle, but he manages to work out roughly where he is. Just as he expects the convoy to turn right and north on the Midway Road and head toward the al-Qara foothills, the Saladin turns south toward the Arabian Sea.

John Woodward is puzzled as well. "Captain? Where are we headed?"

"I've an informant down on the beach," Captain Fenwich retorts. "I want a word with him before we head up the Midway Road."

A mile later they crest a slight rise and see the Arabian Sea and a broad yellow beach. The surf is high. Fishermen in khaki shorts and checkered shirts are landing a small jolly boat. As soon as the prow rubs across the sand, they jump knee-deep into the water and begin to haul a net through the waves to the beach. A flock of heron stands opportunistically nearby, watching for stray fish. Patiently, a black flamingo circles overhead, sleek wings motionless as he crests an updraft of hot air.

It is calm and beautiful. For a moment, the Adviser fantasizes a scene of art deco holiday hotels with pink stucco and sprawling verandas and beach umbrellas and waiters in white shirts bringing drinks to thin, bronzed, expensive women in string bikinis.

There are no resorts in South Arabia, he reminds himself.

Maybe I should buy land in Dhofar! Someday the British will win the war and then there will be a Holiday Inn here.

A short distance down the beach, the convoy rumbles into a small native village—a dozen frail frame houses of light wood and woven palm fronds. Women are standing around a well, wearing brightly colored print dresses with black cotton *abayas* over their heads. As the convoy shambles to a halt, they cover their mouths and noses with their shawls, gazing at the soldiers with brown, curious, frightened eyes.

Open to the sun and sky, there is a one-tree school in a nearby field. Beneath a coconut palm, an aged Koranic master squats on his haunches. The children sit cross-legged around him, small boys in front and a scattering of little girls in back.

Seeing the convoy, the boys abandon their lessons and come rushing up to gape at the Saladin. They are all wearing the standard white cotton *dishdasha,* a garment that begins as a man's shirt and falls to the ankles like a dress. Somber in their black gowns with white embroidery and silver necklaces, three bold girls wander down to stare at the Land-Rover. They all have silver rings in their ears and the palms of their hands are rouged with henna.

With dark, serious faces, they regard the Adviser, who smiles at them. I would have liked being a father, he thinks. My child might have been a little girl. She might have been beautiful like Ellen . . . or homely like me. It wouldn't have mattered.

"Wait here!" Captain Fenwich jumps down from the Land-Rover and takes Ali Rashidi with him to translate as he strides over to the coconut tree to consult with the schoolmaster. Startled, the little girls hold hands and run away.

The Saladin's motor goes silent. There is a moment of quiet, except for the wind and the sounds of heron squawking excitedly as sardines and mackerel and small sharks come spilling out of the nets. The men are clubbing the larger fish to death and stacking them on a cart while teenage boys are organizing the sardines in rows on the sand to dry in the sun.

"That SEP told me his people use dried sardines as cattle fodder," the Adviser rekindles the conversation.

It is still hazy, but there is a glare off the water, and John Woodward takes a khaki field cap out of his pocket and pulls it down over his eyes. The Land-Rover is cramped, and the sergeant major arranges his long legs over the back of Ali Rashidi's seat. "It's Dhofar's one great claim to originality. During World War Two, my father passed through Oman and came home talking about a god-awful place called Dhofar where they fed cows on sardines. That was the first time I heard of the province."

"I first ran across it when I was studying Greek," the Adviser recalls. "There is an old mariner's manual from the first century A.D. called *The Periples of the Erythraean Sea*. The author called it the Frankincense Coast. In those days Dhofar was rich."

"What were you doing studying Greek? Unusual training for an intelligence officer."

"I spent my university years in a Roman Catholic seminary." The Adviser usually keeps this embarrassing autobiographical fact to himself, but he is becoming comfortable with John Woodward.

"Studying to be a priest?"

"That was the idea at the time. I quit before I took Holy Orders."

"What made you think you wanted to be a clergyman?"

The Adviser sighs quietly, half-wishing he had never raised the issue. "In a Catholic orphanage, the nuns propagandize you relentlessly about becoming a priest. I left the seminary when I discovered how much I liked women."

"I am familiar with the problem." Woodward chuckles. "You know, every intelligence officer I ever met was an ex-priest or a randy defrocked curate or something. What is it with you people?"

"We have an unusually well-developed capacity for accepting the improbable," the Adviser jokes. "If you can believe in the Immaculate Conception, you can believe in American foreign policy."

"And do you?"

"What? The Immaculate Conception?"

"No, your foreign policy. And ours."

"I used to," the Adviser admits. "Fervently. Then after a while, it just became a job. We're on this side. The people up on the *jebel* are on the other side. I asked that prisoner what the *adoo* believed in and he said they pretended to be Marxists so that the Russians would give them guns. What they really want is for all the foreigners to go away so they can get on with feeding sardines to their cows."

"You must believe in something," Woodward objects quietly.

"I once did. I don't know anymore. Maybe this is the stage in history where it's become a habit for all of us. Pretending to believe in things."

Down on the beach, there are sudden shouts and the alarmed squawking of small birds as the black flamingo dives boldly into the center of the net, seizing a silver fish with his beak. With a desperate flapping, the huge bird tries to regain the air with his prize, but the fishermen furiously attack him with their clubs and smash his wings.

With a shudder the Adviser closes his eyes, wishing to see no more. I have already seen too much, he thinks.

Sitting comfortably in the shade of the coconut tree, Captain Fenwich spends a solid thirty minutes chatting with his informant.

Sweltering in the back seat of the Land-Rover, the Technical Intelligence Adviser waits with diminishing patience. He whiles away the time getting to know John Woodward, who has a house in York, a historic thatched cottage he intends to restore during his retirement. They talk about the pleasures of hiking on the North Yorkshire moors, and the six best brands of north country brown ale. And about women, with the sergeant major admitting to one previous divorce. He is filled with gloom over the prospects of being jettisoned by the second Mrs. Woodward, a comely younger woman named Jenny.

At eleven, the Adviser notes the time and feels his temper rise. I bring them solid reasons to fear that their position is in danger, he fumes. After some hesitation, the commanding officer correctly decides to dispatch a scout unit along the presumed axis of enemy attack. Instead of obeying this simple and specific order, the scout commander displays his contempt for my information by wasting half the morning interviewing an elderly schoolmaster.

"Is this a deliberate insult?"

"Yes, but it's aimed as much at me as you," Woodward comments dourly. "Our lad Bernie doesn't much fancy having either a brigade sergeant major or an American spy looking over his shoulder."

"What's he got against you?"

"I upset Bernie's notions about the natural order of officers and enlisted men. He has a third-class degree from some vile polytechnic in London and I got a first at York University."

"What the hell are you doing in the Army with an honors degree from a good university?"

"I read cultural anthropology at York. Unfortunately, knowing a lot about native cultures and folk rites and primitive peoples didn't get me a job on civvy street when I took my degree. We still had National Service in those days and when I was called to the colors, my father got me assigned to the Yorkshire Fusiliers, where he'd been a sergeant major himself under Nigel's father. He maneuvered me into a job as Nigel's batman and somehow the Fusiliers became home."

"At the very least, you could have got a commission."

"People talked about it from time to time"—Woodward suddenly seems evasive—"but my father spent his life teaching me to be a sergeant major. When he died, I thought about applying for a commission, but . . . I don't know. Working-class people who become officers are usually misfits like Bernard Fenwich."

They both fall silent, watching the captain get to his feet, shake hands with the elderly schoolmaster, and make his way back to the Land-Rover.

"No prob!" He avoids their eyes. Ali Rashidi starts the Land-Rover's big engine and wheels them around to follow the Saladin back up the Midway Road.

"That was your big informant?" The Adviser points at the schoolmaster. The children have returned to their lessons now. The old man has opened his book and is once again reading to his pupils, one finger inching from right to left as he follows the words on the page, his other hand describing arabesques in the hot coastal air.

Without turning his head, Fenwich nods. "People tell him things. He and I have a quiet word from time to time."

"A quiet word?" The Adviser's patience fragments. "You slip

discreetly into his village with two four-ton trucks, one Land-Rover, forty heavily armed soldiers, and a Saladin? And then have a quiet word?"

"What are you trying to say?"

"Where did you learn your intelligence-gathering techniques? Everybody south of Baghdad must know you're in bed with this guy, and nobody is going to tell him anything they don't want you to know."

"He's been reliable in the past!"

"Really? And today what tantalizing secrets did he whisper in your willing ear?"

The convoy is picking up speed now, whizzing north on the Midway Road about thirty miles per hour, and Captain Fenwich is forced to turn in his seat and shout. "He confirmed what I've learned from other sources. The *jebel* is quiet, and there are no reports of *adoo* activity."

"Except for the antiaircraft missile they shot at my plane and that Katyushka attack on the airport and the saboteurs who blew up your commo station at Mirbat! Jesus, what does it take to make you guys nervous? A burning bush? A voice from the heavens?"

"Look, Captain America, the *adoo* are just kissing us good-bye, using up leftover ammunition," Fenwich growls. "There is a handful of hardcore fanatics out there and we can expect to have sporadic terrorism for some years to come. But I've got informants all over the *jebel,* and if there were a significant force of enemy troops in the area, I would have heard about it a long time ago. Now sit back and enjoy the view. Because that's all you're going to see today!"

The Advisor glowers, but for the moment, there seems to be no alternative. Bernie Fenwich lights another cigarette and relays his position to Um al Gwarif over the Land-Rover's radio link. The Adviser realizes that he is going to have to start being nice to Captain Fenwich if he ever intends to bum a cigarette.

He distracts himself by looking at the scenery. The Midway Road skirts the edges of Salalah, taking them past row after row of mud-brick buildings, mostly covered with white stucco. The brightly painted windows are all barred against life's uncertainties and shuttered against the midday heat. The roof tops are uniformly flat, with spouts emerging from the balustrades to carry away water from the monsoon rains.

"Not very many people around," the Adviser observes. A few heavily veiled women trudge by, always in pairs, their faces averted from the passing convoy.

"Maybe it's the heat," Woodward speculates. "And we could get some rain in the early afternoon."

A moment later they are back in open country, climbing through the lush green al-Qara foothills. It is an impressive landscape. The Adviser wonders why good governments seem to flourish in boring, featureless land while great scenery stimulates dictatorship and civil war.

They ride for a long time. Captain Fenwich stays in periodic contact with Um al Gwarif, and while the static makes it difficult to hear from the backseat, it seems clear that nothing very exciting is happening anywhere in Dhofar. The first and second regiments have moved into positions at the foot of the *jebel,* screening Salalah and Um al Gwarif, but their forward patrols have discovered nothing.

Did I get it wrong? In anguish, the Adviser prepares himself for professional disgrace. In the after-action critique, he thinks, the Dhofar Brigade headquarters staff will observe that I was sent down here to deliver some maps, not introduce a whole new strategic dimension to the war. My chum Bernie will inform the Americans in Muscat that I have exceeded my instructions and the Embassy will send a rocket to L.R.R.G. headquarters.

The Admiral, having decided after my last disaster that I required a therapeutic desert, will now determine that I need an office in Washington where my creative urges can be kept under control.

Death. A desk in the basement of the Pentagon is death. I will remain a GS-14 until the end of my days. Buy a town house in Arlington. They will put other people's reports in my in-box, and I will initial them and put them into my out-box. I will date a succession of increasingly elderly secretaries and drink heavily in the evening. . . .

* * *

Suddenly the macadam ends. The Saladin kicks up an enormous cloud of dust, making them all cough. The earth all around them is bright red, and the ground is rough, all gullies and ravines, seared and torn by erosion.

"Right, people, time to get a little careful!" In a supremely casual tone, Captain Fenwich clicks on his microphone, instructing the driver of the Saladin to decrease speed. Ali Rashidi downshifts into third, creeping closer to the armored vehicle for protection, and the two Bedford troop transports close up ranks.

"What's going on?" The Adviser feels a chill of apprehension. Sergeant Major Woodward is checking the magazine on his jimpy, and Captain Fenwich is standing on the seat and leaning over the hood to feed a cartridge belt into the breech of the Browning automatic rifle.

"This is the point on the *jebel* where the population begins to change," Woodward explains quickly. "The coastal people are regular Omanese Arabs who are mostly loyal to the government, at least since the present sultan took over. Up here, you find al-Qara tribal people and even on good days the al-Qara are never really happy to see us. Look, there's a few."

Following Woodward's outstretched finger, the Adviser looks to the west and sees three men gathering twigs and branches in a field of camel thorn. They are thinner than the well-fed Arab scouts, and instead of the standard *dishdasha,* they are barechested, wearing only a short kilt around their loins. The wood collectors ignore the convoy as it passes them.

For a long time they roar up the *jebel,* encountering neither local Arabs nor al-Qara tribesmen. The land is becoming progressively steeper and less even. Colonel Fine had said something about keeping the Midway Road open so that the al-Qara folk could deliver their cattle to the Salalah market, but no one seems to be moving anything up or down the road today.

"If this is enemy country, then maybe we should slow down," complains the Adviser. The metal in his environment is making his compass crazy. It is now difficult even to read his map because the Land-Rover is bounding from rut to rut as it groans up the steep incline in second gear. The mud track twists and turns, following the irregular contours of the mountainside.

The road divides again and again, with perfectly plausible alternative tracks going off on either side, but they are going so fast the Adviser cannot work out which is the main trunk. And the terrain around them is incredibly rough, making it hard to find visual reference points.

"What's the matter, Captain America? Nervous?" Fenwich grins.

I'm lost, the Adviser admits to himself. I could orient myself easily enough if he would slow down enough to let me use my compass and read my map, but at this speed I'll never figure out where the hell we are. Are the others lost?

Ali Rashidi has concentrated all his energy upon clinging to the back of the Saladin, hardly glancing left or right. Sergeant Major John Woodward looks worried and keeps scanning the horizon with his binoculars, but Captain Fenwich—who after all is the Dhofar Brigade intelligence officer—seems supremely unconcerned.

"Why are we going so fast?" the Adviser demands.

"Makes it harder for snipers," says Fenwich.

"How do we know where we're going? Have they got a map in the Saladin?"

"Napalm knows the way!"

"Napalm?" the American screams. "You've got four vehicles and forty men roaring through enemy territory being led by a raving lunatic?"

"Look, he may be a nutter, but he knows this mountain like the back of his hand," Fenwich explains. "And he's not as crazy as all that, y'know. You tell him where you want to go and he gets you there. Besides, you're the only one who thinks this is enemy territory. Seen any *adoo* recently?"

"We've seen hardly anyone," the Adviser counters. "And it's making me nervous. Is the *jebel* always this deserted? We should be deep inside al-Qara country by now, but we haven't seen a tribesman for some time."

"Just as well," Fenwich comments dryly.

"The al-Qara have devils in their hearts, Captain America," Ali Rashidi confides, mistaking Fenwich's insult for an honorific. "They are communistical people!"

"Until a few years ago, the *adoo* got most of their hardware from Chairman Mao," Captain Fenwich adds. "But the Chinks lost interest, and now we're seeing more conventional Warsaw Pact gear being filtered through Iraq. There's no question about the *adoo* political orientation."

This is nonsense, and the Adviser feels compelled to say so. "Revolutionaries get their hardware where they can, and when you go into rebellion against Great Britain, you can't shop at Harrods anymore! In Latin America, the right-wing death squads all have Russian weapons. The Soviets sell them to Egypt, who lose them in battle to the Israelis, who sell them to anybody with hard cash. So you don't need to be a Marxist-Leninist to own a Kalashnikov. Look at your own platoon!"

"Under interrogation, the *adoo* routinely confess to being communist."

"A couple of days with your famous five techniques and a prisoner will admit to being a Martian if that's what you want to hear. I got the impression from that SEP that the al-Qara are more nationalist than communist."

"If they're not communists, why are they rebelling?"

The vehicle lurches and almost slides off the road. The Adviser clings grimly to the roll bar as he pursues the argument. "They're tired of living poor in a repressive dictatorship, I suppose. If the old sultan had taken better care of them, they might have become loyal subjects."

"What's that supposed to mean?"

"Well, I've only been in Oman for a week, but the place is pretty clearly a dismal dictatorship. Sultan Qabus doesn't permit political parties or elections or civil rights. If you're out here to build democracy . . ."

Fenwich raises his hands in an elaborate display of irritation. "This is exactly where you sodding Americans always get it wrong! You tell your men that they are fighting to defend democracy. The moment they discover that they are risking their lives to save some dictator's arse, they stop fighting and you lose the war."

"That's simplistic!"

"I'm a simple bloke! Look, your English soldier is a professional and we carry out British government policy. Her Majesty desires that we come here and shoot these Arab gentlemen. Last year, we went to Ulster and shot some Irish gentlemen. Next year we go back to Germany and prepare to shoot some Russian gentlemen. It has nothing to do with building democracy."

It is taking all the Adviser's energy just to hang on to the Land-Rover, and he searches for a dignified way to disengage. "That's pretty cynical, Fenwich. I'm not sure I could live in your world."

"It's the real world, Captain America, and you Yanks aren't comfortable outside of Disneyland. England has lasted a thousand years because it has always produced men who were willing to go out and kill for it! Not your fake democracy or civil bloody rights or MacDonald's fucking cheeseburgers, but England!"

"Now listen, you son-of-a-bitch!" The Adviser leans forward, holding onto the door frame of the bouncing vehicle with one hand—"I've taken just about as much insolence from you as . . ."

"Is there going to be a Disneyland in a thousand years, Yank?" Bernie Fenwich is delighted to have infuriated his guest. "There will still be an England, but for my money North America will be a rubble heap of plastic trash! Administered by Canadians!"

"Look, I don't know where we are!" John Woodward suddenly interrupts, trying to see the TechIntel map the Adviser holds on his lap.

"Every time you bastards get into a fight with the Germans, we have to come over and save your asses!" The Adviser relinquishes the map. It contains classified information that Woodward is not cleared to see, but he is too agitated to care.

"First you wait until all the serious fighting is done. Then you buggers turn up and claim it was you who won!"

"Gentlemen!" shouts John Woodward. "Where are we?"

Shaking his head, the Adviser reclaims the chart and peers at it. The dust and smoke from the Saladin make it difficult to see and his throat is raw from shouting. "I thought Napalm was supposed to be infallible! You guys keep telling me this is your war and your corner of the desert. So we don't really know where we are?"

"I'm not precisely sure," Woodward confesses. "This is the first time I've been up the Midway Road in a couple of years and it looks all different. Captain, I wonder if Napalm hasn't taken us off the main road?"

"Impossible!" snaps Fenwich, but he seems uncertain. "I've been by here a dozen times. There's a big village just ahead."

"Look, we must be right . . ." The Adviser studies the chart, feeling panicky. "Could we slow down? Aren't we . . . no, we passed that point, uh, did anyone see a big, deep *wa'adi* off to the left?"

"We passed the *wa'adi*. So if we're here, then maybe Captain Fenwich's big village is Bait al Muktar?" Woodward is looking over the Adviser's shoulder, and he reaches down to indicate a tiny spot on the map.

"We're nowhere near Bait al Muktar!" Bernie Fenwich asserts. "And what difference would it make?"

Woodward shakes his head angrily. "With the greatest respect, sir, if our American guest does turn out to be right about the location of the Nine June Regiment, then we'll be arriving at their headquarters in time for lunch."

"What?" Fenwich is confused. "Rashi, is this where we took that *adoo* prisoner?"

"I am not knowing, sir!" Abruptly aware that his Anglo-Saxon leaders are lost, Ali Rashidi stamps on the brake and the Land-Rover careens to a halt, its back wheels skidding through the mud.

"Why are you stopping?" Fenwich thunders, but the two Bedfords are forced to stop as well, jamming on their brakes and lurching to a halt. They have been tailgating all morning and the Adviser looks over his shoulder in time to see the rear Bedford go into a skid as its driver struggles to avoid a collision. The four-tonner skates for a few yards and then slides off the road. It remains upright, but its left rear wheel is no longer touching the ground. The Adviser sees the big wheel spinning freely, a foot from the bottom of the ditch.

"It's off the road!" Fenwich glares at the Adviser as if this were somehow the deliberate doing of the Long Range Reconnaissance Group. "Bloody hell! We'll be an hour pulling it out of that ditch!"

Ali Rashidi is unapologetic. "It is time to be praying, sir," he reminds the unfaithful that one of the five daily prayers demanded by the Moslem religion is supposed to take place at noon.

"You and your sodding prayers!" Captain Fenwich picks up the microphone and hails the Saladin. "Hold up, people! We'll pause here for prayers and lunch."

"Is this a good place to stop?" the Adviser asks. Ahead of them, the Saladin reverses directions with a catastrophic grinding of gears, and he can see Napalm grinning as he stands on the hood of the armored vehicle.

"We don't seem to have a lot of options, do we?" Fenwich is furious. "Looking for a place with hot-and-cold running water, were you? Howard bloody Johnson's?"

They do not have much choice, although the Adviser regards this as the worst prayer-and-picnic stop he has ever seen. It is still not clear where they are. The road is narrow at this point and twists up and off to the west so that they cannot see what lies immediately ahead of them. There is a dense forest of young pine to the right, providing an ideal ambush site.

They have a clear field of fire only to the southwest where the terrain falls away into a large pasture. The grass is closely cropped as if sheep or goats had been eating there. There are no animals here today and no sign of human habitation except for a handful of huts about a mile in the distance.

As soon as all the motors have gone silent, Captain Fenwich calls Dhofar Brigade Headquarters at Um al Gwarif on the radio, using a pair of earphones for privacy. He fails to mention that he has a vehicle off the road and simply announces that his Scout Platoon has encountered nothing suspicious and is stopping for tea at Mile Twelve of the Midway Road.

The Adviser calculates that they passed Mile Twelve several miles back but Fenwich is consulting a British Army ordinance map and the American decides to avoid another nationalist shouting match. Having communicated his position, Fenwich listens silently for a moment, and then turns to the Adviser.

"Well, Captain America, your great Dien Bien Phu Offensive is a bust so far!" His contempt is withering as he relays the news from Um al Gwarif. "The RAF have a couple of Skyvans up, and they've seen nothing. The First and Second Regiments have both been patrolling aggressively without encountering a trace of enemy activity. We're back on line with Muscat, and they tell us the whole country is quiet. Did you forget to tell the Popular Front they were supposed to be attacking today?"

"I will be delighted to be proven wrong. You seem to have some difficulty mastering the concept, but I am actually on your side."

"The way things are going, I'd rather you were on the other side!" Fenwich stalks off to inspect his disabled Bedford.

Feeling stiff and battered from the violent ride up the *jebel,* the Adviser climbs down out of the Land-Rover and stretches. With a deep sigh, Woodward lays his jimpy on the seat and jumps down on the other side, doing a quick round of calisthenics to loosen up his lanky frame.

"The next time he calls me Captain America I'm going to shoot him," says the Adviser.

"Well, you could call him 'Bernie.' That's what Colonel Fine calls him, and he hates it."

"Our friend Bernie seems to take a relaxed view of security," the Adviser observes. "There could be an enemy unit around the next corner! Does he intend to post perimeter guards or would that be considered unsporting?"

"He'll let the men pray first." Woodward seems embarrassed by the officer's behavior. "Omanese troops find it difficult to comprehend why they should guard against the unexpected whilst communicating with their omniscient creator."

"What? Look, anyone could creep up on us!"

Woodward laughs. "You were once in a seminary. Think theologically! From the Islamic perspective, no one could harm us without God's permission. These are primitive Moslems, and they believe absolutely in an omnipotent intelligence up there who is deciding right now whether or not the Scout Platoon will be ambushed today. Hence it makes more sense to implore him not to let it happen than to trust in a fallible perimeter defense."

The Adviser groans; in his experience, the deity who watches over the Defense Department is prone to periods of transcendental underachievement. But Captain Fenwich's troopers pour confidently out of the two Bedfords and spread their reed prayer mats out on the dirt road. A few require a cigarette before consulting with the Almighty, but Ali Rashidi quickly orients them northwest toward Mecca.

Napalm joins the scouts as the prayers begin. He does not speak, even to murmur his favorite word, but he performs the complicated Islamic choreography of squatting, standing, bowing, kneeling, and pressing of forehead to the ground. When the homage to Allah is completed, Napalm sits down cheerfully in the middle of the bivouac area, smiling beatifically as the scouts contend for the honor of sitting next to him and sharing their food.

The scouts all seem to have brought the same basic lunch, a circular envelope of unleavened *pitta* bread stuffed with ground beef and peppers. There is a big wooden box filled with dates for quick sugar, and a bucket of hard-boiled eggs is making the rounds. One of the lance corporals is passing out dessert, chunks of *halwa,* an incredibly sweet fudge made of ghee, starch, brown sugar, cardomom, and honey. Peter Reston's Arab friends were always bringing the stuff around to the house in Oxford.

"There are British Army field rations for us in the Land-Rover if you want a nosh," Woodward mentions.

"No, my stomach is still grappling with that British Army breakfast." The Adviser shakes his head, more concerned about finding himself on his chart. He turns to the southwest and points to the circle of houses at the far end of the pasture. "John, if we are where I think we are, that settlement down there has recently been abandoned."

"Is that what your satellite says?"

"You're not supposed to know about our satellites!"

"I'm afraid we've been wicked." John Woodward smiles. "Down in Um al Gwarif we create a potent brew called McGinty's Brown Ale, which we once administered to your predecessor in large quantities. After an imperial gallon or two, he got pissed as a newt and told us all about Big Bird."

"You'd better have a cold one ready for me if we ever get down off this mountain!" The Adviser laughs. "Okay, all summer long, Big Bird has been detecting heat from that little village, consistent with human occupation and maybe some livestock. In last night's Big Bird run, the place went cool, as if everybody took a walk. Assuming we've got the right place."

Looking over his shoulder, Woodward glances at the TechIntel chart. "Look at those contour lines! If that is the right village, we should be able to stand in the middle of it and see the ocean. At least that would tell us where we are. Do you want to go down and have a look?"

"Yeah. Because if we really are here, then Bait al Muktar is right around the corner, and Bait al Muktar got real hot recently. Let me borrow your field glasses." The Adviser scans the horizon attentively. There does not appear to be any danger, since the settlement consists only of six huts in a rough circle and one larger building, probably a barn, some distance away. There are no trees or bushes anywhere near and no sign of people or animals.

"Do you think we need an escort?"

The correct answer ought to be yes, but the Adviser's instincts rebel and he shakes his head. L.R.R.G. officers typically work alone. Woodward is clearly a soldier's soldier, but a gaggle of Bernie Fenwich's troopers would increase their visibility without decreasing their vulnerability. "No, let's go by ourselves."

In fact, neither man senses danger. No competent enemy would take refuge in a hut in the middle of an empty field with no concealment or means of escape.

Woodward goes through the formality of asking Fenwich's permission, but Bernie is preoccupied with the task of getting four tons of Bedford back on the road. The Yorkshireman returns with a smile. "Alright then, it's going to be Captain America and Sergeant Dauntless, alone against the Popular Front!"

"Listen, Sergeant Dauntless, intelligence officers are not expected to be heroes. If we meet a three-year-old *adoo* girl with a frisky puppy, we run away."

Woodward chuckles as they climb through the ditch on the right-hand side of the road and walk downhill through the empty pasture. "Whatever you say, but you strike me as a man with a fair amount of combat experience."

The Adviser shakes his head. "I've been in combat zones often enough, but even when I was on active duty with the Army

I did intelligence work. And I've been trying to avoid combat situations ever since I shifted to civilian status with the Long Range Reconnaissance Group."

"Doesn't your L.R.R.G. do covert operations for the Department of Defense?"

"Once in a while, but mostly we just take long walks." The Adviser is actually telling the truth, although he finds it an uncomfortable sensation. "We got our start back in the early sixties when a SAMOS satellite produced photographs of a huge hole being dug by a Soviet team in the Algerian Sahara. The photo interpretation people couldn't figure out what the imagery meant. In frustration, a Defense Department analyst went on vacation to Algeria with his civilian passport and walked out into the desert until he found the mysterious hole in the sand."

"An ICBM site?"

"No, the Russians were helping the Algerians dig a well for water. Our guy said he was a hydraulics engineer from Winnipeg. They gave him a guided tour and let him take pictures with a Kodak. We've been pretending to be Canadians ever since. Nobody hates Canadians. Anyway, the Secretary of Defense created the L.R.R.G. to go and look at things that satellites couldn't identify. Then we got involved in advising people like you on how to use TechIntel. And sometimes we do covert intelligence collection operations when there's something of purely military significance and the CIA can't be bothered."

"Where did you learn your Arabic?" Woodward inquires casually. The Adviser is vaguely aware that he is being pumped. For the first time, it occurs to him that an English sergeant major with an honors degree in anthropology must have spent some of his career in intelligence.

"I've been in the Middle East a number of times before, but I studied Koranic Arabic last year at Oxford." This is more classified information, but the Adviser is proud of his Oxford master's degree.

"Since when does Uncle Sam send spies to Oxford? Or were you there to keep an eye on the Greenham Common situation?"

Woodward is on the target with his first shot and the Adviser is stunned at the quickness of his intuition.

"I can't comment on what I was doing," he hedges. "It is true that the Pentagon was nervous about the possibility of terrorism or sabotage developing out of the fringes of the Committee for Nuclear Disarmament."

"Seems a little paranoid." Woodward snorts. "CND was always a peaceful movement, and the protestors at Greenham were all women, weren't they? How could they have interfered with the mighty United States Air Force?"

"Well, the awful truth is that the Peace Women had paralyzed that base. Cruise missiles are designed to be towed on mobile launchers to secret locations in the countryside where the Russians can't find them. With the women blocking all the exits, the Air Force could never test the system, and when they did get a missile team out, the women trailed it and compromised its deployment assignment. Nobody wanted to say so out loud but CND had completely neutralized Greenham Common, and the Pentagon was desperate for information."

"So you . . ."

"It was a complicated situation." The Adviser realizes that he has already said too much. "But . . . uh, well, I loved Oxford. The countryside is perfect for hiking."

Woodward backs off, and for a few minutes they walk along silently. The day is becoming a little cooler. A *kareef* is blowing from the south, a moist monsoon wind off the Indian Ocean. It is easy going downhill over even ground. The Adviser notices goat turds among the weeds, but they are dry, suggesting that the flocks have been gone for several days.

Four hundred feet above them a thick-bodied bird circles slowly, disturbed in his search for lunch by their intrusion. It feels lonely here, as if there is not another human being on the planet.

"So you really like hiking?" Woodward rekindles the conversation, his jimpy slung carelessly over his shoulder.

"Yeah, I love it. I'm even enjoying this." The Adviser thinks immediately of those long Sunday strolls with Ellen, walking up the Oxford Canal from Port Meadow or along the Cherwell River from Magdallen Bridge.

"So am I. Listen, come visit me in Yorkshire when we're finished here. Come in the spring, and we'll hike over the North Yorkshire Moors."

"I'd like that. I, uh, I really would like to come." The American is moved by the offer, suddenly realizing that Woodward could be a chum. Life in the L.R.R.G. made it difficult to accumulate friends, at least friends on the outside. Field officers like himself customarily got to know the Reconnaissance Group headquarters people in Washington and London, but staffers were a different breed, all gossip and rank consciousness, angling for the next promotion and screwing each other's secretaries. Field officers like him were habitual loners, changing countries frequently as new assignments came along.

"Good. Consider yourself invited."

"Do you have a lot of buddies in Yorkshire?"

"Not many," Woodward confesses. "In the British Army, it's difficult to make friends with civilians because you move every few years. And a sergeant major is always an isolated figure in a regiment. You make the officers nervous, especially if you have a degree and you have too much power over the other ranks to make any friends among the enlisted men. How about you? Are you a social animal?"

The Adviser shakes his head. "Most Technical Intelligence Advisers my age have long since taken desk jobs back in Washington or at one of the bigger embassies. I've always liked field assignments, but they keep you moving around so much you never get to know anyone very well."

"Are you married? Or is that a secret?"

"No, I guess I'm a perennial bachelor. When I was living in Oxford, I considered leaving the Reconnaissance Group to marry an Englishwoman," he blurts out. "But it didn't . . . ah, materialize."

"Perhaps she'll give you a second chance? Bring her up to romantic Yorkshire and I'll give the two of you a room with a large, soft bed and a view of the River Ouse."

"There isn't going to be a second chance." The Adviser quickly shifts the conversation away from himself. "How about you? Do you think your Jenny will have you back when you come marching home?"

Woodward sighs. "It doesn't look like it. When I told her I was going to come back to Oman with Nigel, she broke every glass in the kitchen and stormed out in a fury."

"Did you go after her? Try and make her see reason?"

"No. Jenny is twenty years my junior, and she comes from a good upper middle class family. In fact, she's distantly related to Dick Barnet, our surgeon here, and he's distantly related to the royal family. I always worried that Jenny would wake up one morning, realize she was married to a middle-aged enlisted man, and leave me for somebody younger and more acceptable socially. I guess . . . I've never said this to anyone before, but looking back, I wonder if I wasn't playing mind games. As things stand, I can tell myself that she left me because I chose to do my duty to the Army and help my friend Nigel through a difficult period. And not because I was getting old."

"You're not getting old!" How easy it is to be sage about other people's marriages, the Adviser thinks. "Do you miss her?"

"Yes. We used to have wonderful conversations. The bedroom business was pretty wonderful too, but I miss just talking to someone clever. Now tell me about this Englishwoman of yours. Was it primarily a physical relationship? Or could you actually communicate with her?"

The Adviser feels his chest growing tight. "We never talked as much as we might have. Because of my work, I could never be honest with her. But I loved her . . . a lot, I guess. A lot."

There is a moment's silence. "It makes me wonder what could have gone wrong for the two of you," says Woodward. He slings the jimpy off his shoulder as they approach the first hut. "Some night I'll fill you up with McGinty's Brown Ale and get the whole sordid story."

No, you won't, the Adviser thinks, but it is time to concentrate on the faint possibility that there could be danger here. He gets the lady pistol out and switches off the safety. He feels silly, stalking gun in hand through an empty village.

They pause at the entrance to the first hut, a round structure about thirty feet in diameter. It is cunningly constructed. The al-Qara native builders first raised a short circular stone wall around a medium-sized tree, and then fastened the tree's branches to the wall to serve as rafters. The roof is expertly thatched and thick enough to keep the rain out.

His machine gun at the ready, Woodward ducks inside and the Adviser quickly follows him. The little house is surprisingly neat, with a well-swept flagstone floor and bunks made of wood and straw matting and big earthenware jugs for water.

"This looks regularly inhabited. I wonder where everyone is."

"We don't know much about the al-Qara lifestyle," Woodward admits. "Some of the *jebel* people are settled agronomists, and others are semi-nomadic pastoralists. These villagers might have temporarily moved their goats farther up the mountain to find better pasture land."

"There's no trace of violence," the Adviser notes as they stroll back out into the sunlight. "And no articles of clothing left behind, which suggests an orderly departure. When our infrared imagery showed that the village was cold, I thought immediately of *adoo* activity. It never occurred to me that it might have been a case of normal migration!"

"Look, there's the sea!" Woodward suddenly points southeast. "That means we really were on the main trunk of the Midway Road after all. Napalm didn't let us down."

The Adviser sees a faint shimmer of blue in the distance, about fifteen miles away. "What it is about seeing the ocean that always makes you feel good?"

"I don't know. It's beautiful here. The al-Qara could be so happy if they didn't fight all the time. I wonder if we're going to see any action today."

"It doesn't look like it." The Adviser sits down on the step of the empty hut and unfolds his TechIntel map. With his lensatic compass, he begins shooting azimuths to all the terrain features he can identify, trying to work out the precise grid reference for the abandoned village. "But at least we know where we are."

"I'll see if I can find some artifacts for my collection." The anthropologist in Woodward is surging to the surface, and he sets off to investigate the other five huts in the circle.

"We're going to get rained on in another minute," the Adviser predicts, but Woodward waves at him cheerfully and disappears.

After a few minutes of close concentration, the Adviser concludes that he has been right about their location while the wretched Captain Fenwich is at least three miles wrong. On the other hand, he reflects, I seem to have been thoroughly wrong about everything else. Wherever the 9 June Regiment is, they don't seem to be here.

Just as well. Feeling sleepy, he puts his back against the mud-and-stone wall of the hut and rests his head against the roof thatching. Woodward is now strolling another fifty yards further downhill to check out the barn that stands at the southern edge of the clearing.

It is comfortable, and there is a little breeze. Grasshoppers and locusts are bouncing around on the grass, but the flies have not found him yet, and the *jebel* seems innocent of mosquitoes. Above him in the sky, the cloud cover is still heavy, maybe now down to a few hundred feet, and that same large-bodied bird is still circling patiently. He wonders what species it is, but his intelligence training never included much ornithology.

The first drops of rain begin to fall, but it is a gentle shower and the sensation is cool and pleasant.

It rained the night we first made love, he thinks suddenly, memories of Oxford stirring after the conversation with Woodward. After dinner at the Victoria Arms, we got soaked by a cloudburst hiking back down the Cherwell River. By the time we'd raced across town to Walton Street, we were wet as two drowned rats.

And it was cold, even for the end of November, and the Walton Street house was empty, since Peter was off for his usual weekend of London sex and CND strategy.

The memory floods back. The living room was chilly and they huddled before the fire, having changed out of their wet clothing. Encompassed in one of Peter's oversized bathrobes, Ellen sipped her red wine while the American drank Bell's whiskey in his pajamas and bathrobe.

After an afternoon of talk and laughter, they suddenly found it difficult to find things to say. The Adviser was thinking hard.

I love her, he forced himself to face the truth. Whatever she thinks of me, I love her and she is forbidden to me by every law in the universe. I've got to find someplace else to live.

Suddenly, Ellen shivered.

"Are you still cold?"

"No." She turned away to pour herself another tumbler of wine, and he caught a quick vision of her thigh. Beneath Peter's bathrobe, she had put on a simple white cotton nightdress and the sight of it inflamed him.

I will tell the L.R.R.G. that they were becoming suspicious of me, he began to plot strategies for disengagement. They'll have to believe me. . . .

In fact, he was under orders to stay put for as long as possible, since the intelligence product from Walton Street was wonderful. CND's anti-American protest movement had already achieved a high profile. As deployment plans for the new Cruise missile went forward, the Department of Defense was increasingly worried about a major protest offensive. The women in the movement were even talking about establishing a permanent peace camp on the public park just outside the gate at Greenham Common.

"Are you sad?"

"I want to go to bed." There was an ambiguity in her words, and she left it there. He stood up, a little excited and wondering if his bathrobe was concealing the fact adequately. When Peter was present, she always kissed him good night, brushing her lips across his cheek. When they were alone, they were careful not to touch.

On this occasion, however, she put her hands on his shoulders and stood on her tiptoes to kiss him directly on the lips, her eyes closed.

He made it a brief kiss. When he pulled away, she turned and darted wordlessly from the room, climbing to the third floor where Peter's study and the master bedroom were located. Going to his own room on the second floor, he listened to the tinkle as she used the toilet a few feet above him, and then the clanging of the chain and the vulgar rush of water as she flushed.

He sat on his bed for a long time, finishing his whiskey and thinking hard. It would be easier to justify leaving if I could find out what CND is going to do about the new Cruise missiles at Greenham Common. A permanent women's camp would be bothersome. Peter would tell me what was in the works if he were here.

But his notes and records are upstairs in his office. There is even a thick file on his desk marked "Greenham Common." I saw it there yesterday when I went in to use his big Arabic dictionary.

I'll find out what I can. Afterward, headquarters will have to accept my judgment that it was time to go.

A reconnaissance of Peter's office was risky, but Ellen had once confessed to being the kind of sleeper who went unconscious two minutes after contact with a pillow.

If I am discovered, I shall say that I was suffering from insomnia and wanted a book from Peter's study to read. There will be no danger. They have never been suspicious of me.

Which was, in itself, strange. The Committee for Nuclear Disarmament was seriously inconveniencing the Defense Department, the dominant branch of the most powerful government in the world. It never seemed to have occurred to these gentle, well-meaning peaceniks that someone would someday come to spy on them, someone who would lie about who he was and what he wanted.

It made him feel guilty, somehow, since extracting information from idealists like Peter Reston was not in the same moral ballpark as defending the United States against Soviet ballistic missiles. But this is the job, he told himself. *They* are the assignment. It's like practicing law. Unless you are a very pure sort of lawyer, there comes a day when you have to stand up in court and defend a gangster or prosecute a really nice guy. It comes with the territory. All part of the game.

He moved carefully up the steps, still in his bathrobe. The light was off at the top of the stairs. There was one squeaky board on the step just before the last one, but the Adviser had committed its location to memory and he stepped over it almost silently.

"Sweet? Sweet, is that you?"

"Ellen?" For an instant, he was confused. Sweet? Am I sweet?

"Is that you?"

He prepared to roll into his prepackaged explanation about sleeplessness and a book on the top shelf over Peter's desk, a volume of the sayings of the Prophet Mohammed. Your authorized sweet is in London, Ellen. Screwing a Labour Party activist with pacifist tendencies and a large private income.

"Oh, Ellen, sorry to disturb you," he began. "It's only me."

"It's only me? Do you know that song? On the other side of the bedroom door," she began to laugh, maybe a little hysterically.

"What song?"

Abruptly, she began to sing:

> "It's only me
> From over the sea.
> I'm Barnacle Bill,
> The Sailor!"

"I thought you thought it was Peter," he replied, standing frozen at the top of the stairs and looking at the half-open door to her bedroom. Peter's bedroom. It was cold in the hallway. He felt awkward in his bathrobe. It's only me from over the sea.

"I . . . I knew it was you. When I said 'sweet' it was you I meant because I thought you might be coming up to see me, and when you didn't come, I was in agony and I started to cry and then I heard you."

"You wanted me to come and see you?" Christ, he thought, she does want me, after all! All these weeks I have been yearning for her, and I thought she only wanted a friend.

"Yes, I thought you might want to . . . come and see me."

Ah, Ellen . . . Make your excuses, he told himself firmly. Claim to be a closet homosexual. Or in love with another woman. Or too dedicated to your beloved professor to sully the honor of his bed. Then pack your bags and go. The Reconnaissance Group will understand. Nobody ever expected you to walk point forever.

These are the rules. I have spent my entire life obeying rules. Orphanages are good places to learn about obedience, and seminaries have regulations for everything. And the Long Range Reconnaissance Group has these subtle, complicated commandments.

And all the rules say I must turn around right now and go downstairs.

"Don't stand out there!" Ellen entreated.

The Adviser remembered that passage in the *Summa Theologica* where Saint Thomas Aquinas contemplates the sin committed by a man who marries a woman under a counterfeit identity. Saint Thomas had rightly deemed the mortal sin to be one of rape, since the bride did not yield herself to this groom, but to another, albeit fictional one.

This would be a kind of rape, he decided, since Ellen has fallen in love with a gentle peacenik. Not a career intelligence officer.

Who will destroy his career if he gets caught breaking the rules about sex and covert sources! This woman is a target, the object of a Human Intelligence Operation authorized by the Secretary of Defense, he reminds himself. She and her common-law husband have been assigned to me for covert scrutiny. I can sleep with every other woman in the world except this one.

"Ellen . . ." He began to tremble, his hand pressed flat upon her bedroom door. You're forty-one years old, he told himself. The L.R.R.G. has been your whole life. The Group is family. She is an outsider.

"Don't make me beg," she whispered. "You got all the way to the top of the stairs! Don't back away now. Am I so awful? Peter jumps into strange beds every time he gets the chance!"

"No, of course, I . . ." He pushed open the door. The room was small, with only a king-sized bed and a chair and a little desk covered with sixth-form essays that needed correcting. There was a pink night-light glowing, the kind timid children have in their bedrooms.

Ellen was under a duvet, a tiny presence in the enormous bed. Peter's bed. As soon as he closed the door behind him, she sat up, letting the covers fall down to her hips, and he saw that she was naked. There were the high, generous breasts he had always imagined. There was the dancer's flat stomach, and the bare, outstretched arms.

"Come to bed. We've been good long enough."

He obediently took off his pajamas, but there was anarchy in his brain. Bless me father for I have sinned. Am about to sin. Thought is soon to become deed. And the word was made flesh. Her flesh and mine.

He closed his eyes and saw himself walking down that long marble corridor to the seminary chapel for the singing of Matins, wearing his black cassock and carrying his rosary beads. He shook his head to drive away the image and thought instead of Peter Reston, his famous radical friend, patiently teaching him Arabic literature and explaining why nuclear weapons had no place in a civilized world.

Peter may have been false to her, he thought. But he was always true to me.

"Sweet," Ellen said again, and he tried to remember whether she had ever used this endearment for Peter. She kissed his face. Mechanically, he took her in his arms, feeling her breasts crushing against his heart, her legs rubbing against his thighs.

He kissed her, and she sighed with pleasure, but nothing was happening inside him and he was still soft. Christ, he thought in despair, feeling a kind of sweaty, prickly heat take possession of his body, all these months I've been aching for her, and now that she's in my arms . . .

"It's okay," she consoled him quickly. "Nothing has to happen. I just wanted to hold you." Exploring, she ran her hands quickly over his loins.

"I'm sorry."

"No, I'm sure it's me. The only other man I've ever slept with is Peter and he always does everything and I just let him, so I'm probably doing everything wrong. Tell me what to do. I'll do anything you ask."

"No, it's just that I feel guilty."

"I don't," she told him. "Tonight, I decided to give myself permission to love you. If you need permission to love me, you'd better get it because it's happened to us."

"Ellen, there are things about me that you don't know."

"I don't care!" She began kissing his chest hungrily. "For once in your life, be a little crazy. I need you crazy tonight."

She touched him again with her fingertips, delicately, and the sought-after craziness began to mount. He stroked her skin, feeling a sudden frisson of pleasure as his hands roamed over her breasts and thighs. It has been so hard not to touch her, he realized. I've used up so much energy just keeping my hands off her. And I like the way she touches me.

It takes getting used to, being touched. But I like it. And I'm hard . . .

With a sudden cry, Ellen threw off the duvet, climbing on top of him with a wantonness he had never suspected in her. As soon as he was firmly inside of her, she began to climax.

"Oh, come inside me!" She shook her head wildly back and forth, her hair, still wet from the Oxford winter rain, flailing in his face, her nipples brushing against his chest. "Please, fill me up, take me, take me, oh sweet, sweet, sweet, sweet . . ."

He exploded uncontrollably, rolling her onto her back and thrusting fiercely into her.

"I love you." It was over for the moment, and they were both warm beneath the duvet. It struck him that he had never said that before—I love you. Some people said it so lightly, all the time, to everyone. Some people found it hard to say it to anyone, ever. You could never say it to the nuns, somehow, and he never managed to say it to any of his previous women.

But it felt good, saying it to Ellen and he said it again. "I love you."

"Sweet," she whispered. "I love you too. So much."

I'm happy, he thought as he lay back against the pillow with Ellen's head on his chest. Sixty seconds of jubilance after forty years of sullen obedience. And by God, it has made me happy, happy, happy.

Chapter Five

SEXT

"Sir!"

The Adviser sits up, realizing with a rush of guilt that he has been utterly lost in reverie. The heat is making him stupid. Remembering that first night with Ellen has aroused him, but now he feels silly, sitting with a pointless erection, upon a peak in Dhofar.

"John?"

The sergeant major is bounding uphill with his jimpy in one hand and his binoculars in the other. The Adviser gets the lady pistol out again, just to be on the safe side, but the village is as deserted as ever, and there is no one to shoot. The rain has stopped, but the clouds are still ominous.

Woodward is breathless and his face is white. "Something has gone . . . very wrong here . . . I don't know where all the women and children are, but there are six men down in that stable."

"What do they say?"

"Nothing. They've got their hands tied behind their backs and they've all been shot in the back of the head. Christ, it was awful!"

There is a quick motley of emotions. At first, the Adviser feels frightened. There are men with guns roaming around this mountain, killing people ruthlessly. Somewhere nearby . . . then it occurs to him that he has been right when everyone else is wrong. If this develops into a major attack, they'll be talking about me in Washington, he thinks. I called it right when everyone else had it wrong. My career is back on the rails. If I can get out of here alive, they'll give me that National Intelligence Medal and a promotion. Next stop, GS-15!

Then he thinks again of Ellen Huntington, and feels ashamed. Ellen's first thought would have been for those poor shepherds, murdered in cold blood, and she would have fretted about the fatherless children they left behind. She would have wept, and afterward organized a jumble sale to help finance their schooling . . . I was always unworthy of her, he thinks humbly.

"How long have they been dead?" The professional intelligence officer in him begins to function.

"Maybe since yesterday," Woodward guesses. They begin to slog uphill, walking rapidly now because the pasture no longer feels safe. "They were already stiff and the birds and insects had got at them, but there was no smell yet."

Of course. The Adviser gazes up at the sky, at last able to identify the heavy, slow-moving bird circling overhead. As he watches, the vulture languidly glides toward the stable where the corpses are waiting.

Lunch for you, big guy, he thinks morbidly as they rush over the stubble. Death and dismemberment for them. A medal for me. A battle for the Sultan's Armed Forces. A little something for everybody.

Suddenly, Woodward halts and points at the top of the hill, beginning to curse like a real sergeant major. "Oh, Jesus wept! He's left us! Oh, goddamn the bastard!"

Up on the ridge, where they last saw Captain Fenwich and his Scout Platoon, there is now only a solitary Land-Rover. As they rush the last few dozen yards to the road, a nervous Ali Rashidi stands on the driver's seat waving at them and shouting "Hallo! Hallo! Hallo, you chaps!"

Woodward is coldly furious. "Where is everybody?"

"The Platoon is going on ahead, Sergeant Major. Captain Fenwich says to bring you along when . . ."

"Come on, let's go!" shouts the Adviser, flinging himself into the back of the Land-Rover while Woodward takes the machine-gun position in the passenger seat. "Bait al Muktar must be a kilometer farther up the mountain!"

Over his shoulder, Ali Rashidi casts a longing glance back down the Midway road toward Salalah. He is a coastal Arab, and the idea of venturing any higher up the desolate *jebel* makes him uneasy. The Land-Rover's wheels spin terrifyingly in the mud for a moment, and when they catch hold, the vehicle takes off with a jolt.

"What's that home brew you guys concoct in Um al Gwarif?" the Adviser calls over the roar of the engine. The road is almost vertical in places, and he wonders how the big, clumsy Bedfords managed it.

"McGinty's Brown Ale." Woodward grins as he feeds a cartridge belt into the breach of the machine gun. He clings to the weapon's wooden stock as the Land-Rover careens from side to side. "When Sergeant McGinty retired to Belfast last year, he left us the recipe. I keep a case on ice for emergencies."

Alcohol is forbidden by the *Quran* and savagely punished by Oman's criminal code. Driving grimly in second gear, Ali Rashidi pretends not to hear.

"Good. We're going to need at least a case!"

The vehicle's transmission whines in agony as the Arab sergeant takes them skillfully over the top of a crest and onto a small rectangular plateau, about a mile wide. Shrouded in gray mist and cloud, the *jebel* still towers another thousand menacing feet above them, but for the moment, they are riding on flat land again.

"There's the convoy!" Woodward shouts. Ahead, they can now see the Saladin and the two Bedfords parked by the side of the road. Napalm is waving at them from his post on the turret of the armored vehicle and the Saladin crew is sitting on the grass, smoking. The rest of the Scout Platoon is gone.

Immediately in front of them is an acre's worth of agricultural land, planted with some kind of green vegetable. The wall is intended to keep animals out, but it has been knocked down in several places and in the distance, three lean long-horned goats are calmly grazing within the enclosure.

"Oh bloody hell, there he is!" Woodward points across the field as they jump down. A quarter of a mile away, Bernie Fenwich and thirty-five men are meandering placidly across the plateau, organized into a uneven skirmish line. They are approaching a small *wa'adi* that runs through the middle of the field.

"Your lad Bernie is seriously stupid," the Adviser comments.

"I know," Woodward mutters. "Nigel has got to send the nutter home before he gets somebody killed."

Another two hundred yards beyond the *wa'adi* is a medium-sized village with about twenty-five low huts surrounding a white, two-story wooden building with a balcony. On the village wall there is a rusty red and white Pepsi-Cola sign with the product's name in English and Arabic. On the far side of the village, the land rises precipitously as the *jebel* ascends into the clouds.

"That must be Bait al Muktar. Why did Bernie go ahead without us?"

"I don't know." Woodward shakes his head angrily. "Bravado maybe, or maybe he wants to deal with anything he finds without our interference."

"During last night's Big Bird pass, Bait al Muktar was generating a lot of heat. Now it looks deserted. Can you see anyone?"

Woodward focuses his field glasses. "No . . . no, there's no one there at all. Christ, I hope we're not going to find another pile of corpses. Wait, I see some children!"

"Are they alive? Let me see."

The Adviser focuses the binoculars on a small patch of grass between the cultivated field and the first thatched hut. There are two children there, rolling a hoop back and forth between them. Four or five years old, the girl is wearing a simple white shift with a pink ribbon in her black hair. The little boy is no more than a baby and he is naked.

"It still worries me." The Adviser lowers the glasses. "Has that field been abandoned? Ali Rashidi, what's growing there?"

The question strains Ali's command of English. "We call them *lubiyah*, sir."

"*Lubiyah.* . . ." The word is not in his mental lexicon, so the Adviser climbs over the wall and discovers ordinary beans, ready for harvest, or perhaps a few days past ready, since some of the pods are starting to split. The soil is so dry that the foliage is wilting, suggesting that no irrigation has been carried out for several days.

"The villagers should be out picking their beans," Woodward reads his mind. "And why don't they mend the wall and chase the goats away?"

"I don't know. How can we contact your dim-witted captain?"

"He has the Panasonic," volunteers Ali Rashidi. "I shall call him from the Land-Rover and then come with you."

"Right, then tell him that he must stop where he is and wait for us, because we have important information." Sergeant Major Woodward then turns to the Saladin crew. "Alright you lot, get off your arses and prepare to deliver supporting fire against that village if we need it!"

As the Saladin's turret swings around to address Bait al Muktar, Napalm leaps down from the armored vehicle. Holding his jimpy easily in one hand, the crazy man climbs over the stone wall into the bean field.

"Do we need more problems?" the Adviser asks quietly.

"He has a sense of where he needs to be." Woodward speaks as if Napalm were not there. "And sometimes he seems to understand when you talk to him even though he's always carrying on that one-word dialogue with himself. He won't be in the way."

"What's his real name?"

"What's your real name?" Woodward counters with a grin.

"I haven't got one."

"Then neither does he. Let's go."

The field officers of the Long Range Reconnaissance Group are obsessive about leaving their operational environment undisturbed as they pass through it, a fixation that impels the Adviser to avoid trampling bean stalks while crossing the field.

He leads them down a path he has detected, keeping to the low ground where possible and crouching whenever they silhouette against the horizon. The four men walk single file with Napalm following Sergeant Major Woodward and Ali Rashidi bringing up the rear. The Arabian sea is behind them. To the north, on the far side of Bait al Muktar, is the *jebel*. The sun is now 10 degrees west of its zenith.

Scornful of caution, Fenwich is standing at the edge of the *wa'adi*, watching them approach, his back to the village, his hands on his hips, a Rothman filter tip dangling from his lips. His scouts are sprawled among the bean plants, crushing the stalks as they smoke cigarettes and drink from their canteens. Only Master Sergeant Mustafa Said seems nervous, prowling along the edge of the gully and looking suspiciously at Bait al Muktar.

From this vantage point, the village appears deserted and innocuous. The Adviser can no longer see any children. The *wa'adi* is a shallow natural gully, five or six feet deep at its deepest, running across the bean field at right angles to Bait al Muktar and petering out at either end. There is no water in it, although the reddish, crumbly soil looks moist and fertile.

The smoke from Fenwich's cigarette tickles the Adviser's nostrils as they draw near. I will be friendly at first, he plots, and bum a cigarette from him before we tell him what we found in the other village.

"Right, Captain America, what's the problem?"

"Listen, Fenwich, we've just come from . . ." The Adviser begins, but he is interrupted when Napalm slides past him, absorbs the tactical situation with a glance, and then jumps six feet down to the bottom of the *wa'adi*. Without a second's hesitation, Woodward does the same. Ali Rashidi looks worried, but he loyally stands next to the Adviser.

Captain Fenwich is irritable. "You should've waited up there with the Bedfords! We're just going to have a look at this village, and . . ."

"You know, that cigarette smells good!" Improvising a friendly smile, the Adviser interrupts. "You don't suppose I could have one, do you?"

The captain seems momentarily stunned. He keeps his cigarettes over his heart in the left breast pocket of his khaki field jacket. He is undoing the button when there are six beefy base sounds in the distance, coming from Bait al Muktar.

BOH-BOH-BOH-BOH-BOH-BOH! A huge staccato noise raps out like a giant passing gas.

Intent upon receiving his first cigarette in nine months, the Adviser fails to react even though terrible things begin to happen around him. Master Sergeant Mustafa Said screams and throws his hands up in the air. His voice soars to a pure, piercing shriek.

Then a confused gurgling noise comes from Captain Fenwich, who falls over sideways into the beans, his feet dangling over the side of the *wa'adi*.

Funny sound, thinks the American. He is still thinking about getting a cigarette when he sees that there is a two-inch hole in Bernie's chest and air from his right lung is frothing bubbles of blood.

Run, his mind commands as old brain instincts surge from the cortex of his skull. Run. Find safety. Hide. Don't die.

He turns, hesitant. Can I get back to the Saladin?

Before he gets his feet moving, an anti-tank rocket spurts out of Bait al Muktar and floats toward the Midway Road. The flying missile seems ridiculously small and slow-moving, like a child's toy. There is only a distant metallic clang when it vanishes into the chassis of the Saladin.

Then the armored vehicle explodes, throwing sparks and flame five hundred feet into the air. For an instant there is a frightening grayness in the Adviser's mind as he pictures the four men inside burning to death.

"Oh Christ! No, oh Christ!" He turns back toward the village as a second heavy machine gun rips into the Scout Platoon. Rounds are impacting all around him now, and the Adviser feels a warm liquid sensation on the inside of his left leg.

I've been hit!

He freezes, standing nearly alone now in the middle of a shell-swept field, until Ali Rashidi hits him with a flying tackle and flings him down the side of the *wa'adi*.

I've been shot and there is blood rushing down my thigh, he thinks. The wound is too high for a tourniquet. This is that magic moment before the pain comes. You feel nothing at first because the nerves have been destroyed, but blood must now be hemorrhaging out of me. It will flow until there is no more, and then . . .

And then nothing, because the pain never comes. Sprawled in the mud, he smells his own strong urine and realizes that he has merely pissed on himself with fright.

He gets to his hands and knees, confused and disoriented. The surviving scouts are all jumping down into the *wa'adi* near him, shouting orders at one another. No one seems to be in charge. With his General Purpose Machine Gun, Napalm has crossed the gully to shoot back at the *adoo*. He seems to be enjoying himself hugely. Visibly less amused, the valiant Sergeant Rashidi has followed Napalm with the Armalite and he is peering through his sniper scope for targets.

"Watch out for the children!" The Adviser suddenly remembers the naked little boy and his playmate at the edge of the village.

No one pays any attention. Unseen in the smoke and dust, John Woodward is shouting in broken Arabic. With terrible Koranic curses, the scouts follow Napalm to the north edge of the *wa'adi* to fire on the village. The Adviser gets to his feet, his body trembling. There is mud on his face and hands and the pungent wetness in his trousers is embarrassing. Absurdly, he wonders when he can wash and change into dry underwear.

Why did I agree to come? All I had to say was no. Now what do I do?

His legs feel rubbery as he stumbles across the ten-foot floor of the *wa'adi*. There is a shivery weakness in his arms when he hauls himself up on a rock to study the battlefield.

The sight is not encouraging. Bait al Muktar is only a couple of football fields away. There is a slightly elevated patch of ground forty yards to their front and a pile of rocks where some ancient wall has fallen down, but otherwise no cover or concealment between the *wa'adi* and the village.

His analysis is quickly done. They are facing an unknown number of semi-automatic rifles plus two heavy rapid-fire weapons, maybe Russian-made Shpagins, dug into trenches just outside the village wall. The *adoo* gunners seem to be battle-hardened professionals, because they are shooting slowly and rhythmatically and covering the entire field with grazing fire, a burst of rounds from one side and then a pause, and then the antiphony from the other side.

"We attack now, yes?" a competent-looking Omanese lance corporal next to him asks calmly. He is carrying an M-79 grenade launcher and has the name "Nassir" stencilled to his uniform jacket.

"Christ, no! They've got us pinned down." The Adviser shakes his head violently, seeing that the firefight is headed for stalemate. The two *adoo* machine guns have slackened their fire in order to save ammunition but they can easily keep the scouts down in the *wa'adi* until sundown.

With a growing sense of desperation, the Adviser realizes that the two forces, without intending to, have managed to trap each other. As long as their ammunition lasts, the Scout Platoon can defend the *wa'adi*, but not leave it, and their only chance for a counterattack disappeared with the Saladin. For their part, the Popular Front cannot escape from Bait al Muktar since the mountain behind them is a sheer, exposed cliff without cover or concealment. The only access road to the village runs along the side of the bean field where the guerrillas would be vulnerable to fire from the Scout Platoon. Gridlock!

"Stop firing!" John Woodward is shouting. As they jump down to the floor of the *wa'adi*, the scouts seem more angry than frightened. Napalm and Ali Rashidi remain behind to guard the ramparts, but they both hold their fire.

"Listen to me!" Woodward claps his hands briskly for attention. "Sergeant Mustafa Said is dead and Captain Fenwich is wounded, but I will lead you! From now on, we must only shoot to defend ourselves or when there is a clear target of opportunity."

"We are trapped, Sergeant Major!" one of the younger men wails.

"The colonel will send help," Woodward assures them. "Until then, Corporal Ahmad will take his squad to the east and secure that end of the *wa'adi*. Corporal Nassir, you have the center with the Second Squad, and Corporal Rachman's men will protect our west flank. Go!"

Within seconds, Woodward and the three squad leaders have organized the platoon. Four scouts are already dead, and their bodies are brought gently down into the gully and covered with a tarpaulin. Three others have serious leg wounds. Ali Rashidi has located the platoon's medical kit and he calmly applies tourniquets and administers injections of morphine. There is no screaming; the wounded are stoic.

"Fenwich might be dead." The Adviser points to the captain's motionless foot hanging over the edge of the *wa'adi*.

"I hope not," Woodward mutters as they ease the body down. "I want the bugger alive for a court-martial."

The captain's eyes are closed, but he groans and sits up. With practiced skill, Woodward strips off the officer's jacket and web belt, removing his pistol and field radio.

"It's a sucking chest wound!" The Adviser feels faint as he looks at the damaged flesh. The enemy round has passed right through Fenwich's shoulder, destroying much of the bone structure and perforating his lung. The American fights off nausea and he closes his eyes, reflecting that the *adoo* gunner missed him by inches. That could have been me, he thinks. That could have been my flesh, ripped and bleeding.

When he opens his eyes, he sees Woodward briskly disinfecting Fenwich's raw skin and applying large elastic bandages front and back to keep the chest cavity from collapsing. There is a jar of old-fashioned vaseline in the medical kit and he smears it liberally over the dressing to seal the lung.

"Here, sit him up!"

Captain Fenwich is gasping and crying, his eyes tightly shut. His skin has turned gray, and he is perspiring. Together, they prop him up against the side of the *wa'adi* to keep his chest cavity from filling with blood.

The Rothmans are still in Fenwich's pocket. It seems unlikely that the captain will be smoking for a while. The Adviser contemplates helping himself, but he is too queasy for a cigarette.

Fenwich is half-talking and half-crying as Woodward slides a hypodermic needle into his arm. Then he uses a magic marker to write "M" for morphine on his forehead, adding the time to avoid the danger of an overdose later. It is just after two in the afternoon. Four minutes have passed since the first shots from Bait al Muktar. The Adviser feels as if he has been on his feet for a hundred hours.

"If we don't get him out of here, Fenwich's going to snuff it," Woodward says. There is a moment of quiet from the *adoo* machine guns.

The Adviser gestures at the field radio. "Can we call Um al Gwarif?"

"We can call Buckingham Bloody Palace if we want, but nobody will fly a med-evac helicopter in here as long as the *adoo* have that rocket-propelled grenade launcher. Did you see what it did to the Saladin? They'd shoot a chopper out of the sky."

The Adviser fights off a wave of panic and starts working on the problem. There is no way out of the *wa'adi* because the west end of the ravine curves in toward the village while the other end simply peters out in the open field, leaving them exposed to enemy fire in either direction.

"Look, this is a stupid accident!" he reasons. "There doesn't have to be a battle here today just because we've blundered into each other. That enemy commander over there is shitting in his Marxist pants right now because he thinks half the Omanese Army is right behind us and the only way out of his box is over our dead bodies. Unless . . ."

"Unless what?"

"Unless we negotiate. Give me a big piece of white cloth and I'll walk up to that rock and offer to hold our fire while they withdraw."

Woodward runs a hand through his short, thick hair and looks around him, studying the situation. "They shot a British officer," he objects.

"And they will shoot the rest of us in due course if we don't organize a truce."

"I'm a soldier, not a diplomat." Woodward shakes his head. "And this is the British Army. I don't think . . . no, Nigel wouldn't have it."

"Nigel isn't here, and the sun has set on the British Empire."

"I don't care. We'll hold out until the sun sets on this particular corner of the old empire." There is firmness in Woodward's voice. "Then things will get better."

"I don't see how they can get any worse."

Suddenly there is a distant *thwump!*, a hollow, metallic sound. "What's that noise?"

"The sound of things getting worse!" Woodward snaps and then begins to shout at the Omanese troops. "In-coming! In-coming! Get down!"

The scouts all dive for cover. The Adviser drops flat on the *wa'adi* floor and tries to wedge himself between a large limestone rock and Captain Fenwich's inert body. His muscles frozen with terror, he listens to the tiny scream as a mortar round mounts five or six hundred yards towards its apogee and then begins to fall toward them.

It makes a sound like a tea kettle whistling until it explodes forty feet behind them in the field, spraying them with clods of mud and pebbles and shreds of beans stalks. The concussion is awful and the Adviser's ears begin to ring.

Woodward's reactions are amazingly quick. He jumps to his feet, checks to see that no one has been hurt, and then throws himself back to the ground. "Keep down!" he cries. "Stay where you are! There'll be another in a minute!"

"Christ, here it comes!" The Adviser hears the second echoing *thwump* as the shell leaves its steel tube. He looks frantically for a hole to crawl into and fails to find one, so he buries his face in the mud and puts his arms around his head to protect his skull. His heart is beating so hard he can hear it.

No, no, no, fucking hell, no, it's going to get us, his mind is shrieking out of control. God, this is awful! God, get me out of here! I'll go back to the Pentagon and sit behind a desk. . . . This is the one! Christ, here it comes!

The round detonates a dozen feet in front of the *wa'adi,* shaking the earth so savagely that part of the gully wall collapses, half-burying him in soft red earth. Fragments of shrapnel rain down upon them, and there are screams of pain from the scouts.

His head clanging with the echo of the explosion, the Adviser is tempted to stay where he is, buried ahead of schedule beneath a blanket of friendly earth, but Woodward is back on his feet instantly.

"Open fire!" he bellows. "Spray the village! Make that mortar team take cover!"

The Adviser gets up, frightened and bewildered. It is hard to see because of the smoke and dust. Rubbing his eyes only seems to make it worse. The scouts are climbing the forward wall of the ravine, pouring reckless fire at Bait al Muktar to keep the *adoo* gun crew from sending another mortar round in their direction. Completely fearless, Napalm actually climbs into the bean field and mounts the jimpy on its bipod to exchange fire with the two *adoo* machine guns.

"What do we do?" Long Range Reconnaissance Group officers are military intelligence generalists, good with satellite maps, great at rough-country reconnaissance, and fair at covert operations. Small-unit infantry combat is another kettle of fish altogether and the Adviser has spent a lifetime avoiding it.

"We've got to stop that mortar team from bracketing us! Ali, loan me your rifle!"

Ali Rashidi surrenders his Armalite under protest. "Don't go, Sergeant Major. . . ."

"Look, they've already got two reference points on their plotting board, and if we give them time to do their geometry, they'll put the next round right on our heads!"

We've blundered into a sizable hunk of the 9 June Regiment, the Adviser realizes, checking off the indicators in his mind. They've got at least two Shpagin heavy machine guns, an RPG-7 rocket propelled grenade system, and a mortar, maybe that Chinese 82-mm model. This means at least a couple of companies of regular troops, or even a mainline battalion, commanded by somebody competently trained in Russia.

What are we going to do? What are they going to do? Feeling helpless, he follows Woodward to the forward edge of the *wa'adi*. "Can I help?"

"They must have a forward observer up there. If I can see him from that rock pile, I'll try to pot him. You and Ali make sure nobody shoots me in the back!"

"John, don't go—" The Adviser begins to argue, but the sergeant major hurls himself boldly over the top and begins to snake through the bean field, crawling on his elbows and knees with the Armalite on his back. Risking a bullet in the forehead, the Adviser clings to the top of the *wa'adi* and watches the bushes move until Woodward reaches the rock pile.

Where, he wonders, do you get balls like that? I was never that brave. Not on my best day.

On my best day. When was my best day? The day Ellen told me that she loved me was my very best day, but I wasn't any braver then than I am now. I haven't had that many best days.

There is a high keening cry in the distance, a kind of alien metallic scream, but the Adviser is watching John Woodward and thinking about Ellen and there is so much racket that he does not focus upon the sound for that crucial window of opportunity when he still might have jumped back down into the *wa'adi*.

"Oh, God, nooooooo!" he wails, realizing that the *adoo* mortar squad has launched their third shell in his direction. At the last second, he ducks, and the blast knocks him down into the bottom of the gully. Landing on top of somebody, he hits his head against the stock of an M-79 grenade launcher.

"Sorry!" Dazed, he speaks to the man whose body cushioned his fall. "Oh God, look, awfully sorry! Did I hurt you?"

There is no reply. As the Adviser is working out how to apologize in Arabic, he realizes that he has landed on Lance Corporal Nassir, who is now missing the whole left side of his face. Blood is spurting out of an open artery in his neck.

"Oh . . . look, sorry . . ." Still apologizing, he crawls away, seeing that five more scouts are nursing wounds from mortar shrapnel. The plucky Ali Rashidi is delivering first aid, but nobody seems to be in charge anymore. Only the cheerfully indestructible Napalm is still returning fire.

The fuckers, the dirty fuckers, they're gonna kill us one by one while they sit over there laughing . . . his thoughts are coming in fragments now, like the moment between dreaming and waking when everything is stark but confused. Abruptly angry, the Adviser seizes the dead Nassir's grenade launcher with the notion of shooting back at the *adoo*. The M-79 is a simple, thick-barrelled breech-loading weapon of American manufacture.

It was twenty years ago when I learned how to fire one of these things, he thinks as he remembers his days as a U.S. Army second lieutenant at Fort Bragg, North Carolina. Haven't shot one since and I was pretty terrible back then. But I've got to help!

"John?" The Adviser climbs to the top of the *wa'adi* and sees that the last mortar had impacted between the *wa'adi* and the rock pile. Woodward's protective pile of stones has been scattered and he is now lying facedown, his body partially exposed. "John, are you all right?"

There is no answer. A bleak despair creeps over him. Oh Christ, he's dead! Just when we were starting to be friends. We could have gone walking on the moors. In time, I might have told him all about Ellen. He was my Virgil. How does Dante get out of hell without a guide?

There is a fragment of quiet. The *adoo* gunners stop firing. The Adviser hears Woodward groan.

Oh shit! What do I do? I thought he was dead.

I'm not in charge of anything here, he thinks as he grapples with a wave of cowardice. My duty is to the Long Range Reconnaissance Group, and I need to exfiltrate this position. Ali Rashidi is the ranking man, and he can take command of this mess. With a little luck, I could snake back through the beans to the Midway Road. I've got a compass and a map, and there's food and water in the Bedfords. I'll wait until dark and then make my way down the road to Salalah.

That's my line, going places quietly and getting there in one piece. Being a hero was Woodward's line.

"John?" he calls again.

"I'm hurt!" Woodward's voice is thin and uncertain.

Oh, I'm not good at this, he thinks, putting the grenade-launcher strap over his shoulder as he crouches fearfully on the edge of the *wa'adi*. Any minute now those Shpagins are going to open up again. I should have gone back to the Pentagon. I don't deal very well with fear. My legs are going to give out. I don't want to do this. I want to live. I keep thinking I want to die, but whenever the opportunity presents itself, I get real nervous.

"Hang on!" Bent over double, he races through the bushes toward the rock pile. One of the *adoo* machine guns fires, but the shells fly over his head as he throws himself down in the mud next to Woodward.

"Hey!" Woodward is half-buried in rocks and pebbles and clods of dry soil. "Is that Captain America?"

"For Christ's sake, John, are you hurt?" The Adviser excavates him, finding a huge patch of blood on the side of his head.

"Something hit my skull." Woodward shakes his head and wipes some of the blood away with his sleeve. "My leg hurts, and . . . damn, I feel old!"

"You're going to live. You're in good shape."

"I'm old. I'm fifty-five, but I felt young until a few minutes ago." There is a high-pitched sob in the sergeant major's voice. He coughs and clears his throat and gets down to business. "Listen, can you see that big house in the middle of Bait al Muktar? Their forward observer is on the second-floor balcony and the mortar team is in the street just below."

"Give me your field glasses." The Adviser wedges the grenade launcher between two rocks and looks through Woodward's binoculars. Bait al Muktar means "House of the Mayor" and the two-story frame edifice must be the house in question. There is a slender figure in combat fatigues standing on the balcony. "I see him . . . no, her! It's a woman!"

The *adoo* forward observer has long brown hair beneath a Mao cap. She puts her elbows on the balustrade and looks out at the bean field with binoculars. For a moment, they stare at one another. She might have come to a party at Peter's house, he thinks. We would have sat on the sofa and talked about politics and ate *halwa* and drunk mint tea. Now we're trying to kill each other.

"They have women as nurses and political officers and forward observers." Woodward is panting with pain. "Would you mind shooting her?"

"I've never killed anybody before. I've always been a sort of a scientist."

"Please!" Woodward exhales heavily. "You need to shoot now because they're going to fire that mortar in another minute and kill us!"

"Maybe you should take it. You're a better shot than I am."

"I can't move, Yank. And how do you know I'm a better shot than you are?"

"Helen Keller was a better shot than I am." Reluctantly, the Adviser picks up the M-79 and points it at Bait al Muktar. I'll never hit anything, he reassures himself.

There is no way of aiming a grenade launcher with any precision. The range is one hundred and sixty yards, and the M-79 is an indirect fire weapon at that distance. The Adviser aims at the center of the woman's body and raises the barrel about forty-five degrees to achieve a high trajectory.

She is on that side, he tells himself. I am on this side.

Then he takes a deep breath, lets it half out, and holds it, the way the Army taught him at Fort Bragg two decades ago. Relax, relax, and squeeze.

Bang.

The discharge catches him by surprise, the way it always did, and he blinks as the grenade soars toward its target. He gets his eyes open in time to see the ordnance explode against the wooden wall, just below the balcony.

Hey, I hit something, he thinks, feeling childishly pleased with himself, like a child at the fair, winning the stuffed teddy bear with a lucky shot.

Then there is a bright, bluish white light as the explosive bursts upwards. A whishing sound. A column of flame engulfs the forward observer. There is fire all around her. For an instant, he watches her body writhe, turning away, twisting, trying to avoid the hurt, but then she crumbles and falls over the railing into the street below.

If I live long enough, I'll be seeing that in my head fifty years from now, he thinks. I've hurt enough women. I should have stayed in the seminary. I would never have loved a woman. I would never have burned a woman alive.

There is a momentous secondary explosion in the village as mortar ammunition detonates. He can feel the hotness on his forehead. The mayor's house goes up in flames and the fire leaps to the thatched roofs of the smaller buildings on either side. The Adviser watches, mesmerized.

What happened to the people who lived there? What happened to that little girl and the baby boy? My specialty is passing unobserved through the world, scrutinizing but not altering my environment. Now I've set fire to a couple of houses. Bless me, Father. For I have sinned.

Woodward gets unsteadily to his hands and knees. His face is pasty white, and he seems wobbly. "You got 'em, Captain America," he says thickly, and then falls over on his side. The open wound in his thigh is oozing blood and his skull is covered with crimson mud.

"John, you're too heavy to carry." The Adviser puts his shoulder into Woodward's stomach and pulls the man onto his back. He tries to lift the dead weight into the air but the raw physical strength is not there and he sinks to his knees.

"Can't . . ."

"We've got to run," the Adviser pleads. "Come on, buddy! Only a few steps and we'll be safe!"

"You go," mutters Woodward. "I'm never going to see my

wife again . . . you call Jenny and tell her I loved her and I'm sorry about everything."

"You're not going to die!"

"Jenny Woodward," says Sergeant Major Woodward. "It's in the directory. Just call. . . ."

One of the Shpagins is firing again, and the Adviser feels the stream of shells sweeping toward them. John is going to die, he thinks. Because he can't walk and I can't carry him and we'll both die if I don't leave him and run. I've got to save myself!

I can't leave him. There needs to be someone in my life I do not desert.

Ellen, he entreats. Help me! Give me strength! Help me!

The quivering in his body stops and this time he gets to his feet with Woodward over his shoulder. At first he is not sure that he can move, much less run, but he thinks about Ellen again. The thought of her makes him strong, and he begins to lumber toward the sanctuary of the *wa'adi*. Halfway there, Ali Rashidi dashes forward out of the smoke and together they cart John Woodward to safety.

"Oh it's you!" There is pleasure in Nigel Fine's voice. "Listen, we will shortly be pinning a British medal on your anonymous Yankee chest. Over."

The colonel's voice is emanating from a flat, rectangular steel box with a retractable antenna and buttons for volume and squelch. The words "National Panasonic Field Communications Unit NP-16" are printed on the control panel.

It's happening! The Adviser feels a grim satisfaction as he squeezes the push-to-talk button on the hand-held microphone. "How are you managing? Over."

"Couldn't be better! My First and Second Regiments are just now mopping up an estimated eight hundred *adoo* in the foothills north of Salalah. They were clearly preparing a major offensive, but we're going through them like a dose of salts. Without your warning, they'd have trapped us in Um al Gwarif. Nice work, Yank! Over."

"Happy to help, Nigel." The Adviser tries to enjoy the sensation of being right, but there are other things on his mind. "Listen! Up here on the *jebel*, the bad guys are still winning. We're two hundred yards due south of Bait al Muktar, facing a sizable unit. At least a reinforced rifle company, maybe two, maybe a battalion."

"Where's Bernie?"

"Badly hurt. I also have eight Arab wounded and five dead. I'm afraid John Woodward is unconscious with a concussion and shrapnel wounds to the leg. Over."

"Jesus! John is hurt?" Colonel Fine's geniality vanishes immediately. "Look, I would be personally very grateful if you can do your best for Sergeant Major Woodward. He's my best friend. Over."

Maybe he's my best friend too, the Adviser thinks. "I'll do everything I can, sir. He's stable, but we need to get him to a hospital."

"I can send a med-evac chopper. Can you get him back to the road safely? Over."

"Sir, the *adoo* killed our Saladin with an RPG-7, and we're pinned down by semiautomatic rifles and two Shpagins. I don't see any way of exfiltrating this position without air support. Where are your Strikemasters? Over."

Nigel makes his mind up quickly. "I'll have a Strikey or two over your position as soon as I can arrange it. Stay on this frequency and talk them in."

"We've got cloud cover at five hundred feet and a little rain. The *adoo* are dug into a trench on the edge of the town, so your pilots need to come in low and slow and clobber them with everything they've got on the first run. Over."

"Roger. Listen, you understand that we can't land those med-evac choppers until the RPGs and Shpagins are out of action? The moment our Strikies deliver their ordnance, you'll need to take the scouts into Bait al Muktar and secure it. Over."

"Yes, of course, although Ali Rashidi is now the ranking man."

"Don't be silly! Ali's a good man, but you're part of my organization as long as you're in Dhofar. You're senior to Ali, and I want you in charge."

"Ah, yes sir. Over. . . ." The Adviser's voice trails off as he digests Nigel's casual order. Secure Bait al Muktar. This is your commanding officer talking. Do it.

"Good luck, Scout Platoon. Out."

The Adviser acknowledges with a ritual squeeze of the push-to-talk button, sliding immediately into a controlled panic. There are some angry *adoo* over there, he thinks, and the Strikemasters will never get them all. The survivors will fight back.

This means a frontal assault against professional soldiers who have semi-automatic rifles, a tactical solution never much favored by Long Range Reconnaissance Group officers.

On the other hand, Nigel Fine's order makes obvious sense. Fenwich seems to be dying. John Woodward is upsetting everybody by staying unconscious, and five of the eight wounded scouts will soon join Mohammed in Paradise without medical attention.

And a helicopter is an inherently fragile machine. One *adoo* with a rifle could shoot the med-evac chopper out of the sky, sending everyone aboard her to hell in a fireball.

The Adviser gets to his feet, feeling tired and depressed and inadequate. He has a headache. His trousers smell of urine. He yearns to brush his teeth. It is twenty minutes after two in the afternoon. There is no wind, and he has been continually exposed to 95 degree heat for seven hours. The air is so warm and moist that inhaling takes most of his available energy. It feels like a century since he last slept.

Everybody is getting hungry. There are a lot of grasshoppers in the *wa'adi,* and the Omanese are eating them like popcorn. One man catches a ten-inch brown lizard and munches thoughtfully on its tail while the lizard writhes in agony.

For the moment, the *wa'adi* is quiet. The Popular Front *adoo* have been firing brief, emphatic bursts across the bean field every ten or fifteen minutes to remind the scouts that they have tactical fire superiority. Napalm shoots back because he is insane, but the others are waiting for the Strikemasters, hoarding strength and ammunition.

"When do the Strikies come, sir?" Lance Corporal Rachman inquires.

"Soon. When they come, we will attack the *adoo.*"

"We will kill them all, sir!"

Maybe, thinks the Adviser. But war has its own sullen arithmetic. Before we kill all of them, they will kill a few of us.

Maybe you. Maybe me.

* * *

John Woodward wakes up at three o'clock, weak but clear-headed.

The indefatigable Ali Rashidi has created a primitive field hospital, rigging up a blue plastic sheet to keep the sun off the wounded. Captain Fenwich has not moved for some time. If he is still breathing, he is doing it very quietly. No one touches him, perhaps out of a superstitious fear that he may already be dead. In this part of the world, an Anglo-Saxon stiff always means trouble.

Ali seems to regard the brigade sergeant major with reverence, however, fanning him with the top secret TechIntel map and moistening his lips with a water-soaked rag and demanding that the Adviser take his pulse at regular intervals. Woodward's athletic heart is doing sixty steady beats a minute when he finally opens his eyes.

"Are we all right?"

"Sorta," the Adviser explains. "You've been out to lunch for an hour. There's a piece of shrapnel in your thigh but it isn't bleeding very much and I've disinfected and bandaged it. There's a nasty wound on your skull but we patched it as well as we could."

Woodward does not respond. His face is still very white, and the Adviser wonders if he is sliding into shock. Then he notices tears welling up in the Yorkshireman's eyes.

"Come on, Sergeant Dauntless, it's going to be okay! Nigel is sending air support and a chopper to ferry you home. Then you hobble back to Yorkshire, buy a large bouquet of roses, and get that woman of yours back."

"She's not coming back. Look, are the Strikies on their way?"

"They'll be here any time now. John, are you getting a lot of pain?"

"It smarts . . . damn, I get wounded once in every war." The Adviser sees that Woodward is crying. "This is all my father's fault. Damn him! He's ten years in his grave and I still hate him!"

"Why?"

There is another moment while the Englishman battles for self-control and then it pours out. "I didn't want this kind of life!

116

I was going to be a schoolmaster, but he said teaching was for poofters. I could have been an officer, but he hated officers so I had to become a sergeant major like him."

"John, listen, hey, I'm sorry, buddy."

"He used to hit my mother!" Woodward is crying openly now. "We were so terrified of him. When he drank. The bastard! I never had the courage to make him stop!"

The man is in agony. The Adviser does not know what else to do, so he hugs him. He has never hugged another man before, for fear that people would think he was gay, but under the circumstances, it seems the only thing to do. Slowly, John Woodward fights his way back to self-control, wiping his eyes with the back of his hand and taking a swallow of warm water from Ali Rashidi's canteen.

"Sorry, mate. I had no business subjecting you to that. I never told anyone about him before. I mean, I really do apologize, seriously."

"S'okay, you seemed too well adjusted to be human. When I come to see you in England we'll get tanked up on Yorkshire brown ale and trade ancient agonies."

"At least this injury will get me out of the sodding army. I'll be home in Yorkshire for Christmas. Maybe it'll snow. It doesn't always, but it's bloody marvelous when it does."

"John, is it still hurting?"

"Everything hurts."

"Do you want morphine?"

"No, just . . . just keep talking. Ah, were you in Oxford last Christmas? You have to tell me even if it's secret. Did it snow?"

"Okay, I spent last Christmas in Oxford. It got cold as a bitch and snowed just before dawn on Christmas day."

"You must have been with your English lady."

"Well, yeah, I guess."

"Tell me about her. It'll keep my mind occupied."

"I can't. It's too hard."

"Tell me the parts you can. What was her name? Was she beautiful?"

"Very beautiful. Her name was Ellen."

It was going to be a real Christmas Eve, the Adviser remembers. With a tree to be decorated with tinsel and stockings on the mantelpiece and roast beef and Yorkshire pudding because it was my favorite English food.

Woodward's eyes are closed tightly. There is a desperation in his voice, but his mind seems clear as he continues the interrogation. "How did you know that it snowed just before dawn? Did you stay up all night?"

"Yes. It was a terrible night. You see, Ellen lived with Peter Reston, the vice-chairman of CND. He was my teacher, and I had been staying in their guest bedroom. . . ."

"The famous peacenik professor? So you were using him to report on CND?

"It wasn't that cold-blooded. . . ."

"I bet it was precisely that cold-blooded," Woodward retorts. "Tell me what happened."

"Peter was screwing a woman in London, and their affair was reaching some kind of crescendo. Early the afternoon of Christmas Eve, he said he needed to run down to London for a quick CND meeting."

"And Reston never suspected you were sleeping with his woman?"

"He was a deeply arrogant man. I used to wonder if he would ever become suspicious, but it never seems to have occurred to him. Anyway, we didn't know whether he was going to pull his usual stunt of being unavoidably detained overnight so he could stay with his London woman, or come back to Oxford. So we sat in the kitchen, waiting and watching the roast beef burn."

"Did she make Yorkshire pudding?"

"It came out inedible. When Peter didn't call, we gave up and ate burned beef and got drunk on gin. Ellen told me that Peter had been the only man in her life. Until me. She said that she had once loved another woman, but that was over a long time ago. And Peter had not made love to her in months and she would never let him do it again because she could not bear to be touched by anyone but me."

"And you didn't explain about being an intelligence officer, did you?" Woodward whispered. "This was meant to be the moment of complete honesty and when she told you about the lesbian affair, you could have said, oh, by the way, I'm one of those contemptible spy chaps you've read about."

"I didn't quite manage it. I said there were aspects of my life that she might find difficult to understand."

And she said I'm drunk and I don't want any mysteries tonight, the Adviser remembers. Just take me to bed. Wish me Merry Christmas. Tell me you love me more than anyone else in the world. And screw me to sleep.

John Woodward's eyes are now closed and he seems to have dozed off. The Adviser is frankly glad, because the next part of the story is hard to tell. For the moment, their little bean-field battlefield seems calm, but he does a quick tour of inspection. Napalm seems to be daydreaming, resting on the stock of his jimpy and gazing blankly at Bait al Muktar.

Sergeant Rashidi is tireless, moving from squad to squad, checking on the wounded, talking to each of the men, watching the flanks of the *wa'adi* for signs of enemy action. He looks up as the Adviser wanders over. "Is he good?" he asks, pointing to John Woodward. "The sergeant major?"

"He's good," the Adviser affirms. "He's resting. And the Strikies are coming, Ali. We'll be okay."

"In God's hands," Ali Rashidi says absently, and goes off to redistribute their remaining ammunition.

With nothing else to do, the Adviser returns to John Woodward's side. It is hot under the plastic sheet, but the sun is afternoon murderous, and he feeling woozy from the heat. The moment he sits down, however, John's eyes pop open. And he looks fiercely at the Adviser.

"I've got it," he says, and the Adviser thinks he has conceived an escape from the *wa'adi*.

"What have you got?"

"I know the rest of the story. Peter Reston didn't stay in London that night. He came home and caught you in bed with his woman."

The Adviser sighs at the memory. "More or less. Reston met his lady friend at CND headquarters and told her that their affair was over because he had realized how deeply he loved Ellen. But that was the day that CND got word that Cruise missiles were being flown secretly into Greenham Common and the leadership called an authentic emergency meeting. Peter got back to Walton Street at three in the morning with a bunch of carnations and a bottle of champagne to beg Ellen's forgiveness for being such a bastard."

"And all hell broke loose when he found you together?"

"No, everyone was very English." In fact, the Adviser had been in the third-floor toilet, having a nocturnal pee. First he heard footsteps on the stairs and then Ellen's voice. Strangely calm, as if she welcomed, finally, a denouement to their drama.

"Don't come upstairs," she told Peter. "There is someone here with me."

Someone. It's only me. From over the sea. Feeling leaden, he climbed into his clothes and went down to face Peter in the living room, expecting shouts and screams and curses, maybe even a punch in the nose. I'm sorry, Peter. I'm sorry. Not knowing what else to say. There are moments for which there are no lines. Sorry. I wanted to be your friend.

"What are friends for?" Peter seemed exhausted. Hysterics are for Mediterranean peoples, and the professor preferred to wear his horns with Britannic dignity. "Just go away, will you?"

"So you left?" Woodward grimaces with pain, perspiration on his brow. "I hoped for a longer story."

"John, let me give you half a vial of morphine."

"Just a half then." The Adviser finds a vein in his arm and gives him three-quarters of a hypodermic.

"The story gets longer." The Adviser wipes the sweat off Woodward's face. "I got my suitcase and my Arabic dictionary and went out to my little Ford Cortina and sat there in Walton Street with the engine running. It was cold."

"But you waited?" Woodward seems woozy now. He is lying still. Morphine acts fast.

"I didn't think she would come. She and Peter had known each other since they were children together in Liverpool, and they had been lovers for a decade. I found out later that he pleaded with her to stay. Offered an exchange of forgiveness. And part of me didn't want her to come because I knew I couldn't structure a life with her as long as I stayed with the Reconnaissance Group."

"Surely after that assignment . . ."

The Adviser shakes his head. "I need a cabinet-level security clearance to do the work I do, and my government likes to know precisely where our loyalties lie. We're not allowed to marry foreign nationals, and a romance with a left-wing anti-American CND peace activist like Ellen would have been out of the question. They'd have yanked my clearance just for sleeping with her. So it was a clear-cut choice."

"What were you thinking?"

"I'd stopped thinking. I just sat in the Cortina and watched the lights go on and off on various floors as they roamed through the house, arguing and packing. Once she peered through the curtains to make sure that I was still there. Then she came out with an old cloth bag and a crockery pot she used for making yogurt. And jumped in. Shivering with cold. And maybe fear, I don't know."

"Where did you spend the night?" Woodward seems groggy and he slurs his words.

"Oxford is too quiet a place to have transient hotels open at three-thirty on Christmas morning. There's a horse pasture called Port Meadow near the Thames and we parked there. We had to run the motor most of the time to keep warm. Every so often a stallion would wander over and look in the window at us. Just before dawn, it began to snow and when the sun came up we saw horses standing at the edge of the frozen canal with snowflakes on their manes. It was very beautiful."

Woodward sighs deeply, comfortable now with the morphine soothing his brain. "I can see the rest of the story," he says in a curious sing-song voice. "When she found out you were a miserable spook, she got mad. But we can sort it all out, Captain America."

"Really, no, John . . . that's not how the story ends."

"The lass just needs a talking to," he mumbled. "Look, as soon as I can hobble around, I'll go to Oxford and explain things to her. When your plane lands at Heathrow I'll be there and so will she."

"It's too late!"

"I'll tell her what a decent chap you are. How you dodged bullets to save me."

"No, look . . . John, are you awake?"

"You deserve to be happy," Woodward murmurs. "We all deserve . . . a happy ending."

Then the sergeant major is asleep, dreaming morphine dreams. The Adviser touches his shoulder, but he does not move.

Numb with fatigue, he gets to his feet. All this telling of truth has tired him. Lies are so much more restful.

Most of the surviving scouts have gone to sleep, trusting that Napalm will warn them if there is an attack. A few feet away, there is another wounded soldier sobbing quietly and holding his stomach.

The Adviser mounts to where Napalm presides over the empty field, his finger resting lightly on the trigger of his jimpy. The houses at the south end of Bait al Muktar are still smouldering.

"The airplanes are coming," he tells Napalm, wondering what the man's real name is and why the British insist upon keeping his identity a secret. "It's just a question of time."

"Napalm," says the bearded man. He turns and points directly at the Adviser. There is no hostility in his voice but he speaks as if there were an urgent message within him. "Napalm, napalm," he repeats. "Napalm!"

"Napalm," the Adviser agrees, and they settle down side-by-side to wait.

I don't know who you are, Mr. Napalm, he thinks. And you don't know who I am. Am I anyone?

I tried to tell Ellen what I was, again and again. That night in the car, not knowing where the words were coming from, I said, look, you don't really know who I am, but if you would like to be married then I want to be your husband.

"Husband?" She turned and touched my chest with her hand. Feeling my heart.

"Yes, your husband. And if you wanted one, I would love a child with you. I would be its father."

And she said yes she would marry me. I'll have your babies. I want to live the rest of my life with you. I love you.

"You don't know who I am."

"I don't care who you are. Who are you?"
"You've always known," I said, but then I lost my courage.

> It's only me
> From over the sea.
> I'm Barnacle Bill,
> The traitor.

━━━━━━━━━━━━

Chapter Six

NONNES

The man from the Long Range Reconnaissance Group puts his ear against Captain Bernard Fenwich's chest and listens. Ali Rashidi watches anxiously.

"Sleeping soundly!" he proclaims, smiling at the Arab staff sergeant with reassuring calmness.

In fact, within the captain's ravaged chest, there is no longer a hint of breath or heartbeat. The wretched man is finally dead. So long, Bernie baby, the Adviser thinks, feeling a tiny tingle of regret. A battlefield is no place for silly people.

Instinctively, he glances at his watch. It is three o'clock. Nine hours since sunrise and five hours before sunset. The cloud cover still lingers at five hundred feet. It is oppressive, like living under a blanket.

"Sir, he will be all right?" Ali demands suspiciously.

"He will be fine." The Adviser has decided to defer Fenwich's demise, partially to avoid upsetting the superstitious Omanese and partially because the RAF will hurry to the rescue of a not-quite-dead British officer. Once they know that Fenwich is dead, they may be less eager to risk their lives for a wounded NCO and a terrified American intelligence adviser.

"Allah kareem!" chorus the scouts. "God is generous!"

He'd better be, thinks the Adviser pessimistically, wishing John Woodward would wake up and take charge. Of the original forty, there are now only twenty-seven scouts left alive and unhurt. Another of the wounded has died, and several more are going to Paradise with Bernie if help does not arrive soon. The *wa'adi* is growing rank because the troopers are shitting in corners and behind rocks. Since there is no toilet paper, the men are using handfuls of sand; the Adviser tries to imagine what it must feel like, and fails. Nor does underarm deodorant seem to be in plentiful supply. Nobody has any water left except the Adviser who has confiscated Fenwich's canteen.

Do I still want to smoke? Robbing a corpse is gauche, even for an American spy, so he leans solicitously over the Captain and pretends to be taking his pulse while slipping the squashed package of Rothmans from Fenwich's field jacket to his own. He is hunting for a match when the National Panasonic squawks at him.

There is a moment of dead air. Then the Adviser hears a faint English voice. "Scout Platoon, Scout Platoon, can you hear me?"

"Yes, come in!" The Adviser's heart begins beating rapidly. The war is about to begin again.

"Are you that American bloke?" The pilot's voice is clearer now. "How is Bernie Fenwich? Over."

"Hanging in there, and so is John Woodward! But we need to get both of them to a hospital!"

"Roger. Med-evac is ten minutes behind us. What are we looking for? Over."

"A town called Bait al Muktar!" In the distance, the Adviser can hear the rumble of approaching aircraft. "Just off the Midway Road, you'll see some burning buildings. Do you have the coordinates? Over."

"Yeah, we see smoke," says the pilot. "Where are you? Over."

"In a gully halfway between the road and Bait al Muktar. The Popular Front unit is dug into a long trench on the south side of the village facing us. Try not to hit the village itself. There are still civilians there."

"Sod the civilians!" says the pilot. "Get your heads down, Scout Platoon. Over and out."

"Ali! Sergeant Rashidi!" The Adviser is already fearful of the violence to come. "Get your people ready! We attack when the aircraft have struck the village."

With their hands over their ears, the scouts press their backs against the north wall of the *wa'adi*, preparing to endure the concussion from exploding bombs. The two surviving lance corporals issue their final reserves of ammunition. Napalm is standing up boldly in the bean field, peering at the sky. He looks worried. The Adviser is learning to worry whenever Napalm worries.

"Napalm! Get down, you lunatic!"

Napalm ignores him, staring at the cloud cover, which seems to have dropped another hundred feet in the past few minutes. The air seems incredibly still and so thick it is hard to see through. The rumble of jet engines grows closer and closer, but the aircraft are still invisible.

"Where are they, sir?" Ali Rashidi is puzzled. The jet roar is powerful but the Strikemasters are still lost in the clouds. Then, very high over the Midway Road, the Adviser sees a trace of jet exhaust, but nothing more.

"Oh Christ!" In a fury, he dives for the National Panasonic, realizing that the pilots are worried about the possibility that the *adoo* have another Grail heat-seeker in the inventory. "Strikemaster! Strikemaster! You're too fucking high! You can't hit anything from outer space!"

There is no reply.

Fighter pilots are funny people, he snarls mentally. Never knew one who wasn't a perfect shit. They start out thinking they're immortal. Then one day our blue-eyed, jut-jawed Anglo-Saxon hero watches his wing-mate crash and burn and realizes it could just as easily have been him. Longevity becomes a serious concern. Bombing runs are henceforth conducted from the safety of the stratosphere.

There are two squat, vague outlines in the high mist as the two Strikemasters fly past the Popular Front position and release their ordnance over Bait al Muktar itself. Suddenly lighter, the jets bound skywards and execute screaming right turns into the cloud bank. Having been as brave as they could for as long as they could. Which was not very brave. Nor for very long.

"Are those daisy-cutters?" He thinks at first that the RAF has dropped their deadly five-hundred-pound anti-personnel bombs. Then Napalm screams his favorite word and the Adviser understands that the Strikies have merely plopped four canisters of explosive petroleum jell on the village.

Just what we needed. With a certain clumsy elegance, a quartet of silver barrels comes cascading out of the sky, tumbling end over end, starting small and getting bigger as they plummet toward the smoldering village.

Napalm! A word to conjure with. All that technology to incinerate a village that is already burning. This is our ultimate response to any problem in the Third World, the Adviser fumes. When nothing else works, we drop fire on their heads.

He watches, crouched at the top of the gully. His mind fills with dread as the napalm splashes into the center of Bait al Muktar, well behind the two-story mayor's house and a long way from the *adoo*. The jell detonates and there is a silent column of horrid black smoke. A moment later, he hears the dull deep crackle as sound catches up to light. What had been a slow little fire becomes a big fast one and flames burst outwards from the center of the village consuming house after house.

Everything in the village is being destroyed except for the goddamn machine-gun entrenchment, he thinks furiously. Which the goddamn pilots couldn't even see from that altitude!

Did they think the village was the target? Or didn't they care? It is not the function of pilots to concern themselves with these mundane terrestrial matters but they have left the Adviser with a serious tactical problem.

There is a riot in his brain as he tries to decide what to do. He gets to his knees and looks through Woodward's field glasses at the Popular Front position in front of him, seeing *adoo* moving about frantically. They are hot and unhappy, but they are still trapped, and the napalm attack has accomplished nothing beyond making them more desperate than they were before. And the Scout Platoon continues to be cut off because there are still angry men over there armed with semi-automatic weapons, ready to cut the Scout Platoon to pieces.

"Must we attack now, sir?" Ali Rashidi seems unenthusiastic about a suicidal dash across the empty field.

"Not yet!" The Adviser leaps to his decision. He is not sure whether it is cowardice or good sense but "The Charge of the Light Brigade" has never been his favorite poem. He picks up the microphone and turns his broadcast strength up to maximum so they can monitor him in Um al Gwarif.

"Come in Strikemaster! Strikemaster wing, this is the Scout Platoon! Over."

"Roger, Scout Platoon. Over." The pilot's voice is uncertain.

"Strikemaster, you missed your target! I need one low-level sortie with cannon and rockets against the south side of Bait al Muktar and I need it now!"

"Scout Platoon, we have given you all the ordnance we could spare. We have another ground support mission. Out."

"Strikemaster, I have two badly hurt British personnel as well as many seriously wounded SAF troops. If we can't chopper them out, Sergeant Major Woodward and Captain Bernard Fenwich will both die! If you can give us one genuine ground support sortie, then there will be no questions raised later about your courage. Over."

This is my last card, the Adviser thinks as the two pilots turn down the volume to debate with one another privately. If they don't come back, I don't know what the hell to do. This is the last time I want to feel this frightened. If I survive today I will let the L.R.R.G. send me back to the Pentagon. Even downtown Washington can't be this dangerous.

"Right, Scout Platoon, we're going to knock your hats off." The lead pilot is back on the air an instant later. "We'll be over you in thirty seconds."

"This time we go no matter what!" he shouts to Ali Rashidi and the two corporals. "We'll never get the Strikies back a third time!"

"We are ready, sir!" Sergeant Rashidi herds the scouts to the top of the gully. The Popular Front guerrillas are still shooting haphazardly but they seemed confused.

Looking south, the Adviser sees the first Strikemaster coming in two hundred feet over the Midway Road. It is a squat, thick-bodied plane with a sharp nose, painted in blotchy camouflage brown and green and carrying a hodgepodge of rockets and bombs under each wing. It looks like a flying junkyard.

The air seems to shatter as the two ugly planes thunder across the bean field at a hundred miles per hour. They are firing a steady stream of 20-mm high-explosive cannon shells into the trench south of Bait al Muktar. The noise is frightening; with his hands over his ears, the Adviser watches each Strikey launch a Sura rocket at the *adoo* position. One missile goes long and detonates inside the town. The other hits a Shpagin and the gun emplacement seems to evaporate in blue flame, along with all its gun crew.

An instant later, the two planes streak over Bait al Muktar itself, and they each drop one five-hundred-pound daisy-cutter into the cluster of burning buildings.

The echoing blast seems to chase the aircraft skyward. Both pilots go to afterburners and climb straight up into the clouds. They don't bother saying good-bye.

The Adviser gets unsteadily to his feet, feeling numb. The noise and concussion is awful, and there are secondary explosions coming from the Popular Front position as ammunition stocks blow up. The air smells bad because acidy napalm fumes are drifting south from the village. The stench of cordite haunts the breeze.

For a moment, he feels too stunned to move. Is the heat getting to me? I shall now faint, he decides, feeling distinctly woozy and trying to encourage the sensation. I will pass out from the intense heat and Ali Rashidi can take command. My medal is waiting in Washington. This can be his chance to get a decoration. Maybe they will make him an officer for leading The Charge of Bait al Muktar.

The scouts are all standing still, looking at him. He realizes they are not going to attack until he leads them. They are accustomed to following the orders of murderous Caucasians, and there is no point now in trying to explain that his role here is purely advisory.

He gets the lady pistol out and studies the Popular Front position. Nobody is firing at the moment, but there are still some live *adoo* lurching around in confusion. Those are serious professionals over there, he thinks. If we don't take them out now, the survivors will get their shit together in another two minutes and defend that position. And then we won't be able to bring in a chopper to take John to the hospital!

"Okay! Okay?" I don't want to do this, he thinks, but he holds the lady pistol aloft and waves it to get their attention. "Follow me!" he cries in the approved Fort Bragg fashion and begins to lope across the bean field. He coughs because the smoke is getting into his lungs and then shouts again, "Follow me!"

Follow me. Oh yes. There is a huge cry from the scouts and an authentic charge begins. They are squat, compact men, built close to the ground, and they pound across the field like stampeding buffalo, shooting into the air and shouting incoherently. For the first fifty yards, Ali Rashidi dances along beside him breathing heavily, scared but determined to be precisely as brave as the Adviser. Suddenly, the Omanese staff sergeant shouts and falls flat on his face. For an awful moment, the Adviser thinks he has been shot, but Ali has merely tripped and fallen. He gets slowly to his hands and knees, waving to signify that he is all right.

In fact, the Adviser himself has been frightened until now, but adrenaline kicks in from some previously untapped source and he suddenly feels triumphant and strong.

"Let's go! Get the bastards!" He is beginning to feel very good about the whole enterprise, particularly since the *adoo* are still not shooting back. I can run faster than these scouts, he tells himself childishly, dashing out in front of the pack. Long legs are good for jumping over bean stalks. If Ellen could see me now. . . .

If Ellen could see you now she'd say that you'd gone crazy, a quiet corner of his brain warns, but after a day of discomfort and piss-in-your-pants fear, it feels good to be striking back at the bad guys.

And by God, we're winning now, he thinks as he gallops across the field, waving the lady pistol. We've got'em now! This is such a pure, uncomplicated emotion, he thinks, and it has sweet fuck-all to do with queens and countries and communists and capitalists. War isn't hell once you start winning: It feels like an orgasm!

This is the awful secret soldiers keep to themselves. To kill other people. And not die yourself. It feels good.

No, you're thinking crazy thoughts, he rebukes himself quickly, remembering a comment Ellen had once made just after they had made love, more roughly than usual. There was a bruise on her shoulder and he wondered if he had caused it.

"I sense rage in you," she had said. Do you think you joined the peace movement because subconsciously you wanted to master your inner violence? When we're making love, it excites me. And then afterward it frightens me.

It frightens me, too, he thinks. Calm down. Calm down. Bless me, Father. For I have sinned.

Only a few shots come from the Popular Front position, but their resistance falters quickly as Napalm sprays the trench with fire from his jimpy. The *adoo* ditch is four feet across. As they approach it a young man with a rifle jumps out.

The guerrilla's intentions are unclear. Instinctively, the Adviser raises the lady pistol and points it at the *adoo,* wondering what to do. Shoot, he commands himself. Take him out! Waste him! Shoot!

No, be not violent. Ellen tried so hard to make you gentle.

No, shoot! He is on that side and you are on this side!

He is still trying to decide when Lance Corporal Rachman cuts the *adoo* down with a burst from his Kalashnikov.

A second later, they all arrive at the edge of the *adoo* trench. The Adviser is panting from the exertion. It is a hot day for a two-hundred-yard dash.

The bottom of the trench is soaked with blood and there are many young *adoo* down there. Most of them are already dead or badly wounded. It's going to be a while before we can get this crowd to a hospital, the Adviser thinks, watching a dozen un-wounded guerrillas climb out of the trench on the opposite side. Shattered by the Strikemaster sortie, they raise their arms in sur-render. Two of them are barefoot young women. They all look dazed and frail in their baggy fatigue trousers and ragged khaki shirts.

It's over! The Adviser feels his body relax. We've won!

His jimpy slung casually over his shoulder, Napalm rolls up, laughing with schizoid satisfaction. The Adviser holsters his lady pistol and thinks about interrogating a few of the prisoners to find out what became of the rest of the 9 June Regiment. He pauses on the edge of the trench, gathering his strength to jump across.

Suddenly, the scouts open fire, cutting the *adoo* down one after another.

It takes fifteen seconds to kill them. When the firing stops there is one woman still unhurt, the last one in the row. She freezes, too frightened to run, watching her companions scream and crumble back into the ditch. The Adviser is too stunned to think properly. It occurs to him that they have spared the girl out of gallantry or because she is pretty.

Perhaps the female *adoo* reaches the same conclusion, because she sinks to her knees and folds her hands in front of her, as if praying in gratitude. She is very young, maybe fourteen or fifteen. She has covered her hair with a black Che Guevara beret, worn rakishly on one side of her head. The Adviser pictures her as she must have been a few hours earlier, on the eve of her first battle for proletarian democracy, posing before a mirror and adjusting that beret to precisely the right angle.

She manages a frightened smile, looking up in supplication as Lance Corporal Rachman leaps over the ditch and stands over her with his Kalashnikov. Rachman is smiling too. They're going to rape her, the Adviser thinks. I won't permit that. Where the hell is Ali Rashidi?

Then Rachman puts the muzzle of his assault rifle against the side of the girl's skull. Time seems to stop. Everyone is watching. There is an awful look on her face when she realizes what is going to happen. She closes her eyes, clenching her hands against her breasts.

"No! Listen, don't you . . ." the Adviser stammers, but Corporal Rachman squeezes off a single round. It blows off the back of the girl's head.

"Oh . . . oh, no!" His body is suddenly cold. His fingers and feet go clammy and there is bile in the back of his throat. No one is paying any attention to him now. The scouts begin shooting down into the trench, killing the wounded and double-killing the already dead. Then they leap down and ransack the corpses for valuables.

Dizzy, the Adviser hops over the ditch. A cloud of smoke blows in from the village. It is hard to see. In the confusion, he finds Napalm standing over the *adoo* girl. What has just happened seems to signify something to him because he seems sad for a moment. Then he shrugs and stalks away, walking back across the bean field toward the Midway Road, losing interest in the rest of the battle.

"Rachman!" In the midst of the confusion, the Adviser spots

the lance corporal and grabs his arm. "What . . . what are you doing?"

Rachman looks at him blankly. "We are killing them, sir." He speaks as if clearing up an obscure technical point. Two men remain behind to loot the body of the dead girl but the other scouts are filing into the village. Up ahead of him in the midst of the smoke there is more shooting. The Adviser wonders how anyone in Bait al Muktar could still be alive to kill.

"You must not murder prisoners! Those people had surrendered."

"We are sending them to hell," Rachman snarls. "When the *adoo* are all dead, we can all go home."

"You can't. I will not allow. . . ." the Adviser breaks off, since he is starting to feel seriously nauseous. Corporal Rachman turns on his heel and marches off into the smoldering village.

The two adolescent scouts crouched over the body of the dead *adoo* girl have ripped open the front of her khaki shirt. They are playing with her tiny breasts, giggling and poking her nipples with their fingers.

Suddenly Ali Rashidi appears, leaping over the *adoo* trench. In a fury, he attacks the two scouts with his Armalite, holding the rifle by the barrel and clubbing them unmercifully with the stock. He is screaming in Arabic, using words the Adviser never learned in Oxford. They cringe and take their beating unresistingly. After giving them a half-dozen good wallops apiece, Sergeant Rashidi stops, panting heavily. His nose is bleeding and his face is scratched from falling among the bean plants earlier.

Whimpering, the two scouts dash into Bait al Muktar to join their compatriots.

"The fighting makes them crazy." Ali Rashidi gazes at the dead *adoo*. "Allah . . . does not like this."

"Allah must be disappointed all the time." The Adviser intended to be sarcastic but Ali Rashidi takes him seriously.

"I don't know why we are these things doing!" He is seriously unhappy. "We Arabs must not do the crazy. We fight because our God want but this is bad things."

There is the sound of shooting from deep inside the village and Sergeant Rashidi turns away.

"Get your people under control," the Adviser mutters. "You and Allah need to take charge of Bait al Muktar."

Ali nods and runs into the village, leaving the Adviser abruptly alone. A harsh wind from the north is blowing smoke and cinders and ash into his face. It is hard to see and even harder to breath.

The vomiting comes over him with savage force. There is nothing left of the British Army breakfast in his digestive tract, but some awful green liquid pours out of him as he drops to his knees.

When the spasm finally passes, he wipes his mouth on his undershirt, crouching on his hands and knees next to the dead girl. There is a strange serenity about her features now. As she lies on her back, she looks like a daring teenager sunbathing topless at the beach.

"I'm sorry," he says in English. His Arabic has turned off and any language, under the circumstances, will do as well. "I don't seem to be able to make up my mind what to do in time to be of use to anybody. I'm sorry.

"I'm sorry," he says again. Without knowing exactly why, he covers her breasts with her torn shirt.

There is a mud wall standing a few feet beyond the *adoo* ditch, breached now in many places by 20-mm cannon shells.

At first the Adviser feels disinclined to enter the town at all, wondering if he should not return to the *wa'adi* to care for John Woodward. On the other hand, Nigel Fine had been emphatic about ensuring that Bait al Muktar was clear of *adoo* before bringing in med-evac choppers.

I'll check to see that it's safe, he thinks dully, not overly anxious to witness whatever horrors Bait al Muktar now contains. Unsteady on his feet, he climbs through the rubble into the town and finds himself on a narrow avenue, paved with flagstones and leading through the center of the shattered town.

The village is still smoldering. All the thatched roofs have been consumed but hard wood rafters are still burning briskly. A slight atmospheric downdraft is swirling eddies of acrid smoke in the street. His eyes are stinging badly and the fire is making the day even hotter. Ash is everywhere and burning twigs are still falling out of the sky.

He wanders down the main street to the burned-out wreckage of the mayor's house, the two-story frame building he himself hit with the phosphorus grenade. I can't blame this on the RAF, he thinks soberly. This is my handiwork.

He forces himself to look through the door frame into the gutted interior. There is a gray blanket of cinders covering everything. A few feet from the door, he sees the bodies of two adults, three adolescents, and half a dozen small children. The blackened corpses are all intertwined. The family must have been huddling together in fear when the building caught fire.

The hut has a strange smell about it, recalling the scent of sirloin over charcoal. It reminds the Adviser of those Long Range Reconnaissance Group picnics in Virginia and the aroma of sizzling steaks.

Abruptly, he realizes that barbecues and burned people smell about the same. The thought shivers him.

This could have happened to us, he thinks, retreating quickly to the street. If the battle had gone the other way. Somewhere in the distance, there is the echo of rapid-fire weapons, but the Adviser is losing interest. He wanders along what must once have been the main street, catching an occasional glimpse of the scouts rampaging down side alleys in groups of two and three. They are in a looting frenzy and no one is in charge of them now, not Ali Rashidi, not the Technical Intelligence Adviser from the Long Range Reconnaissance Group, and certainly not Allah.

There are bodies everywhere, dozens and dozens, and even dead donkeys and dogs. He realizes that most of Bait al Muktar's population must now be dead or in the process of being hunted down and slaughtered. A few of the casualties are young men and women who might have been combatants. There are sides in life, he tries to tell himself. I am on one side. They were soldiers, fighting on the other side.

But the formula fizzles; the majority of the human casualties appear to be simple al-Qara tribesfolk, old women and little kids who don't look as if they were ever on anyone's side. Most of them have been burned by the napalm or sliced up by shrapnel from the daisy-cutters. A few are unhurt except for bullets in the chest, courtesy of the Scout Platoon.

I can't take any more. He tries to number the times since arriving in Dhofar that he reached the same conclusion. I've been saying this since three in the morning, but I really can't take any more. My brain is going to quit. Minds were never designed to absorb things like this.

In other wars, the Adviser has seen men react to terminal awfulness by sinking into a comfortable fugue state, curling up in a fetal ball and ignoring the world until someone takes them to a hospital and fills them with blissful therapeutic drugs.

That's what will happen to me. Any minute now. I can't take any more. I need to go and lie down. I need to get drunk. To be unconscious for a long time. To wake up in big bed with smooth white sheets and a bathroom with hot-and-cold running water and a wise, gentle nurse stroking my forehead with her fingers.

The way Ellen used to do.

A dizziness comes over him. Nearby is the partially collapsed wall of what was once a house, providing a place for the Adviser to sit. I will rest here for a moment, he thinks. Then I will go back and wait with John until the helicopters come. This day is almost over and soon I can go back to the Um al Gwarif Hilton. It will be cooler after dark. Today's ration of hard things has already been chewed and swallowed.

"Arjook said akqi?"

He is too numb to jump when a child's soft voice assails him from the interior of the devastated house, but his hand drifts slowly toward the lady pistol.

Ridiculous, he thinks. If there is someone back there with a gun, I'll be dead in another second . . . he turns cautiously.

"Arjook said akqi?" The voice is pleading, insistent, asking, "Please help my brother?"

The smoke and dust make it hard to see. The ruined house is a pile of rubble: mortar and stone and shattered boards and fragments of brightly colored cloth and broken clay pots and shards of glass and crockery. Somewhere in there is a child.

He rubs his eyes and gets them focused well enough to see a little girl, no more than three feet tall and perhaps four or five years old. It is hard to tell with Arab girls because they need to grow up so fast.

"Don't be afraid," he tells her, although she does not seem afraid. She is a beautiful child with dark, wide, luminous brown eyes. She is wearing a simple cotton shift that extends from her shoulders to just above her knees; the frayed garment was once white but now is soiled with soot. The girl's ears are each adorned with a single silver earring.

The scouts would kill you for that silver, the Adviser thinks, suddenly realizing that this was the same little girl he saw just before the fighting began, playing on the edge of town with a little boy. She has long black hair, secured at the back with a dirty pink ribbon.

"My brother is hurt." Lifting her bare feet carefully over the rubble, she approaches the Adviser and takes him by the hand. You are a big person, her manner implies. Sorry, but you are in charge. There isn't anyone else.

Briefly enjoying the sensation of having her soft hand in his, the Adviser follows the child past some fallen timbers into a protected corner. Lying on a burlap bag is a baby boy, perhaps eighteen months old, naked and badly burned by splashed napalm. The child's face is untouched but his right arm and right leg have both been horribly seared and his elbow bone is visible. His skin is fiery red where it has been scorched and black where the napalm has eaten away the flesh.

The Adviser feels the nausea returning. I hope the child dies quickly, he thinks, forcing himself to bend down and look at it closely. The smell of charred flesh is terrible and he tries to breathe through his mouth.

"Will he be all right?" asks the child. "His name is Suleiman."

"I don't know." Little brother seems to be in shock. His eyes flutter open and closed. His breath is shallow and rapid. He is drooling and his tiny body is twitching.

"Is this your house?" he asks, wondering if any of her relatives could conceivably be alive.

"No, our house was burning," she answers methodically. She has a deep voice for a little girl. "We came here to the house of our uncle. Then the fire fell out of the sky."

The whole family must be dead, the Adviser calculates. It's up

137

to me to do something. Not knowing how else to proceed, he strips off his khaki shirt and spreads it next to the boy. He picks him up by his unwounded arm and leg and lays him down in the shirt, so that he can carry him without doing any more damage to the blistered flesh. When the Adviser tucks him under one arm, the boy whimpers and then begins a steady muffled sobbing.

"Hold my hand," he commands, since he worries that the girl will be shot by the scouts unless she is clearly under his protection. The nearest medical kit is back at the *wa'adi* and he pulls her along quickly behind him, now anxious to be out of Bait al Muktar. At the end of the street, the little girl suddenly points to the wreckage of the mayor's house, the one struck by the Adviser's phosphorus grenade.

"That is the house of my father. It has stopped burning."

Oh lord, it was her family I killed, he realizes. The girl is pulling away, wanting to see the interior of her house, but the Adviser holds her hand tightly. "There is no one there! They have, uh . . . gone away."

"Where?"

"I don't know. I will take care of you."

"Who are you?"

"I am just a friend. What is your name?"

There is a long puzzling pause. The child seems terribly bright. Surely she knows her own name?

"My father called me *'bint.'* "This perplexes the Adviser even more, since *bint* is just the ordinary Arabic word for girl and not a real name at all.

"But what was your proper name?"

"I am just Bint," she explains in a matter-of-fact tone. "My father has too many daughters and he could not think of a name for me. Will you help us?"

A child with no name! The Adviser is powerfully moved. Bint, we are special, he thinks. People without names can invent their own. And change them as needs be.

"I am on your side," he tells her as they cross the bean field. The baby boy has lapsed into unconsciousness. Bint is too small to walk easily through the vegetation so he picks her up. Trustingly, she puts both arms around his neck and holds on for dear life.

I am on your side, child, he thinks furiously. There are no other sides.

The Dhofar Brigade's med-evac chopper is an ancient Agusta-Bell 205, similar in design and function to the "Huey" known and loved by a generation of Vietnam veterans. The pilot brings her in slow and sideways, looking for a flat spot in the bean field near the *wa'adi*. A British medical officer with captain's pips is dangling from the hatchway, his eyes sweeping the landscape as he counts casualties.

The Adviser has placed the wounded baby boy next to Woodward in their makeshift aid station. The little girl is terrified by the roar of the Agusta-Bell engine. She squats next to her brother, holding his hand and crying out in fear every time the Adviser moves away.

"Hey, Sergeant Dauntless, it's time to go." Gently, he wakes John Woodward, wondering if and when they will see each other again.

"Huh?" When his eyes open, Woodward gazes blankly at the Arab girl. "What a beautiful child!"

"John, we've secured the village." The Adviser is curiously proud of having led the charge of Bait al Muktar; he wishes Woodward had been conscious to see it. "We're going to fly you back to the Field Surgical Team in Um al Gwarif."

"Don't let the scouts . . ." He lifts one arm and points at Bint, but the sergeant major is too full of morphine to carry on a coherent conversation.

"Don't what?"

". . . get her." His eyes close again wearily.

A second later the medical officer leaps down from the Agusta-Bell and tumbles down into the *wa'adi,* carrying a medical bag. A short, stocky young man with spectacles and close-cropped hair, he manages to look competent and frightened at the same time. Ali Rashidi by his side, he moves rapidly from casualty to casualty, performing a rapid triage as he snaps instructions to his stretcher-bearers. Under Rashidi's direction, the walking wounded among the scouts begin to pile onto the Agusta-Bell and the Adviser wonders how many people they intend to crowd aboard a machine built for twelve passengers, and whether or not there will be room for him and the children.

"Hello, I'm Dick Barnet." Reaching the far end of the *wa'adi,* the physician offers his hand and the Adviser shakes it. Barnet has that imperial accent that English families acquire after nine generations at Eton. "I hear you've been frightfully brave. Are you all right?"

"I'm fine, but we just lost Captain Fenwich. Could you glance at Sergeant Major Woodward and see if we have the bleeding in his leg stopped?"

With a fine eye for protocol, Barnet first runs a stethoscope over Fenwich's chest and touches a vein in the captain's neck. He shakes his head and moves quickly to the sergeant major.

"He ought to be okay, but I'd better call Jenny," says the physician after a quick inspection.

"You know Mrs. Woodward?"

"She's my mother's aunt's great-niece. Smashing girl."

"I thought she was divorcing him?"

"She is but she shouldn't. Listen, how much morphine has John had?"

"Three quarters of an ampule, about forty-five minutes ago."

The doctor waves urgently for a stretcher team. "Let's get him on board. I can get that shrapnel out but we need to move sharpish. In this climate, that wound will go septic in a jiffy."

When the stretcher team has carried John Woodward away, the Adviser unfolds his field jacket to expose little Suleiman.

"Can you look at this boy?" The child's eyes are open, and his body is quivering. His burned flesh looks worse than ever, and Bint begins to sob at the sight of it.

"Oh shit!" Barnet pronounces the word to rhyme with "bite." Gently, he turns the baby over, looking at the trauma on his side and back. "Did our chaps accomplish that?"

"The Strikemasters did a napalm run."

"There's not much I can do." Barnet digs in his medical bag and produces a large morphine hypodermic. "I . . . I don't know. I'll leave this with you. If he wakes up again, give him the whole dose."

"Can't you fly him out with the others?"

The doctor looks distressed. He gets to his feet and takes a few steps away. The Adviser can see that the answer is going to be no. "I'd break the rules and take him if there were a minimal chance of doing him any good. But he needs a whole medical team all to himself and about eight hours of immediate surgery and even then it would be iffy. I'll be operating for the next twenty-four hours straight on the military patients whom I'm obligated to treat first, and this lad'll be dead long before I could look at him."

"What can I do?"

"There's a civilian hospital in Salalah." Unhappily, the doctor walks back to where little Suleiman is lying and looks at him again. "They might be able to save him if they're not too busy with other casualties. You've been out of touch up here all day, but there's been a lot of fighting down on the plain. The Salalah Hospital frankly is a long shot. You might do better to use the morphine."

The Adviser holds up the hypodermic. "Isn't this too much?"

"I hate this!" Suddenly, the doctor's shoulders shake and his voice quivers. "It's like being a butcher."

"The morphine," the Adviser begs. "Isn't it too much?"

"Of course it's too much!" The doctor stamps away toward the helicopter. "That's the whole bloody point, isn't it?"

The Adviser watches the helicopter lift off, its overburdened motor straining to rise out of the bean plants. He worries about Woodward's safety, since there are far too many passengers aboard the Agusta-Bell, and flying a chopper down to sea level through the circling mists of the *jebel* will not be easy.

Led by Lance Corporal Ali Rachman, one squad of scouts wanders back across the field, dragging bags of plunder from Bait al Muktar. Still smoking, the village is now almost completely level.

They'll have killed everyone, he realizes. Bint's whole family must be dead, except for poor little Suleiman.

"Hallo, Captain America, sir!" Returning victorious from glorious battle, Rachman jumps down into the *wa'adi*. He looks sinister and violent.

"I'm not a fucking captain anything, you bastard!" the Adviser shouts, remembering the murder of the *adoo* girl. Anxious to get away, he rewraps the wounded baby boy in his field jacket and tucks him under his arm. Bint eagerly takes his free hand and they cross to the gully's south slope and climb up.

Cold and resentful, Rachman follows them to the surface of the bean field. "Hey, you got nice girl, eh?" He bends to look at the terrified Bint, his hands reaching out to touch her ears.

He wants her silver earrings! The Adviser has the lady pistol out in a second, pointing it at the lance corporal. "Get away from her! Touch her and I kill you! Do you understand?"

For a moment it looks like trouble. Rachman's face darkens and he runs his fingers over the stock of his Kalashnikov, swinging it boldly around to aim at the Adviser's stomach. At least twenty scouts are watching the encounter with interest and the American contemplates the ease and safety with which they could murder him in the middle of this obscure bean field and then blame it on an anonymous *adoo* sniper.

The Adviser is frightened but stubborn. Deliberately, he switches off the safety on his lady pistol and presses the weapon against Rachman's chest. "Go away!" he says.

"Fuck you!" The lance corporal pushes the barrel of his own weapon into the Adviser's gut.

"Rachman!" There is a harsh shout from a few yards away and they both look up to see Ali Rashidi standing at the edge of the *wa'adi,* aiming his Armalite directly at Rachman. "It is time to be praying."

Very slowly, the lance corporal lowers his assault rifle, his face softening into a grin. "Nice little girl, Captain America." He makes a circle with the thumb and index finger of his left hand, and then jabs the middle finger of his right hand in and out of the hole. "You like, huh?"

"Go fuck yourself!" The Adviser backs away with little Suleiman in one hand and the pistol in the other and Bint clinging to his leg. Corporal Rachman laughs again and then turns back to join the praying.

This day keeps getting longer, the Adviser thinks as he trudges toward the Midway Road. Bint still cannot keep up the pace because the bean plants are up to her waist so the Adviser hoists her again into his arms. I'm getting tired. Got to be careful here. The old brain isn't working very well.

Carrying the two children across the field is exhausting and he is breathing heavily when he reaches the Midway Road. The keys to the Land-Rover are missing, presumably because Ali Rashidi has them in his pocket. One of the Bedfords has been badly damaged by Shpagin fire, but the other, parked behind an embankment, is untouched and the key is in the ignition.

I'll swipe the truck and drive the child to Salalah, he decides. The Scout Platoon can walk. Then it occurs to him that he no longer has his map of Dhofar Province. Oh Christ! I left it back at the *wa'adi,* next to the Panasonic!

For a moment, the Adviser panics. How could I have done that? A TechIntel chart is classified well above top secret and even the existence of satellite thermal infrared maps is considered sensitive. Under the L.R.R.G. regulations, it is his solemn obligation to retrieve the map. Otherwise, he faces a commission of inquiry with disciplinary sanctions to follow.

Little Suleiman begins to cry again, making birdlike noises as the coarse fabric of the Adviser's field jacket abrades his burned flesh. To hell with TechIntel, he thinks. I'll say there was a moment when it looked as if we might be captured and I burned the map. I've got to get this kid to Salalah.

But how am I going to find Salalah without a map?

He is working on the problem when Napalm wanders up to the Bedford, drinking water from a canteen. The man looks tired and depressed and he is filthy, his bare chest covered with gray soot from the village. There is bean field mud in his beard and hair, and Bint cries out at the sight of him.

Mad or not, he's our only chance, thinks the Adviser. He found his way up here and he can find his way back down.

He rushes forward, the two children in his arms. "Napalm! Listen, hi, how are you?"

Napalm gazes at them without responding. Ignoring the Adviser, he quickly puts his canteen to Bint's lips. The girl shrinks back at first and then gulps the warm, heavily chlorinated water.

"Look, look at this little boy." The Adviser holds Suleiman out to the deranged Englishman. "We have to take him to that hospital in Salalah."

"Napalm." Napalm inspects the child and splashed a few drops of water from his canteen onto Suleiman's head, touching his forehead with his blunt index finger. "Napalm, napalm, napalm . . ."

The Adviser is mystified. "What are you doing? Listen to me! We can't be crazy now. There's been enough crazy for one day. Do you know where the hospital is? The hospital in Salalah?"

"Napalm."

"Listen, you bastard, I know you're in there! You can go back to being demented tomorrow, but now you have to be sane enough to get us down to that hospital! Take us to the hospital. In Salalah!"

Napalm seems moved. He stares intently at the Adviser and his eyes redden, as if he is about to weep.

"First, tell me your name!" begs the Adviser. "Don't say 'napalm.' Tell me who you are."

Shaking his head, the big man turns and throws his jimpy onto the passenger seat. "Napalm," he says, climbing into the cab of the Bedford and starting the engine.

Is this a decision? The Adviser darts to the rear of the truck, finding that the tailgate is down. The back of the Bedford is a rubble heap of military paraphernalia: bed rolls, mess kits, ammunition boxes, reed prayer mats, medical supplies, shovels and extra machine guns, canvas tarpaulins, jerrycans of water, and that big wooden box of dates.

I need to make a bed for Suleiman, he thinks, setting Bint on the floor of the truck and climbing in after her with Suleiman in his arms. Locking the tailgate in the upright position, he drags the children to the front of the passenger compartment and arranges the wounded child on a prayer rug.

"Go," he shouts to Napalm through the opening into the cab. "Take it easy on the bumps."

Despite the roar of the motor, Suleiman is asleep or unconscious. The Adviser wedges the boy's tiny body between two ammunition boxes to keep him from rolling back and forth.

Smoothly, Napalm brings the big lorry around in a circle and heads downhill toward the coast. As they go into the first turn, the smoking skyline of Bait al Muktar appears briefly in the distance, framed by the Bedford's open hatchway. Bint looks at her doomed village and begins to cry.

"Baby, no, it's okay, girl," he soothes her. There are wooden benches on either side of the vehicle, but the Adviser sits on a prayer mat with his back braced against the bulkhead of the cab. Then he lifts a frightened Bint onto his lap. Instinctively, the child rests her head against his chest, bringing her knees up against her stomach and covering her face with her hands.

"Peace, peace," he whispers in Arabic. "It's alright, little girl. Everything's going to be alright."

Bint's sobbing subsides and she closes her eyes. He can feel her tiny heart beating against his chest.

It's over now, he thinks. We'll take Suleiman to the hospital and I'll have done all that anyone could have expected of me. There must be an orphanage or a shelter for homeless children in Salalah and when I've made sure that Bint is safe I can go back to Um al Gwarif. I wonder where John Woodward keeps his stock of McGinty's Brown Ale? I need a drink. And then sleep.

"My house is burned," the child murmurs unhappily. "Where will I go to live?"

"Don't you have relatives somewhere?"

Bint shakes her head. "All my father's brothers live in Bait al Muktar."

"Does your mother have relatives?"

"My mother went to Paradise when Suleiman was born. She was an Arab woman from the Yemen. I might have relatives over there but I don't know who they are."

Then you are a proper orphan indeed, the Adviser meditates gloomily. The People's Democratic Republic of Yemen and the Sultanate of Oman are virtually at war over the Dhofar rebellion. It seems unlikely that they have an orphan exchange treaty.

It is hot and stuffy beneath the Bedford's canvas top and the Adviser tries to let his battered body relax, resting against the steel partition between the cab and the passenger compartment. Bint's pink ribbon has come undone and her dark hair is now sprayed untidily over her shoulders. Tentatively, he strokes and smooths her hair and refastens the silk band. He is worried at first that she might misunderstand the gesture, but she sighs and snuggles up to him more closely. It occurs to him that he will miss her.

"How is it that you speak such good Arabic?" he asks.

"Everyone in the village speaks Shheri, but my mother always talked to me in real Arabic." Suddenly, she looks up at him, her brown eyes flashing. "How many sons do you have?"

"None."

"You must get another wife," Bint advises him seriously. "My father has three wives. Do you have a little girl?"

"No."

He is unsure what else to say, but the answer seems to be satisfactory because Bint closes her eyes again, murmurs something indistinct, and drifts into an exhausted sleep.

I almost had a little something, he thinks, closing his eyes and letting his mind wander back to Oxford. Maybe a little girl. Until I met Ellen I never thought about being a father—not that kind of father.

It was amazing that it took as long as it did. Since we made love every day. Sometimes twice. In that little North Oxford flat on the Woodstock Road. And never took any precautions.

It was a Sunday morning, he remembers, three months ago. June it would have been, because this is the end of September. And Sunday morning because the church bells woke us up, and she jumped out of bed and dashed down to that Boots Pharmacy on Cornmarket Street. She came back with a package and disappeared into the bathroom for the longest time. I listened to Radio Three and turned it off when the Sunday Service came on.

Then she came out, smiling and frightened, and said something about litmus paper changing color. She was wearing that old pink cotton bathrobe.

"I'm going to have your baby."

It was a brittle moment. Ellen stood at the kitchen table, her hands cupping her breasts, as if waiting for them to fill with milk.

"My baby?"

"Yes, of course, your baby," she giggled. "You complete fool! Who else?" She had gray-green eyes and they were glistening with tears.

"I'm happy."

"Are you really happy?"

"Yes," he swore, "I'm happy, by God, I'm happy," and he swept her into his arms to avoid the interrogation. A baby. A wife. A family. Yes, I am happy.

"What will we do?" she asked.

"We'll make plans," he vowed, holding her tightly and kissing her hair. And thinking, now it begins: complications without end.

His mind worked furiously. I have three options, he thought for the hundredth time. First, I could inform the Reconnaissance Group that I intend to marry a foreign national whose political beliefs are inconsistent with my continuing to serve the U.S. government in a classified capacity. They'd cart me back to Washington for a long, hostile debriefing to determine whether I'd compromised the CND operation. How would I explain my absence to Ellen? When the Reconnaissance Group turned me loose, I'd be out on the street with a woman who was both suspicious and pregnant, without a job, or prospects for getting a job.

Second alternative? I could say nothing and—for the moment— let things go on as they are. The L.R.R.G. is ecstatic with my reports from Greenham Common and nothing has to change instantly. But I now have a proper master's degree from a proper British university, and if we marry, I would have right of residency here in Britain. I could teach or work for an oil company in the Middle East. There is some money in the bank, and once I've got a proper job, I could quietly resign from the Long Range Reconnaissance Group without saying anything about her to them or them to her.

And we could live happily ever after. I will become an authentic peace activist. I will go to demonstrations.

With my wife. And my child.

"You're going to be a wonderful father," she said. "I've watched you with children. You have so much to teach ours."

"Yes, yes, I'll teach him Arabic."

"Maybe she'll be a girl. You could teach her about peace."

I could teach her about deceit and deception, he thought. Unless I chose my third option, which involves saying, oh, by the way, I'm not actually an idealistic draft dodger. I was once a captain in the Army. With two tours in Vietnam. A Bronze Star and a Purple Heart and three Army Commendation Medals. I am now a senior officer in an American intelligence unit called the Long Range Reconnaissance Group. I was sent here with the mission of penetrating the Committee for Nuclear Disarmament.

Penetrating you was an unauthorized private initiative.

"Ellen, there are some things about me, some disagreeable things," he began.

"You snore," she said, and kissed him hard, her lips apart, her tongue exploring the interior of his mouth. "And I love you anyway! Could anything be worse than that?"

"There are worse things than that. And I love you too much to deceive you."

"There are things in my past too. We'll drink gin again some night after the baby comes and get drunk and confess all our dirty little secrets." She sighed and put her head on his shoulder and hugged him. He felt her breasts pressing against him. This goes beyond honor, he decided. If I could keep her by confessing all, then I would do it. If I can keep her by saying nothing, then I shall be silent.

I will say nothing to anyone about anything. My whole life has been an exercise in keeping secrets. Why should anything change now? Once I have a job, I can simply walk away from the government. Being an intelligence officer is not like being a priest. Those vows were never meant to be eternal.

"I have to ask you something," Ellen was saying urgently. "Before it gets to be too late in my pregnancy, I want to spend a few days a week down at Greenham Common with the other women. You know, we've started that camp. The Women's Peace Camp. I'll hate being apart from you, but I need to do my bit."

"Greenham? You want to go to Greenham?"

"Sweet, what I love most about you is how you make me feel free. I want to spend some of my freedom at Greenham with my sisters in the movement!"

Oh. His mind went into high gear. This could be part of the solution, he thought. Ellen could be my pipeline into the heart of the Woman's Peace Camp. If she could produce some high quality intelligence, it would ensure that I was left here in Oxford until I get things sorted out.

"I'll be so proud of you," he said quickly. "I'll miss you, but if it'll help stop those warmongers in the Pentagon . . ."

And so I let her go to Greenham Common, he thinks as Napalm takes the Bedford around a sharp turn. With my baby inside her. All unwitting and unaware, she became my agent, the best I ever ran.

I would drive down to Greenham Common for lunch and take her to that awful Little Chef Restaurant near Newbury and feed her fish and soggy chips while she told me all her news.

"This evening we're going to barricade the camp. We're going to dance and sing all night and spook the Americans. On Wednesday we'll lie down in the road and block the convoy. One of our sisters has seduced a sergeant named Jackson and he's told us about a rear entrance to the camp. We're going to sneak in Friday night and paint peace symbols on a Cruise missile. We're deciding now whether we should try to sabotage it as well."

She told me everything—in plenty of time for me to tell the Long Range Reconnaissance Group, and for them to tell the Greenham Common commanding officer. The rear entrance was suddenly chained shut, and Sergeant Jackson got sent to Alaska.

But the CND kept great mobs of angry women at every entrance and exit and Greenham Common stayed non-operational. The women built a huge slum city at the front gate with tents and plywood shacks and camp fires and outdoor kitchens. They had babies there. They prayed and sang and laid down in front of the mobile missile launchers every time the base authorities tried to move them in or out.

And the Pentagon was frantic. Every day more Cruise missiles were flown in from America, and they couldn't be deployed. The Air Force military police at Greenham Common were growing violent. One day, one of them could go berserk and start shooting the women.

Being there was hard for her, because the police harassed the peace campers unmercifully, using loud speakers to keep them awake all night. She wasn't used to sleeping in a tent and I was worried she'd lose the baby because she needed sedatives to get to sleep. I should have insisted she come home or stayed there only during the day. But night was when CND held its war councils and hatched its darkest plots against the Cruise. I needed her there at night.

Could I have played it differently? Suppose, the moment she said she was pregnant, suppose I'd told her who and what I was, what would have happened? Would she have left me there and then?

Probably. Nobody partied with Benedict Arnold after the war. Bless me, Father. For I have sinned.

But damn, it would have been good, he thinks, feeling an emptiness in his chest. Being the father of a child. A little girl like this one. I don't suppose it will ever happen now, but it would have been good. I'd have put a lot of energy into being a father. Hello, Daddy, she'd say in the morning when I came to wake her up. Or would she call me Papa? Hi, Papa! Hi, Pop. Hello, Dad. Where's Mommy? Mommy's still sleeping, my darling daughter, but Daddy will get you breakfast this morning. Thank you, Daddy. I love you, Daddy. I love you too. My daughter. I love . . .

Bint is asleep, but he is crying and cuddling her when the shooting starts.

He cannot tell who is firing at them or why or from where, but it is that old Shpagin sound and in the last fleeting moment of sanity, he remembers that they never did account for that second Russian-made machine gun when they stormed the *adoo* position. Some of the 9 June people must have slipped out of Bait al Muktar before the Strikemaster raid.

Bint wakes up, screaming in terror as bullets come tearing through the Bedford's canvas top. From the driver's compartment there is a crash of glass as the front windscreen shatters. Napalm howls, a deep-throated savage yell.

Christ! Not again. I can't take any more! This has got to stop! The Adviser gets to his hands and knees, indecisive and uncertain. All he can see over the tailgate is sky and mist high on the *jebel*. Do I have to act? Couldn't I just lay here and let it all happen? I was meant to be an observer of life, not a participant. The Bedford is swaying violently from side to side as it waddles its way down a steep incline and military gear is tumbling all over the Bedford's interior. The big wooden box overturns, spilling sticky brown dates across the floor.

Save Bint.

And Suleiman. I can't go on losing children. The little boy seems safe enough where he is but the Adviser puts the girl into the half-empty date box, closes the cover, and pushes it into the far corner of the passenger compartment under one of the wood benches.

"Stay there!" Frantically, he begins to pile anything he can find on top of the box: blankets, prayer mats, empty ammunition boxes, canvas tarpaulins, and stretcher poles.

The firing halts momentarily as the *adoo* gunner gives his barrel a moment to cool. Napalm jams on the brakes and the Bedford skids, the giant rear tires screeching sideways over hard-packed earth and throwing up a cloud of red dust. The Adviser loses his balance and falls backwards, his head slamming into the bulkhead of the troop transport.

"No, no, Christ! Watch out!" Stunned, he bounces off the metal partition and rolls down the aisle between the two wooden seats toward the tailgate. There is a jumble of loose equipment sweeping along with him and he flounders toward the back of the truck, scraping his knuckles as he tries to hang on to something solid.

"What's happening? Don't stop, Napalm! For Christ's sake, keep moving!" He hauls himself up on the tailgate and tries to see where the fire is coming from. We're headed downhill, he thinks desperately. Even if the Shpagin knocks out our engine, we ought to be able to coast out of range if Napalm can only keep it on the road!

From under the chassis, the Adviser hears a grinding from the gearbox and the truck slows even more, dropping to a few miles per hour and rocking from side to side.

Is he going to stop and fight? Can't we get through? I can't see anything. The Adviser gets to his feet, puzzled, blinded by exhaust smoke and dust, and leans out the back of the Bedford, trying to see.

Just then, Napalm gets the Bedford into first gear and stamps on the gas.

The big four-tonner surges forward with such unexpected force that the truck drives right out from under the Adviser, tossing him onto the road like a sack of potatoes. He hits hard on packed mud, his left shoulder striking first, and then his nose, as he lands facedown. The impact drives the breath out of him and he rolls over and over until he comes to rest on his back. Dazed. Looking at the sky.

Everything hurts. In the distance, the Shpagin is firing again, but he cannot tell whether it is shooting at him or at the Bedford. His mind is working sluggishly, producing only brutish, elemental little thoughts. I've broken my back. Have I been hit? I'm going to die. Don't leave me here. Ny nose hurts.

There is more shooting. At first, he takes vague comfort from the dense cloud of dust and smoke swirling up over the road since it seems to provide him with temporary invisibility. Then little turfs of dirt begin to fly up around him and he understands that the *adoo* are firing at him.

Animal instinct assumes control. Run! He gets up on his hands and knees, fighting an atrocious pain in his shoulder and back. Is that a bullet wound? He tries to inhale but his chest screams at him. The red dust makes him cough and that hurts even more. Where's the truck? Napalm must be streaking for Salalah by now. Long gone. Leaving me behind.

The firing stops again, but a breeze has reorganized the dust enough to allow him to be seen. Got to get off the road, he thinks. Find a ditch somewhere and lay down. He gets unsteadily to his feet, holding onto his nose, because it hurts worse than anything else.

Then, close at hand, there is a roaring, grinding noise and he raises his eyes in time to see what looks like a red cloud rushing toward him. He is massively disoriented but the blur seems to be coming from downhill and it is moving far too fast to escape. For an instant, he gazes upon the apparition in despair. This is surreal, he thinks. A cloud of death. What is it? Does it matter?

At the very last minute, just before it hits him, the Adviser realizes that the red shadow is merely the Bedford in reverse, churning up dust and spouting exhaust fumes. Napalm is coming back to get him. He has just time to turn away. Oh no. No.

The truck's rear fender catches him square on the ass with incredible force and flings him into the air.

I'm flying, he thinks. I'm never coming down. I have been launched.

Things become confused. He is not sure where he is. It is hard to breathe. Someone seizes him around the waist.

"Napalm!" a voice entreats. The tone is somehow priestly. The Adviser is lifted into the air. There is a harsh acrid smell. I don't remember landing, thinks the Adviser. There is more shooting, the angry twanging of bullets striking metal.

"I can't see," he says. "My nose hurts."

Then a man screams. Very close. Was that me? Did I scream? Am I shot? Or was it another?

"Into thy hands, Lord," someone says.

There are no hands, thinks the Adviser. Who spoke? Consciousness is leaving me. My nose hurts. Bless me, Father.

It's only me. Good-bye.

Chapter Seven

VESPERS

I am.

Yes. No, surely this time I must be dead.

Who spoke? Into whose hands?

"We started at two hundred seventy-two for six," says a man who sounds like Prince Philip. "Bimini and I took a seventh wicket stand to fifty and then . . . Healy, what's the score over there?"

"Eighty over forty-five," responds a working-class accent. "No, sixty over . . . no, it's dropping." There is a long pause. "Fifty over nothing. Nothing over nothing."

There is another silence and then the sound of footsteps across a cement floor. From a distance, the royal voice now has a tone of authentic mourning in it. "The poor mad Rev! Well, it's for the best. We could never have fixed him."

"What happened then?" Both pairs of footsteps return to the Adviser's side. His body tenses.

"They lost three wickets for seven inside seven overs without a run on the board." Prince Philip now seems uninterested in his own story; his voice is sad and husky. "Good old Bimini went on to get his century."

The Adviser lies still and silent, allowing his mind to move upwards like a swimmer floating to the surface of a quiet pond. He can detect light above him but he keeps his eyes shut for the moment, wishing to understand his environment before entering it. The conversation is without meaning. He senses that he has been asleep for a long time because his bladder is once again full. The room seems cool but he does not know where he is, or why he is wherever he is.

I am stark naked, he realizes. Lying on my back. And Bimini

got a century. Not just any century but his very own century. Lucky old Bimini.

What does this mean?

Still only semiconscious, he begins to improvise ad hoc realities. Maybe I'm in Oxford. Prince Philip could be here on a royal visit. This might be the Radcliffe Infirmary. Did I come here to see Ellen?

My sweet, there will be no more secrets now. I can explain about the helicopter.

Then . . . and then I fainted and fell down stairs and had to be taken to the emergency room. With a broken nose. Another patient on my ward is named Bimini, and he has lived to be a hundred. Prince Philip is congratulating him on living so long on the National Health Service.

This isn't working. My nose hurts. What made me faint? What did I find at the Radcliffe that sent me tumbling down a flight of stairs? To break my nose. Something . . . I can't remember.

The room feels big. It is warm. The Adviser keeps his eyes shut as he tries to sense his body. He can feel his penis lying limply on his stomach, and he worries briefly that some stray thought of Ellen might give him an erection in the presence of Prince Philip. His legs are slightly parted and his knees both hurt. One ankle is throbbing. His stomach is empty. There is a powerful ache in his left shoulder and a terrific pain in his nose.

There is silence now except for a faint high-pitched clanging, ringing sound. The Adviser listens carefully, realizing only slowly that it is coming from inside his head.

My ears are ringing. For me and my gal.

"Someone screamed," he says aloud.

"Welcome back, sleepy head." There is new pleasure in Prince Philip's voice. "Can you tell me your name?"

Ah! Interesting question. The Adviser cannot recall what is currently written on his ID card. "You tell me your name first," he counters inventively, trying to remember where and when he heard this voice before.

"I'm Dr. Dick Barnet," says Prince Philip. "Do you know where you are?"

"Is this the Radcliffe Infirmary?"

"We should be so lucky," says Barnet. "You're in the Field Surgical Team station at Um al Gwarif. Province of Dhofar. The Sultanate of Oman. Does any of that ring a bell?"

The memory bell begins to ring slowly, clanging in time with the one inside his head. The Adviser opens his eyes to see the pale, earnest face of the same physician who came to Bait al Muktar in the med-evac chopper.

"I thought you were Prince Philip."

"He's my mother's third cousin by marriage," says the physician seriously. "How are you feeling?"

Hovering behind Barnet is a young corpsman in a white uniform. There are blood stains on his sleeves. According to a tag on his chest, his name is Healy.

"Okay, I guess. How is John Woodward?" The Adviser remembers the wounded sergeant major being flown away in a helicopter.

"Good. We just took a hunk of high-grade Czechoslovakian steel out of his thigh and patched up his head. He'll be fine."

"What's . . . what's wrong with me?" As his eyes begin to focus, the Adviser sees a plastic bottle hanging over him with a tube running to a needle in his left arm. He is alarmed to see Corpsman Healy taking his blood pressure while the physician investigates his chest with a stethoscope.

Barnet taps his sternum a few times before he is satisfied. "Everything sounds fine in there. You have a thoroughly broken nose. I've set and bandaged it, but it could heal crookedly and require surgery, so have your embassy physician look at it when you get back to Muscat. You also had a dislocated left shoulder. We got it back in place while you were unconscious but it'll ache for a while. There are abrasions and deep cuts and bruises all over your body which we've cleaned and bandaged. I can't see anything else wrong with you, but they'll be checking you over thoroughly at Muscat hospital. Your embassy is sending a helicopter to take you home."

"To Oxford?

"To Muscat! Weren't you assigned to Muscat? Listen, count backwards by fives from one hundred."

"One hundred, ninety-five, ninety, eighty-five, eighty . . . what's happening outside? There was a battle. . . ."

"Which we've just about won, thanks mostly to you. Colonel Fine is out with the First Regiment now, but he says he'll be along to see you Wednesday in Muscat. Our ambassador wants to present you with a medal."

Great. The Adviser tries to feel cheerful about the prospects of being decorated by the British Ambassador, but his body hurts too much.

"There's a ringing in my ears."

"It's called tinnitus."

"Will it go away?"

"Not until you do," says Barnet. "Letting people drop mortar shells on you is not recommended therapy for eardrums and you may have some hearing loss. Do you want to sit up?"

"I gotta pee. What happened to my clothes?"

"We've thrown them away. When you were brought in, we assumed you'd been shot, so we cut off your clothing looking for bullet holes. Take it easy now." The corpsman gently moves the Adviser's legs off the examining table while Barnet takes his forearms and hoists him into a sitting position. His back and shoulder hurt badly, making him whimper with pain.

There are two other tables in the examining room and two other patients. One is covered with a sheet, with only his brown feet extending. With a chill, the Adviser wonders if it is one of the scouts. On the other table is Napalm, gazing steadily at the ceiling and looking as cheerful as always, although he is not moving. There is a crisp white sheet drawn up over his waist.

"Is he all right?"

"Who? The Rev?" Barnet studies Napalm sadly for a moment and then pulls the sheet up over the bearded face. "The poor man's finally at peace. He crashed the Bedford a mile outside of Salalah. You were unconscious in the back and he was already terminal when the ambulance team got him here. He had a chest full of bullets. God knows what kept him going."

The Adviser's short-term memory is still not functioning very well, but he feels a powerful pang of loss, realizing that he had liked Napalm as well as you could like someone with a one-word vocabulary. "Why do you call him the 'Rev'?"

The two medical men exchange a quick look. "Well, it was supposed to be a bit of secret," Barnet finally confesses. "But we called him 'Rev' because he was a reverend. Until he became rather peculiar, he was our chaplain here at Um al Gwarif."

"A chaplain? This is the guy who ran around shouting 'Napalm' and shooting people!"

The physician shrugs. "I don't think the Reverend Geoffrey Wentworth remembered very much about being a priest in the Church of England."

Barnet is shining a light into his eyes. The Adviser is still trying to piece together the sequence of events that brought him to the Field Surgical Team station at Un al Gwarif. He now remembers the battle at Bait al Muktar and then Napalm driving the Bedford. Why? Where were they going?

In disjointed segments, memory returns. "At the end . . . he knew who he was!" Suddenly, the Adviser recalls seeing Napalm make a sign on the forehead of a child. Did that really happen? Or did I dream it? No, it happened.

"He'd been around the twist for a couple of years," says Healy.

"Up on the *jebel* he baptized a child," the Adviser insists. "I didn't understand what he was doing at the time, but he used water and made the sign of the cross . . . where . . . where are the children?"

Oh my God! Bang, it comes back in a terrible rush. The children! Bint and Suleiman! Where are they?

A sense of urgency sweeps over him. I've been lying here, indulging in recreational unconsciousness and all the time . . . He tries to climb down off the examining table. There is a piercing pain in his upper back.

"This one's off his nut as well," says the corpsman.

"Could be shock," Barnet agrees as they push the Adviser back down onto the examining table. "Get him covered up."

"Look, there were two children in the Bedford with me!" the Adviser shouts. "We were ambushed and I was thrown out. Napalm must have been shot when he came back to get me. Somehow he managed to get me into the truck. But what happened to the children?"

"Calm down, sir," says Healy gently. "We got a report that one of our Bedfords was lying on its side just off the Midway Road a mile outside of Salalah. I went out with an ambulance and found you and the Rev and a smashed-up lorry. There was nobody else there. You've had a proper clout on the head and you've been comatose for an hour so the old brain might be playing tricks on you. Do you have children of your own, sir? You and the missus? Thinking of your own kids, are you?"

"There were two children with me!"

"You know, he could be right," Barnet says thoughtfully. "When I first saw him up on the *jebel* after that firefight, he had two Arab kids with him. One was in a bad way."

"Napalm and I were taking them to Salalah."

A buzzer rings from an adjoining room. With a gesture of fatigue, Barnet looks at his watch and moves away. "Okay, I've got another round of surgery. They're ready for me in the theater."

Feverishly, the Adviser is making plans. "Listen, John will know what to do. He can go with me to find the children. Tell him . . ."

"Frightfully sorry, old man," Barnet turns at the door, putting on a stern voice. "Sergeant Major Woodward is going to stay flat on his back until we can fly him to England. Healy will take you back to your tent to rest until that chopper comes. You are not to go hobbling off on any mad quest for two Arab waifs!"

"But what's going to happen to them?"

"The little boy was dying!" The doctor looks bleak. "If you'd used the morphine I gave you, he would have been happily out of it by now. You only managed to prolong his agony."

"I was trying to get him to a hospital. And I could have taken the girl to an orphanage where she might have been adopted by some good family."

"There are no orphanages here! If she wasn't shot during the ambush or killed in the crash or murdered by the scouts or kidnapped by the *adoo,* then I suppose she'll wander around until someone takes her as a slave. This is not a kind country, my friend, and she isn't your responsibility!"

"Then whose responsibility is she?" the Adviser shouts. "Who's out there right now worrying about her?"

Abruptly, Dick Barnet turns and hits the door with his fist, his face twisting. "Don't you think I haven't felt that way? Why do you think I went to medical school? But I've learned that you have to take responsibility for the people assigned to you and let the others go. Or a place like this will drive you mad! Why do you suppose poor Geoff Wentworth spent the last two years of his life screaming 'napalm'?"

"How should I know?"

"Because he could never accept that things could be so wrong. Because he grieved for every stray cat in the universe."

"She was a little girl. Not a stray cat."

"She wasn't assigned to you. You did your best and it didn't work out."

"She was assigned to me! She was!"

"Who assigned her to you, Yank?"

"I don't know. She did, I guess. She assigned herself to me."

Barnet's face softens. Pausing at the doorway, he motions to Healy. "Give him ten mils of diazepam and keep him here under observation for a bit."

"What's diazepam?" the Adviser demands.

"Valium. Happy Juice. It makes the cosmos seem more reasonable."

I was responsible for Ellen, thinks the Adviser. I was responsible for Bint.

"I keep losing people." he says.

"I know the feeling." The doctor turns away. "I know."

Although the cosmos remains substantively unreasonable, the Happy Juice does make him relaxed and drowsy.

The Adviser lies on his back, his mind empty. Somewhere between sleep and wakefulness, he looks at the ceiling while Healy tidies up the examining room. The corpsman seems to be quite a happy person—he hums under his breath as he works.

The phone rings briskly and Healy comes to a position of attention while answering it.

The Adviser listens vaguely. "No, missus," Healy is saying. "He's in the recovery room out cold at the moment and the doctor wouldn't have me trying to wake him. He's going to be fine. We'll have him on the blower to you as soon as he comes around."

There is a long pause and the tiny faint buzz of a woman's insistent voice. The Adviser is nearly asleep again when he hears

Healy say, with some embarrassment, "Him? Well, we don't know his name, but he's right here. You could ask him yourself."

Suddenly, Healy is offering him the phone. "It's Mrs. Woodward. Calling from York."

"Who?"

"The sergeant major's wife. On the line from England." Healy places the phone between the Adviser's ear and his damaged shoulder so he can talk and listen without moving. There is a lot of crackle on the line, and it takes him a moment to distinguish the interference from the sound of weeping.

"Hello?"

The caller gets her sobbing under control. When it comes, her voice is strong and the accent is upper middle class and well educated. "You're that American gentleman? Dick Barnet just called and said you saved my husband's life. I had to thank you."

"You're Jenny Woodward? John's wife? I thought . . . well, he said . . ."

"Yes, I moved out when John insisted upon following the Wretched Nigel back to the Middle East." She sighs. "But I've been miserable ever since, and when Dick said that John had been wounded I realized that my husband was the most important person in the world to me. Do you think he'll have me back?"

"I think he will." John's going to get his happy ending, the Adviser thinks, feeling absurdly pleased. "When he was wounded today and thought he might die, he gave me instructions to call and say that he loved you. We were out in the middle of a bean field with guys shooting at us, and he kept going on about how I could find your name in the phone book."

"Oh." This appears to devastate her, and there is a moment's silence on the crackly line. "I've been so awful. Will you talk to him for me? Tell him how sorry I am and how much I love him. Please, he'll listen to you."

The Adviser is faintly puzzled. "Sure, but why should he listen to me?"

"John told Dick Barnet that he had only known you a day but he thought you might become his best friend. And you risked your life to save his. So you bring him back to me and back to Yorkshire," Jenny Woodward orders.

"Alright."

"And come yourself!" commands Mrs. Woodward. "We love you."

"Being as how we chopped your clothes up," says Corpsman Healy graciously, "Captain Barnet wants you to take this spare uniform what he left you. Dressed as an officer, like, you'll have all the lads saluting."

"Will it fit?" Barnet is four inches shorter than the Adviser and rounder around the middle. "I've got a change of clothing back at my tent."

"We can't let you run around starkers, can we?" Healy detaches the intravenous drip, deftly removing the needle from the Adviser's arm. "Is your shoulder feeling better? That Happy Juice is also a muscle relaxant."

"I think it's wearing off." Feeling depressed, the Adviser sits up, swings his legs off the examining table and stands. His back does hurt less although he is momentarily dizzy and sways until Healy catches him expertly. There is a full-length mirror behind the door, and it shows him how catastrophically banged up he is.

"Jesus, I'm a mess!" Both of his eyes are blackened and there is a huge bandage covering his nose. His left shoulder is streaked with deep parallel crimson scratches painted yellow-brown with tincture of iodine. The palms of both hands are covered with white gauze and so is his left knee.

"Could be worse, sir." Healy points to Napalm's silent form. "You might have wound up like the poor old Rev there."

The Adviser nods. "I suppose so. You know, I rather liked him."

"A strange bloke, he was. Now your original Reverend Wentworth was a right pompous, preachy bastard. Then he turned into Napalm, and we all got to like him. He was a lot happier after he went mental, you know. Sanity isn't all it's cracked up to be."

Sanity is ghastly, the Adviser muses. I was crazy to think I could keep Ellen. I thought I could be cunning enough. And resourceful. And strong. All of that was crazy. But I was happy crazy. Me and the poor mad Rev.

To cover the Adviser's naked loins, the Dhofar Brigade has

produced a fresh pair of boxer shorts and Healy helps him put on a clean pair of socks. Barnet's trousers are too short at the ankle and too wide around the waist but the Adviser puts them on anyway, rescuing his wallet and pistol from the pile of filthy, sliced-up clothing beneath the examining table.

He takes an experimental step or two, deciding that there is nothing fundamentally wrong with him beyond an ache in his upper back and that painfully broken nose. If John could arrange to loan me a Land-Rover, he calculates, I could drive out to where Napalm crashed the Bedford. And find the children. Maybe Suleiman is dead, maybe not. And little Bint must be out there somewhere. That's unfinished business. I've got to find them.

"Before I go, I want to see John Woodward."

The corpsman shakes his head. "Like I told his missus, we put the sergeant major under to get that shrapnel out of his leg and he's still sleeping."

"I know, but I could stay overnight here and see him when he wakes up. We could tell that American chopper to pick me up tomorrow."

"They called your embassy in Muscat at five, sir. It's just gone seven and the chopper will be here any time now. You can come back as soon as you're out of the Muscat hospital." Healy is leading him firmly toward the door. "Come on, sir, it's all been arranged. Can you walk? Or shall we use a wheelchair?"

"I can walk." As he stumbles toward the door, more unfinished business occurs to him. "Listen, this morning I interviewed an SEP named Mahmoud. Captain Fenwick had him dangling from a chain back in your intelligence shop. Mahmoud gave us some crucial information, and he saved a lot of British lives today."

Healy seems abruptly uncomfortable. "Well, you see, sir, that was actually the first thing Colonel Fine thought of when he realized that SEP had told you the truth. 'Let the wog out,' he says to me. 'And give'em a proper British Army breakfast!' So I went down and checked his vital signs and we had him taken under guard to the officer's mess. When I left him he was tucking into a platter of scrambled eggs and fried bread and bangers and boiled kippers. He was fine then."

"Then? What do you mean?"

"Well, the guard went out for a fag and he came back and found your SEP on the floor turning blue. Wasn't our fault, sir. He choked on the kipper."

"Then he's dead?"

"By the time they got him back here, he'd gone to wherever Mohammedans go, sir." Healy points to the other examining table. There is a brown foot extending from beneath the sheet. "That's him back there."

The Adviser feels his knees buckling, but Healy has a wheelchair beneath him in an instant. "There we are, sir! Sir, if you'll just relax. . . ."

Christ! Feeling a sense of leaden gloom sweeping over him, the Adviser closes his eyes as Corpsman Healy swings the wheelchair expertly out of the examining room and into a long empty corridor. Healy hums as they roll along, perhaps to kill the silence. The Adviser can think of nothing to say.

This is not my fault, he tries to tell himself. Poor Mahmoud simply failed to chew his kipper. The nuns always exhorted us to chew our food properly before swallowing. It was a venial sin of gluttony to gulp your food. A mortal sin in Mahmoud's case. This is not tragedy. It's just stupid.

A moment later they are outside. Leaving the climate control of the headquarters building, the temperature leaps by 30 degrees Fahrenheit and the humidity soars to the top of the scale. It is sunset.

Ali Rashidi apparently managed to get that valiant old Land-Rover down off the *jebel* because it is waiting for them in a courtyard, and Healy helps him into the passenger seat. Someone even thought to take the black American Embassy briefcase of super-secret TechIntel charts from Colonel Fine's safe and put it under the seat. Leaving it thus unattended is a world-class security violation, but the Adviser is too depressed to care.

Healy takes him gently over the bumps to the south side of the garrison and it seems that years have passed since he last saw his humble little tent, although not much has changed at the Um al Gwarif Hilton.

In preparation for the arrival of the American Embassy chopper, the helicopter pad has been illuminated. Next door, the latrine is empty because all the troops are in the foothills mopping up the remnants of the 9 June Regiment. Napalm's orphaned Morris Minor Traveller sits forlornly in front of the mad Rev's empty tent.

Down the road at the Vehicle Maintenance Shed, three mechanics are lethargically sweeping up after a hot day's work. In the junkyard behind the shed, the Adviser sees the remains of a Bedford four-ton truck. The canvas top has been burned away and the cabin is a twisted mass of punctured steel. The two front tires are blown and the vehicle tilts steeply to one side as if the suspension were destroyed.

Healy follows his gaze. "It's a write-off!" he comments. "They towed it back to be cannibalized for parts."

"There was no one inside? You're sure?"

"When we got there with the ambulance, there was just you and the Rev," Healy assures him patiently. "Now let's have you horizontal, sir."

Inside his tent, someone has made up the cot and swept the plastic floor. The girlie magazine has disappeared. The Adviser's duffel bag is standing at attention in one corner. After making him lie down, Healy produces a small package wrapped in brown paper and tied with string. Inside is a red plastic thermos of massively sweetened tea, a bar of Cadbury's chocolate, and four cress and grated cheddar cheese sandwiches with the crusts trimmed off each slice of white bread.

"Thanks. Listen, Healy, you don't need to wait. I'll just rest here, and when the chopper comes from Muscat, the Marines'll get me on board."

"You'll be all right then, sir?" Corpsman Healy stands to attention and delivers a little speech. "Right, well, the lads, you know, the other ranks, they wanted me to thank you for them. They say you warned the colonel that the *adoo* were going to attack. And saving the sergeant major's life, well, that was, uh . . . good and all, because Mr. Woodward is a better bloke than all them officers put together and we hope you like the sandwiches."

The Adviser is authentically moved, although he desperately

wants the corpsman to go away. He stretches out on the cot and closes his eyes. "Thanks, Healy. Look, I'll, uh, see you when I'm back the next time."

"Right you are then, sir. Good-bye." A moment later, the Adviser hears the Land-Rover depart.

Getting back on his feet is more of a job than he expected; the pain sears through his left shoulder whenever he moves. After some experiments in applied agony, he rolls off the cot onto his hands and knees and pulls himself erect with the tent pole. Then he burrows in his duffel bag for a small flashlight.

Outside, it is dusk and the sun has retreated behind the *jebel*. The mechanics have gone to dinner and the Vehicle Maintenance Shed is deserted. It is a fifty-foot walk up the road and past the shed to the junkyard. Every step is painful.

Playing the flashlight over the Bedford, the Adviser sees that the vehicle has been shattered by gunfire; there are hundreds of huge, gaping holes left by Shpagin shells.

Amazing that Napalm survived long enough to get me here, he thinks, circling around to the tailgate and shining his light into the passenger compartment. Amazing that I survived at all . . . with a deepening sense of futility, he observes that the back of the Bedford has been swept clean. There is nothing there now, not even the wooden benches.

The junkyard is an acre of sand, covered with steel scrap and dismembered, broken vehicles, but only a few steps from the back of the Bedford, he finds a mound of familiar rubbish: empty ammunition boxes and spare machine-gun barrels, a pile of shovels and pickaxes, and a jumble of blankets and reed prayer mats. In the fast-fading light, the Adviser rummages bleakly through the rubble. Surely by now . . .

Then, in the midst of the random debris, he spots his own tan cotton shirt, the one he took off in the bean field outside of Bait al Muktar and used to cover little Suleiman. With a sick, sinking feeling, he gets down on his knees in the sand and unwraps the cotton garment.

The little boy is there, but making no sound now, not moving nor crying. His body is already a little stiff. His eyes and mouth are open, as if he died with a scream on his lips.

"Oh God!" Despairing, he looks around, but there is no sight of Bint and he realizes that the search is hopeless. She might have been thrown out of the Bedford during the ambush on the *jebel*. Or she might have crawled away after the crash and disappeared into the countryside, perhaps hurt or already dying. In any event, she is not here or she would long since have been seen. A dead baby boy wrapped in a shirt would be easy to miss, but someone would have noticed a pretty little girl, alive or dead.

He picks up Suleiman and cradles him in his arms. "I'm sorry, little boy. Didn't mean to put you through all of that. Sorry we couldn't seem to make the system work for you. I was unconscious for a while, and you were lying here dying. I'm sorry."

Sorry. Sorry. Sorry. I spend my life saying sorry, he thinks. To people who are not here to hear.

Near to hand is a shovel with a broken shaft. The Adviser's back hurts too much to do a proper job and the sand is harder than it looks. Six inches down he hits an unexpected layer of clay. After a few more minutes of painful excavation, he gives up. Scarcely a foot deep, it is the shallowest of graves.

The child's body seems lighter now, as if weight had fled with life. There is a bad smell of charred flesh coming from Suleiman's skin and the Adviser holds the little corpse away from his nose.

"Good-bye, Suleiman." He places the child in the hole and scrapes some soft sand over him. The ex-seminarian in him feels the need for ritual here, for eulogies and prayers.

Listen, he speaks in his mind, determined not to grovel as he attempts one last transcendental communication. I'm not sure I even believe in you anymore, and if it turns out that you do exist, I think you owe us all a huge apology. If you are still even vaguely in the business of looking after defenseless people, then take care of my friend here. He never hurt anybody.

He listens inside his skull, hoping for anything, a slackening in the fury of his emotions or a sense of peace or resignation or rest. As usual there is nothing.

Nothing! Even the Happy Juice worked better than this, he thinks. And here we are in the Middle East! Tortured spirits crying in the desert are supposed to get some kind of hearing in these latitudes! Maybe some giant voice booming out of the heavens. Thou Art The Technical Intelligence Adviser From

The Long Range Reconnaissance Group. With Whom I Am Pissed Off.

It's not funny. There is a bad feeling coming over him now, a hard vicious depression, a sadness so deep and visceral that it is almost physical.

Is this battle shock? I've been upset before after bad days in the field, but never anything like this. Desperately, he searches for some way of making himself feel better since the unhappiness is giving him strange thoughts.

A cigarette, he thinks, remembering those Rothmans he swiped from the dead Captain Fenwich. Smoking cigarettes is a kind of incremental suicide. We will approach this step by step.

It takes him a moment to work out that Fenwich's Rothmans are in the pocket of his field jacket now six inches beneath his right foot, buried in the sand and wrapped around the body of a small dead Arab boy.

So, no cigarettes, he thinks. All day long I've been trying to go off the wagon and each time something goes wrong.

Shit, they're just down there. I want a cigarette!

You've gone mad, he tells himself, scratching away at the child's sand-covered grave until he finds the tail of his shirt. Squeamishly trying not to touch the baby's body, he runs his hand up along the row of buttons until he reaches the collar and then finds the upper right-hand pocket.

The half-filled packet is still there with Fenwich's matches tucked inside the plastic wrapper. Once he has the pack in his hand, he brushes some sand over the child's body and sits up to enjoy his smoke.

The filter tips are squashed and bent. The first two matches fail to ignite and he burns his index finger with the third because his hands are shaking. On the fourth try, he succeeds in lighting the Rothman.

This will make me feel better, he thinks, drawing the tobacco smoke deeply into his lungs.

Instantly, his chest explodes with coughing as the unaccustomed harshness of raw tobacco assails his lungs. The sudden movement wrenches his damaged shoulder and he doubles over in pain, gasping for breath.

"No, no, no," he moans. Even sitting up is too much effort

now and he sprawls on top of Suleiman's grave, still choking and coughing.

Before he can organize his emotional defenses, he starts crying. Not some manly moisturizing of the eyes, but a real hard sobbing. I should have done my crying in Oxford, he thinks as the tears stream down his face. Instead I'm here in a junkyard in Dhofar, crying for you, Suleiman. Nothing personal, kid, but you happened to be here and dead when I needed to cry.

How long has it been? He counts backwards on his fingers. Eight days? No, today is Sunday and it was a Thursday, so that's eleven days. And this would be my eleventh night without her.

There were so many watershed moments when I thought I could alter everything with the right word. If I had ever devised the right word. How could I have known when it was my last chance to get it right?

Thursday. He remembers it as happening in a long shattered sequence of unconnected moments. Fragments of broken time. The call came at three. That did not leave me enough time. At first I assumed she would be ringing from that phone booth just up the road from Greenham Common. The one painted red. With all the glass panels missing. There was always a queue of peace women there, jangling fifty-pence coins, waiting to phone husbands and lovers and children. We had the booth wired. So did Scotland Yard and somebody else we couldn't identify. Maybe the Russians. When she talked to me, she talked to half the spies in Europe.

Thursday at three. A week ago last Thursday. With more time, I could have organized an appropriate response to what ought to have been no more than an operational hiccup.

"It's a secret," she said. "It's going to happen tonight!"

"Don't do it," I said. "Those soldiers have orders to shoot."

"They won't shoot! This is Britain. The Government would never let them shoot down a bunch of English ladies."

This is not the old Britain, I ought to have said. We Americans own you now, and our Security Police have orders to defend those nuclear weapons by any means necessary. If you break through that fence and approach an operational Cruise missile, they will open fire. They are ignorant, savage adolescents. To them, you are Marxist lesbian terrorists, and they yearn to kill you. Behind the barbed wire, they speak of nothing else. I have been there. I have seen them caress their M-16s and talk about going to full automatic. And mowing you down.

Instead, I said nothing. Or almost nothing. The habits of a lifetime. Even in the orphanage, the nuns always counseled quietude. If you have nothing useful to contribute, young man, keep your mouth firmly sealed. The goldenness of silence.

"I don't think it's a good idea. Sabotage is violent and CND has always opposed violence."

"This is only violence to a fence! By tonight, there will be thousands and thousands of us here, and they're bringing ropes to pull that fence down, barbed wire and all. Isn't that silly? All this time it has looked so formidable and now we discover that the poles are only planted a few inches deep. And there are dozens of missiles sitting on their ramps in the field. I'm here in Newbury, buying all the screwdrivers I can find."

"You're not at Greenham Common?"

This was the crucial bit of bad news. Had she been calling from the usual phone booth at Greenham Common, the L.R.R.G. London staff would have monitored the call and told the base commander to move his missiles and reinforce his fence. Scotland Yard would also be listening, so the British would send in more police and the episode would be self-limiting.

"No, I'm calling from the Post Office in Newbury," she said. "Apparently if you jab a screwdriver into the nose cone . . ."

"Don't!"

But she said she had to go. There were other women waiting in line. I should come and bail her out if she got arrested. With the baby coming, she didn't want to spend the whole night in some damp cell. And I was not to worry.

"You can't go sticking screwdrivers into the nose cones of thermonuclear weapons." I began to explain about the presence of conventional explosive triggers in atomic warheads and Permissive Action Links, but she was gone. Off the line. Off to buy screwdrivers for peace. Disconnected. Our last civilized conversation.

Gone.

It is very, very frightening, but the Adviser now finds himself thinking about the feasibility of taking the lady pistol out of his holster and shooting himself in the brain.

He is a methodical man, and tries to calculate the amount of pain involved. There ought to be none, really, a bang in the head and then oblivion. But he has always sensed within himself a tendency to compromise, and he fears that he would split the difference between suicide and nonsuicide by sort-of-but-not-quite shooting himself in the head, turning the pistol in slightly the wrong position at the very last moment and producing a ghastly wound that would leave him in ghastly pain, a paralyzed, incontinent, drooling semi-vegetable. But not actually dead.

Nevertheless, he wonders, what exactly do I have to live for? The embassy chopper will take me back to Muscat. If my shoulder really is bent out of shape and I flunk my physical, I will be chained to a desk in Washington forever. The Pentagon is looking for someone to catalog all the railroad lines and rolling stock in Africa. That could be my next job. If I survive the medical exam, they'll keep me in Oman until the fighting stops and then send me off to . . . to what? Back to the Hindu Kush, explaining maps to the Mujahiddin? Back to Ulster, collecting bomb fragments for analysis? Back to the Sahara, where I will be asked to . . . what? To infiltrate the Khartoum Bowling League? What?

No. If not this, then what? If this is no longer an acceptable life for me, then what kind of life do I want? Do I have the strength? I was so happy with Ellen. Do I have any reason to think I could resurrect that emotion with someone else? If not, then what is the point?

Why didn't the Happy Juice work? I'd never make it as a drug addict. Woodward promised me a crate of McGinty's Brown Ale, but I'd only wake up tomorrow hung over and depressed.

I don't want to shoot myself, he thinks, but he takes the lady pistol out of his holster and sets it carefully on his knee.

I don't want to shoot myself. I'm frightened of the pain. But I feel so alone . . . How did I get this alone? I've always been alone, but until Ellen happened to me it seemed natural. I'm frightened. Death frightens me. So does staying alive. What am I going to do?

He picks up the pistol again. Switches off the safety. Take this in stages. There will be little pain and soon over. Bless me, Father. For I have sinned.

"Assalam Aleikum."

Someone speaks. The Adviser stops crying and looks up, but now it is quite dark in the junkyard and he sees no one. But someone spoke. Was it a child's voice? Speaking Arabic, someone just said "Peace be with you," which is how Arabs say "Hello."

For an instant he contemplates the possibility that he is hallucinating. Has the Happy Juice kicked back in? Or did I generate that voice from inside me because I need just now to have someone come along and say, Peace be with you, Mr. Technical Intelligence Adviser. You are a man in need of peace. Well, have some.

"Allo?" It is a child's voice, but the Adviser is careful not to let his hopes rise.

"Hello?" Embarrassed that anyone should have seen him in such a state, with tears on his face and a gun in his hand, he puts the pistol back into its holster and staggers painfully to his feet. "Who is it? Where are you?"

"I am here."

"Bint? Is that Bint?"

Following the flashlight's faltering beam, he lurches through the rubble, unable to imagine how a four-year-old child could have remained undetected all this time.

Is she hurt? It occurs to him that it would be a miracle for the child to have survived the ambush without injury, since the *adoo* had sprayed the Bedford with hundreds of rounds. I don't want another dying child, he thinks. I have resigned from the dead baby burial detail.

"I am here in the dates." The voice is calm, even assertive. The Adviser clambers over a pile of sleeping bags and a broken ladder until the beam from his light sweeps over a large bare wooden box. The little girl's head is protruding over the edge, that stubborn pink ribbon still enfolding her black hair. Large and luminous, Bint's eyes regard him with puzzlement, and he wonders if she can recognize him beneath all the bandages.

"You're still there?"

"You told me to stay in this box."

Yes, of course, the memory returns to him now. In extremis, with the *adoo* shooting up the Bedford, he had thrust her into the box where the Scout Platoon kept their supply of dates. And told her to wait.

And you waited. You trusted me.

"Bint!" Forgetting his own injuries, he bends to lift her from the box, but his damaged shoulder protests immediately and he drops to his knees with an involuntary yelp of pain.

"Are you hurt?" She gets out unassisted. Standing beside him with one arm around his neck, Bint brushes the hair out of the Adviser's eyes and wipes his face with the sleeve of her dress, the adult in her administering strokes to the child in him.

"It's all right. I fell out of the truck and hurt my shoulder."

"Where is my brother?"

He senses that she must already know that answer to this question, but children need adults to confirm the obvious. It takes him a minute to compose an answer, because it is not easy to carry on a brisk conversation with a four-year-old Arab orphan when all you have ever read is the *Quran*.

"Your brother is in Paradise."

The little girl seems sad but unsurprised. *"Maktub,"* she whispers. *"Maktub"* means "It is written." Then she closes her eyes and tears begin to flow down her cheeks.

"Oh, little girl, little girl, sweet little girl," he murmurs, putting his arms around her and hugging her as she cries for her brother who has gone to Paradise. She puts her face into the cleft of his neck and hugs him back. Her skin is sticky from all the leftover dates.

For a long time she rests in his arms. Then she disengages, getting to her feet and taking a few steps away from him. Daintily turning her back, she squats, hoisting her soiled white cotton shift above her hips. She pees copiously into the sand and then returns to him as if nothing had happened.

"I am thirsty."

"Come with me." Feeling absurdly happy, he offers his hand. Dutifully, Bint takes it and they make their way silently out of the junkyard and down the road to the Um al Gwarif Hilton.

Suddenly he remembers Barnet's comment about there being no orphanages in Dhofar. *What am I going to do with her?*

Inside the tent, the Adviser switches on the battery-powered lamp and makes Bint sit down on the cot. Unwrapping the lunch that Healy left, he fills a plastic cup with sweet, warm British Army tea.

"Chai?" His memory produces the universal Middle Eastern word for tea. Bint eyes the liquid suspiciously until he tastes it himself and smacks his lips approvingly.

With surprising delicacy, she takes the cup in both hands and raises it to her lips. *"Shookran,"* she thanks him and sips. Then she accepts one of the cheese and cress sandwiches, nibbling it with bright, even teeth.

Except for a bruise on her thigh, the child does not appear to be injured. Her lips are cracked with the heat and her hands and face are dirty. She is exhausted and starving, but the Adviser finds her as lovely now as when he first saw her in the ruins of Bait al Muktar. Her skin is relatively light, about the color of the milky tea she is drinking. Her nose is acquiline and delicate and her brown eyes are clear and intelligent. In repose, her face seems cheerful, as if there is a smile always waiting to burst forth.

Her family must be local aristocracy, he decides. Have been. Must have been local aristocracy.

From the jug on the side table he pours some water into the basin and when Bint finishes the sandwich the Adviser moistens a handkerchief and begins to wash her, starting with the smudges on her face and hands and then moving down to her ankles and feet. She sits still and submits to the clean-up, unafraid and a little amused.

"That's what my mother used to do," she giggles as he scrubs between her toes. "Fathers don't do that."

"In my country fathers sometimes wash their daughter's toes," he informs her, having lately contemplated the implications of fatherhood. Like a good feminist, Ellen always referred to their baby as "her," and he had begun to make room in his life for a little girl, worrying about female names and wondering about frocks and petticoats. When everything came unglued, he felt that Ellen had cheated him out of a little girl.

"What country is that?"

"The United States. I come from America."

"What does America look like?"

The Adviser finds himself short of words, since he has seen so little of his native land. Orphans never travel, except occasionally to new orphanages, and seminarians stay put until lust drives them out of the cloister into the Army. The Department of Defense sent him overseas nearly twenty years ago and kept him abroad for most of his adult life. On his occasional visits to Washington he is invariably collected at Dulles International by one of the L.R.R.G. headquarters people and taken to a town house in Arlington, Virginia, where Reconnaissance Group field officers stayed. There would be trips to the Pentagon for briefings and debriefings and usually a discreet party in his honor at the commanding officer's home over near Dumbarton Oaks in Georgetown. Then back to Dulles for the return flight to someplace foreign.

"It has very tall buildings," he begins, reflecting upon the strangeness of his profession. No other job makes such demands upon your patriotism. You risk your life year after year to defend a nation's interests. Then you wake up one morning and realize that you no longer remember what the place looks like. All the apple orchards are now malls and the field where you once played is a parking lot.

"Are there many goats in America?"

"No, we have lots of cows but not very many goats."

"Oh, it must be very rich." Bint sighs. "Does your father have many cows?"

Does my father have many cows? Out of habit, the Adviser prepares to invent a farmer-father with herds of cows and flocks of sheep, but something holds him back. I'm tired of internally generated realities, he thinks. Even if I never see this little girl again, I would like to tell her nothing but the truth.

"I have no father and no cows," he begins. "But I have enough gold to buy a few goats and perhaps a cow."

"Goats are better," Bint suggests practically. "They never get sick. And I am very good at taking care of goats. I never let them get lost."

"Then perhaps I should buy a goat," says the Adviser hopelessly. "You could watch it for me."

"What's going to happen to me?" she demands. "This is a good tent. Do I live here now? Where is my father?"

For a moment, he is tempted to say that he will take care of her, now that her real father is no longer able. But he holds back, sternly reminding himself that it is wrong to promise what you have no hope of delivering. That was the central error in my relationship with Ellen, he lectures himself. I offered all those emotional commitments to myself and to her, covenants I was in no position to fulfill. What did Barnet say about poor Napalm? That he grieved for every stray cat in the universe. . . .

Bint begins to cry, and the Adviser covers his confusion with a commitment-free hug and then offers her another cheddar and cress sandwich. But you're a little girl, he thinks, not a stray cat. What is going to happen to you? Perhaps there is an orphanage in Muscat. But an orphanage, God, even if there were a shelter for abandoned children, is that good enough for you? I know all about orphanages! Can I send you to an orphanage?

Like my mother sent me? Why did she do that? I wouldn't have minded if we were poor, or if I were illegitimate. If I could have stayed home with her. Whoever she was. And now, I'm supposed to take you off to an orphanage. Because I can't take care of you. But what you need . . . well, you need a father with a couple of goats. And someone to wash your feet when they get dirty.

Outside, there is the sound of a vehicle coasting to a halt. The Adviser welcomes the interruption, whatever it is, since he is reluctant to explain to Bint that her family is dead.

He gets uncomfortably to his feet, the pain in his shoulder smarting like an old insult. Outside, he sees loyal little Ali Rashidi pull up in the familiar Land-Rover with John Woodward in the passenger seat.

"Sergeant Dauntless!" The sight of the indestructible Yorkshireman fills him with sudden assurance that everything will work out all right. John will give me good advice, he tells himself. John will know what to do with Bint.

"Hey, Captain America!" Woodward puts crutches under each arm and hobbles painfully toward the Um al Gwarif Hilton. He is wearing a ludicrous pair of shorts because his injured leg is massively bandaged and braced to hold it stiff. John's unshaven face is gray with pain.

"I just had a conversation with a splendid-sounding woman named Jenny. I've been ordered to convince you to take her back."

"I know. Jenny got through to me a few minutes ago." Woodward produces an embarrassed grin. "She is rather a splendid woman and . . . well, she's moving back into our house in York, and she'll be there when I get home."

"That's wonderful!" The Adviser feels a surge of authentic happiness. "So no divorce?"

Woodward laughs. "Actually the papers already went through so we have to get remarried as soon as I'm out of the hospital. Why don't you come up for a holiday? You can be my best man."

"I'm honored." The Adviser is so moved he can barely speak. No one ever asked him to be a best man before. "John, I'm so glad for you. Listen, should you be running around? Didn't Barnet just operate on you?"

"He'll flail me alive if he finds me out of bed, but it really was just minor surgery."

"What does he say about the leg?"

"Apparently everything is going to be fine, but they're sending me to an Army hospital in York. Barnet thinks I may need more surgery on my leg. At the moment, I can't feel my big toe. How about you? What's the matter with your nose?"

Reminded of its bent status, his nose immediately starts hurting. The Adviser touches it gingerly. "It's broken, and my shoulder's out of whack. I can't stand up straight. Hobble in and let's sit down. Ali, you come too!"

"No, it is time for evening prayers." Looking uncomfortable, Ali Rashidi fetches a large paper bag filled with brown bottles from the Land-Rover, which he deposits at the entrance to the Um al Gwarif Hilton. "I will come back later to say good-bye."

Woodward chuckles as Ali Rashidi strides off into the darkness. "Our pious Moslem friend doesn't want to witness two infidels drinking liquids upon which the Prophet has frowned. Do you remember my talking about McGinty's Brown Ale?"

"Brown ale? You climbed out of a hospital bed to bring me a six-pack of home brew?" From the paper bag, the Adviser extracts a large corked bottle bearing a hand-lettered label that says in large letters, MCGINTY'S BROWN ALE. Beneath it is the ultimate in commercial honesty, IT MAKES YOU DRUNK.

"Your health, old son!" Woodward uncorks a bottle for himself. "No, mostly I came because our lad Healy was worried that you might wander off alone in the darkness to look for that little Arab girl."

"And you wanted to talk me out of it?" After a long, gurgling swallow, the Adviser closes his eyes with pleasure. McGinty's Brown Ale is young and yeasty and terribly alcoholic.

Woodward looks momentarily hurt. "No, if you'd really made up your mind, I was going to go along and help. Where would Captain America be without Sergeant Dauntless?"

"Come and look." Profoundly moved, the Adviser pulls back the flap and helps the wounded sergeant major into the tent. Bint is curled up asleep on the cot with her dark hair sprayed across the pillow.

Woodward sighs with pleasure. "So you already found her. God, what a beautiful child!"

"Actually, she found me. She was hiding all this time in the rubble over behind the Vehicle Maintenance Shed. John, what the hell am I going to do with her?"

With an exhausted sigh, Woodward sinks into a chair, putting his half-finished bottle on the table between them. He seems hesitant about saying the obvious. "I suppose . . . well, I don't wish to meddle in that terribly clandestine existence of yours, but you could take care of her yourself."

"I'd thought of that, but even if the million practical difficulties could somehow be solved, I'm hardly fit to take on the responsibility of a child. Just before coming here to Oman, I fucked up my own life so totally that it left me without a lot of confidence that I could manage anyone else's."

There is a long pause. Woodward grunts and rearranges his damaged leg. With a grateful gulp, the Adviser drains his McGinty's Brown Ale and opens another bottle.

Woodward breaks the silence. "You need to tell me what happened in England before you came here."

"I can't." The Adviser gulps his ale quickly. "I'm too ashamed. It's too awful and too classified."

"You never confessed to anyone, did you?" Woodward leans forward and grips his arm fiercely. "Listen, you need to get this off your chest. Tell me precisely what happened to you and Ellen and I promise to forgive you, even if she won't."

"You're going to forgive me? Did they appoint you acting chaplain when poor Napalm went mad?" The Adviser opts to treat the suggestion as a joke.

But Woodward is deadly serious. "This is the Middle East. We're all priests out here and the only sacrament we have left is forgiving each other. What happened?"

The Adviser puts his head in his hands. This is just like going to confession, he thinks. Bless me Father for I have sinned.

"It's very simple," he whispers. "Remember that Women's Peace Camp down at Greenham Common? Well, Ellen began spending three or four days each week there as one of the antinuclear protesters."

"Wasn't there a fuss there a couple of weeks ago? I remember hearing something on the Beeb—"

"The women decided to pull a section of fence down with ropes and storm the base and sabotage the Cruise missiles."

"Jesus! Didn't they realize they'd be shot?"

The Adviser sighs and closes his eyes. "At Greenham Common, things were a little crazy by this point. Some of the women were looking for martyrdom and wanted to force the troops to open fire. Others had convinced themselves that the Americans would never be allowed to use their weapons against middle-class English women. I was frantic because I knew that the Air Force Security Police had standing orders to shoot any unauthorized person approaching a nuclear weapon."

"So you called the authorities?"

"It wasn't that simple. My operations protocol for emergencies was to communicate with Reconnaissance Group Headquarters in London over a special enciphered telephone system called the Gray Phone network." The Adviser is dimly aware that he is reciting classified material to a foreign national, but military secrets are starting to lose their sacredness for him. "We use the

Gray Phones for conversations classified at one of the levels above top secret."

"There are levels above top secret?"

"All the really interesting stuff is above top secret. Anyway, to get to a Gray Phone, I had to drive to the nearest American military installation, which is an Air Force base called Upper Heyford, just north of Oxford. Once I was there it took a long time to get a decision because the embassy had to contact Third Air Force Headquarters in Germany and they had to talk to the Pentagon. It was a bad day for a crisis because the Greenham Common commanding officer was on leave and his deputy had just had a heart attack."

"So who was in charge?"

"Nobody. There was a hysterical captain on duty at Greenham Common but the Reconnaissance Group decided they needed an on-the-spot report, so I was ordered to fly to Greenham and see what was happening to our precious Cruise missiles."

There is the sound of another bottle of McGinty's Brown Ale being uncorked. Woodward's voice is gentle but insistent. "You didn't much care about missiles by this point, did you?"

The Adviser shakes his head violently. "No. You see, Ellen was pregnant, and all I could think about was her and the baby in her womb. I was terrified she'd get herself shot by some trigger-happy Air Force Security cop. I kept closing my eyes and seeing a bullet going into her stomach."

The batteries in the table lamp are fading. Woodward is silent, patient, waiting for the story to reach its denouement. The Adviser is sorry he ever began. This is the point at which the memory gets hard, he thinks, fearing that his voice might soon crack.

That day was a nightmare in installments, he remembers. Everybody was giving vague orders, setting me up to take the blame if things went wrong. And moving so slowly! The sun was already sinking when they bundled me and a squad of military police into that helicopter. I have always hated helicopters.

And we bounded into the sky and flew over Oxford and down the M-34 to Newbury and then over to Greenham Common Air Force Base. There were dozens of other choppers landing because the British were frantically bringing in riot police. It was already dark when we got there and the women had lit a hundred fires on the common in front of the base. There were thousands and thousands of protesters there, and I kept thinking, she's out there somewhere, the only person in the world I care about. With my baby in her belly. I have to save her without being seen.

"You're almost there, mate." Woodward places a full bottle in the Adviser's hand. "Have another McGinty's Truth Serum and get it over with."

"My chopper was just approaching when the women pulled the fence down and crawled over the barbed wire and swarmed onto the base. It was the Pentagon's ultimate nightmare. A Cruise missile is inherently very fragile and there were thousands of women there armed with screwdrivers. We touched down in the open field between the protesters and the missiles. I used the VHF commo net to tell the Security Police to load one magazine apiece with blank rounds."

"The radio said it was live ammunition."

"That was just a rumor. A lot of people were hurt that night, stumbling around in the dark, or resisting arrest, or just beaten up by the police, but nobody was shot."

"How did the rumor start?"

"I started it," confesses the Adviser. When the peace women kept coming, I went to the door of the helicopter with a bullhorn and warned the demonstrators that the Security Police would open fire if they approached the missiles. When they didn't stop, the Security Police fired one thirty-second salvo of blank ammunition at them. Thinking they'd been shot at, the majority of the women stopped in their tracks or ran away. There were just a few who kept coming."

Just a few. And she was one of them. What was she thinking? If she wanted to live with me and have my baby, what made her run into the muzzles of our guns?

Even then, he thinks, with just a minimal amount of luck it could all have been avoided. It was pitch black out there, and everyone got even more confused when two hundred British riot police showed up and started chasing four thousand screaming women around in circles. In all that chaos, she should have turned and run for her life and our baby's life.

Instead of storming up to the helicopter with a flashlight. And shining it directly in my face.

There I was, flanked by two big MPs with machine guns, shouting into a megaphone and threatening death to anyone who offered violence to our lovely thermonuclear weapons. There were cries and screaming all around us and firing, and Ellen must still have thought we'd used live ammunition against them. I must have looked like Heinrich Himmler on a Nazi state visit to Auschwitz.

Then the Security Police stopped firing because the Riot Squad had taken over and there was a moment of comparative hush. It was quiet enough for me to have said something to her, if I could have thought of anything to say. And silent enough for her to say to me what little she had to say.

You betrayed us all, she spoke clearly. I'll never have your baby.

She might have been puzzled, wondering what her peace-oriented, draft-dodging lover was doing in an Air Force helicopter, ordering soldiers to fire on defenseless women. But she seemed to understand instantly what had happened. Who I was. Why I had come.

Her face went white, and the corners of her mouth turned down.

"What did she say when she saw you?"

"She said that I had betrayed everyone. That she was never going to have my baby. I thought she meant she was going to have an abortion."

"What did you say?"

"What was there to say?"

But you might have tried, he continues the debate within himself. You might have jumped down from the helicopter and taken her in your arms. My dear, I always said there were certain aspects of my past which might require elaboration.

I might have taken her prisoner and locked her in a little room until she accepted my point of view. I might have . . . might have done something. Anything.

Instead I did nothing. I stood there, frozen, paralyzed, staring. For a moment she looked back at me. As if waiting for me to devise a suitable lie that she could pretend to believe. It would have been better if there had been hatred in her eyes because hate can give you strength. But there was nothing but sadness there.

"Was she arrested?"

"Very gently. A policeman came along and took her arm. Most of the women were practicing civil disobedience techniques, going limp and forcing the cops to drag them off to the vans. But Ellen just walked away, arm-in-arm with this policeman as if they were old friends out for an evening stroll."

"So you were—what do they say in your business?—you were 'blown'?"

"It's called 'Identity Compromise,' and there's a procedure we're supposed to follow. I used the Greenham Common Gray Phone to report to L.R.R.G. headquarters that I had been recognized by a radical peace activist. My cover was now unsustainable because Ellen would presumably tell her sisters in the movement that American intelligence had infiltrated CND."

"Did she?"

The Adviser shakes his head. "No, it's strange, but she never betrayed me. The day before I flew out of Heathrow to come here, the Reconnaissance Group operations people submitted their Compromise Survey Report on the incident. Based on intercepted conversations at CND headquarters and the tap on Peter Reston's phone, their conclusion was that she never told anyone about me. But that was later. At the time, we had to assume that my operation was over. I was told to report immediately to London."

In the far distance, there is the faint sound of a motor, announcing the approach of the helicopter from the American Embassy in Muscat. Bint awakens slowly and sits up on the cot, pulling her dress down over her knees and looking gravely at John Woodward. When the sergeant major smiles and pats her cheek, she favors him with her most dazzling grin and snuggles comfortably onto the Adviser's lap.

"Did you go back to the flat in Oxford?"

"It was against orders, but I wanted to see if she would come home, or call."

"Did she?"

"No. At three in the morning, a social worker from the Emergency Room of the Radcliffe Infirmary rang to say I should come immediately to his office."

"What was wrong with her? Was she losing the baby?"

"That's what I was worried about. I imagined her waking up with me sitting by her side and holding her hand and she would realize that I loved her no matter what, and we would start all over again."

I remember it all, the Adviser shudders. That hospital waiting room at three-thirty in the morning. The smell of disinfectant. The staff nurses and sisters working behind the counter, offering courteous, distant smiles. The social worker was a sallow young man with frizzy gray hair and half-frame glasses who took me into his office. He said that the patient became unconscious in a police cell at the Cowley Road Police Station. Did I know of any reason why she might have been unusually depressed?

No.

No? And what relationship was I to Miss Huntington? Fiancé? There is this form to be completed and while the hospital prefers next-of-kin, we are prepared to accept the signature of a fiancé because it is nearly dawn and some of us have been working all night. And I must accept his regrets. It appears that Miss Huntington had a prescription for the sleeping pills. Otherwise there would have been a longer form to complete.

It began to sink in. A cold awful feeling coming over me. Three forty-five in the morning. I am explaining that I had not seen the patient since before she left for Greenham Common to participate in an anti-war demonstration. And what did he mean about regrets? Who regrets? What happened to Ellen? To my Ellen? To my sweet Ellen? What happened?

"She is a casualty of World War Three." The social worker clearly liked peace activists and disliked Americans. "If your government could keep its bloody missiles somewhere else . . . Could you sign here?"

"She's dead?"

"Oh. I thought someone else had explained." The frizzy-haired social worker was embarrassed. "They are supposed to tell you at the front desk. The mortality experience seems to have been induced by consumption of prescription sleeping pills. Of course we will list the overdose as accidental. No point in upsetting her parents. Although she emptied the whole bottle, so it could hardly have been . . . Well! You need to sign this form with this pen down at the bottom of this page, where we have placed that little red cross. And your profession, please."

Your name. Write your name in block letters and then give us your signature. By the little red cross. To show that someone has been notified. Of Miss Huntington's mortality experience. Your name please? And your profession?

Signing next to the little red cross. A special name for death certificates.

> It's only me
> From over the sea.
> William Barnacle,
> Sailor.

"You've drifted away." Sergeant Woodward nudges him out of the trance. "She was dead?"

"Sorry. Of course, it was suicide."

"I'm so sorry. Did they ask you to identify the body?" John's voice is sad, as if he had hoped for a happier ending. The noise of the approaching helicopter is louder now. Bint looks up in alarm, looking from face to face as the two men converse in their strange foreign language. She is a clever girl, the Adviser thinks. She knows something is wrong. And going to get wronger.

"Yes. When they showed me her body in the morgue, I ran out and fainted and fell down a flight of stairs. When I recovered, I walked to the Oxford train station and caught the early morning local to Paddington Street Station and went to the embassy. My old Ford Cortina must still be sitting in the infirmary's parking lot. I keep leaving things behind."

"They're coming for you now." John Woodward pulls himself upright and reaches for his crutches. He seems to have gone cold; did the story make him angry? "Better gulp the last of that ale. Then you can leave us behind too."

The Adviser is dismayed. "You . . . you demanded to hear what happened! You insisted on knowing the truth, and now all you can do is tell me to finish my beer? Did I do wrong? What should I have done? Who was to blame?"

The sergeant major shrugs and hobbles out of the tent.

"Mostly you, I suppose, although Ellen might have been stronger. Of course, there at the end, she must have felt completely alone. She must still have thought you'd ordered the security guards to open fire with live ammunition. She was pregnant. She had rejected a man who loved her in favor of someone who betrayed her. So I suppose it was mostly your fault."

The Adviser is so angry that he scarcely feels the pain in his shoulder when he jumps to his feet and rushes outside, still carrying Bint in his arms. He realizes that McGinty's Brown Ale has had its desired effect; he is a little drunk.

"You said you'd forgive me!"

"I do, but you need to forgive yourself and do penance." Slouched over his crutches, Woodward looks up at the American Embassy chopper. The pilot is coming in slowly, aiming for the cross at the center of the helicopter pad.

"Penance?"

"And repentence. You need to resolve not to go around betraying friends anymore. You need to care more about people than Cruise missiles. Perhaps for your penance, you should look after this little girl."

"That's hard." The Adviser's mind is whirling. He's turned against me!

"Penance doesn't work unless it's hard," Woodward decrees as the helicopter settles on the pad. It is a huge U.S. Marine Corps Chinook, big as a house. "Well, here's your ride."

Frightened at this immense machine, Bint squeals with fear, fastening her arms around the Adviser's neck and clinging so hard she exacerbates the pain in his shoulder.

As soon as the chopper is down, the pilot slides back the hatch and leans out, scrutinizing the landscape for danger. He is a black Marine Corps warrant officer with severely pressed camouflage fatigues and an enormous automatic pistol strapped to his web belt. Finding his environment acceptable, he kills his engines. A pair of crewmen lower a ladder and climb down with a stretcher.

"Where's the patient?" asks the pilot.

"It's me." The Adviser realizes that he is still wearing Dick Barnet's British officer's uniform with captain's pips on each shoulder. "I had to borrow some clothing."

"Not to worry!" The warrant officer looks at him critically.

"We'll get you to the hospital in one hundred and ninety minutes although . . . Where exactly are you wounded?"

"I have a broken nose." The Adviser feels humiliated by his lack of appropriately grievous injuries. "I got bounced around a little and knocked unconscious. The Field Surgical Team here called you guys before they realized I wasn't seriously hurt."

"Fucking Brits think we run a taxi service." The warrant officer looks suspiciously at Bint, but decides not to acknowledge her presence. "Listen, I wanna get going. They got combat going on west of here and somebody shot off a Grail this morning. The embassy told me you had classified documents."

"My briefcase is in that tent along with my duffel bag and there's me and uh, well just me and this little, uh, very small girl here."

"What do you mean about the kid?" The Marine warrant officer nods authoritatively to one of his minions, who darts into the tent to collect the Adviser's duffel bag and the black Reconnaissance Group briefcase.

"Look, we had a battle today. The sergeant major can tell you all about it." The Adviser turns to John for moral support, but Woodward shakes his head, leaving him on his own. "You see, we were trying to take out a Popular Front forward observer, and I burned this child's house down. Then we called in an air strike and destroyed the whole village."

"The whole village? Really?" The Marine gazes at the Adviser with frank admiration. "That's pretty good, sir!"

"Yes, and having successfully orphaned her, the least I can do is make sure that she reaches some kind of shelter."

"Is she a U.S. Department of Defense civilian, sir?" The pilot displays ostentatious courtesy; he wants everyone later to testify that he was patient in the presence of a patently loony civilian.

"No, she's an Omanese orphan!" The Adviser decides that he too can exhibit patience. "Since we managed to wipe out her family, I do feel some sense of responsibility."

"This is a war, sir," the pilot observes tightly. "Bad things happen in wars."

"I know, but there needs to be someone who comes along afterward to pick up the pieces. It's a question of not betraying people you care about."

"Sir, she's not a dependent, is she?" The Marine has brown, cold, incredibly steady eyes. In his mind is a list of persons authorized to fly in his helicopter: active duty U.S. military personnel, Defense Department civilians and their dependents, and officers of allied armed forces, although there is a special form that needs to be completed for them.

"A dependent!" The Adviser hears a shrillness invade his voice. "I slaughtered her entire tribe! I would have thought that makes her extremely dependent."

"The primary mission here is to get you and this classified stuff back to the Muscat. I'm sure the local folks will take care of this indigenous civilian."

"She's not an indigenous civilian. She's a little girl!"

"Listen, mister! You called for the United States Marine Corps! Remember us? We're the folks who land on unfriendly beaches and shoot bad guys! If you wanted a daycare center, you shoulda called Mother Fucking Teresa! Now give that kid to the limey and get your ass on this bird, 'cause we're leaving!"

"I'm not going!" The Adviser plays his last card. "I'm going to take care of this child. If we can't bring her with us, then I'm not going!"

"What do I tell the embassy?"

"Tell them . . ." The Adviser searches for an elegant final statement, something sharp and withering and memorably cruel that they will always remember, but he is transfixed by the angry incomprehension on the pilot's face. "Just tell them I don't want to do this anymore. Tell them I'm not coming back."

You're mad, he tells himself. They'd make you a GS-15. And give you medals. One from the British Ambassador. One from the Secretary of Defense. And if you don't go back, you'll be unemployed! What else do you know how to do?

But fury overpowers him, and he gets his wallet out of the back pocket of Dick Barnet's trousers. He is operating with one hand because he is still cradling Bint in the other, and in his clumsiness he manages to spill the contents of his wallet onto the sand, credit cards in his current name, the one he hasn't been able to remember since breakfast. And driver's licenses for states where he has never driven. Library cards for libraries where he has never browsed for books.

In the midst of the documentary flotsam of his trade, he locates his Department of Defense identification card and throws it defiantly onto the flight deck of the Chinook. Naturally, the name on the face of the ID is a L.R.R.G. special, but it is the gesture that counts.

Massively unimpressed, the pilot mutters a command and one of his acolytes dumps the Adviser's duffel bag back out of the helicopter. They retain possession of the classified documents briefcase.

The twin motors fire into life. Alone in his cockpit, air-conditioned against the heat and insulated from the dust, the pilot slips a cassette into a tape player on the dashboard of the control panel.

The engines are now roaring unbearably and no one can hear his music except the pilot himself, but it seems to be rock and roll because he is tapping out a quick beat with one finger as he studies his gauges. Then he puts an enormous cowboy hat on his head and caresses the stick.

Stirring Um al Gwarif with a potent wind, the pilot ascends like an irritable archangel into the night sky, and vanishes.

The lights around the landing pad extinguish themselves automatically when the American Embassy aircraft disappears.

Suddenly, it seems quite dark and very late. In the monastery, the Adviser thinks, it would be time for Vespers. Were I still a seminarian, that's what we would be doing just at this moment. Saying our evening prayers.

"That's twenty years of my life gone."

He feels Woodward's hand on his shoulder. "I know, but you did well. One can never look properly into another person's life, but it sounded right."

The Adviser's knees feel weak, and he sits down at the edge of the helicopter pad. Climbing down out of his arms with a languid stretch, Bint gets to her feet and points at the Um al Gwarif Hilton.

"Can I eat that chocolate?"

"Go and eat, daughter," the Adviser consents absently.

The child looks at him for a long moment, standing with her arms akimbo and her head tilted to one side. *"Shookran, Babba,"* she says, speaking only after she has thought the matter through. "Thank you, Daddy." And she darts off toward the tent.

Thanks, Daddy. The Adviser's brain is empty. What did that mean? I can't puzzle things out anymore. Twenty years. I have been an officer of the United States government for two decades. I have thrown it all away for a little Arab girl who calls me father.

Do I have an identity outside the Long Range Reconnaissance Group? Except for John, my only friends are other L.R.R.G. field officers, and they will never talk to me again because everything about them is secret. And I will no longer be part of their clandestinity.

Ali Rashidi emerges from the darkness. The Adviser guesses that the astute little sergeant has observed the whole scene from the shadows, trying intellectually to integrate everything he sees into a verse from the *Quran*. We Westerners must seem exotic creatures to them, the Adviser thinks. We appear with our lethal weapons systems and wipe out whole population groups for crass political motives.

And then weep over cute orphans.

"I find your map." Ali Rashidi produces the TechIntel thermal infrared chart of Dhofar abandoned by the Adviser in that *wa'adi* outside Bait al Muktar.

"Thanks, Ali." Back at the embassy, the TechIntel Control Officer will discover this map missing and go bananas.

"You are dropping these paper." Anxious to be of service, Ali is on his hands and knees, gathering up the paraphernalia that spilled from the Adviser's wallet.

"It's all junk, Ali," he mutters. "Throw it away . . . No, wait, there's just this." Leaning forward, he rescues a torn photograph, half a snapshot taken by Peter Reston one day at the Victoria Arms on the Cherwell River just outside Oxford.

Peter lingers unseen in the picture, the way photographers sometimes do, providing only the subtext. The original shot included the Adviser himself, sitting to Ellen's left, but when he looted the picture from her desk nine days ago, he tore himself out for security reasons.

In the background is the terrace of the Victoria Arms and Ellen is wearing a summer frock. Her shoulders are bare, and the dress is cut low in front. On the wooden table in front of her is a half-pint glass of Younger's Number Six Scots Ale. She is looking toward the jagged edge of the photograph, where the Adviser once was but is no longer, and seems to be asking a question.

He cannot remember what the question was or how he had answered. At the time he had been listening absently and looking down the front of her dress.

"Is that Ellen?" Woodward peers over his shoulder. "She was beautiful."

"Keeping her picture like this was against the rules. I should throw it away but it's all I have of her."

"There are no rules now," says Woodward. "You're free."

"I don't feel free yet."

"Amateur psychology is only slightly better than professional psychology, but I suspect you still need to settle things with Ellen. Ali and I will leave you alone for a few minutes. Talk to her one last time."

"How can I? She died nine days ago."

"You've been talking to her nonstop for nine days, haven't you? Up on the *jebel* today, I noticed you a couple of times with your lips moving and no words coming out. You were talking to her then."

Feeling embarrassed, the Adviser nods. Yes, there has been a certain demented dialogue. "What do I say?"

"Say you're sorry. Forgive her and ask her to forgive you. There's not a lot else you can say. What's crucial is that you say good-bye."

Woodward moves away, although it is hard for him. His crutches keep sticking in the sand and Ali Rashidi has to help him back toward the Um al Gwarif Hilton. John got out of a hospital bed only an hour after surgery, thinks the Adviser. He did it to help me. I must be worth something.

Feeling a little stronger, the Adviser focuses on the torn photograph. Ellen, he speaks in his mind, you would have forgiven me if there had been a little more time. There would have been a lot of anger but I would eventually have managed to say what needed to be said. Ultimately, you would have understood—and forgiven me. If you could have survived that moment . . .

But you didn't, and I must now forgive myself on your behalf. Because I have this child to care for now, and I can't be a father if I go on hating myself. I've got to like me enough to persuade her that I am worth loving.

And I forgive you for killing yourself. Life is always better than death and you were responsible for two lives when you took those pills. Three if you count mine. You must have felt all alone. But life is better than death. I sat tonight with a gun in my hand and chose life. You sat in the Cowley Road Police Station with your bottle of pills and chose death. I wish you hadn't.

I really wish you hadn't. You'd have loved this child. She is called Bint. What do you think of that as a name? Bint. She could have been ours. We deserved a daughter. I will love her as if she had been yours. Mine.

Ours.

I've got to go now, Ellen, he says, getting to his feet. Barnacle Bill has to take care of his little girl. Good-bye, Ellen.

Sleep well, sweet.

His shoulder has mostly stopped hurting and his nose now aches just a little.

And I'm not quite so depressed. Perhaps it's the McGinty's, he thinks. Peter Reston was always quoting that A. E. Housman poem. How did it go?

> Brown ale does more than diazepam.
> To justify God's ways to man.

No, that's not right. It doesn't even rhyme properly.

What's John doing? As he makes his way across the road toward the Um al Gwarif Hilton, he sees the sergeant major coming out of Napalm's tent, putting a sheaf of papers into his pocket. Woodward then unlocks the Morris Minor, puts the shift into neutral and puts the key into the ignition. The motor immediately begins to purr.

"John, listen, I need your advice." He hobbles over to join his friend. "I want to adopt Bint. I want to raise her as my daughter."

Woodward switches off the motor and nods emphatically. "As long as you understand that you need her rather more than she needs you."

"Can you help?"

"Perhaps, well, perhaps my Jenny and I could be her honorary auntie and uncle." Woodward abruptly seems awkward. "We never managed to have a nipper of our own, and . . . well, it would be my assigned function to spoil her rotten. Jenny could advise on the clothing front. Do you know anything about skirts and blouses?"

"Isn't there a chain of stores called Laura Ashley?" It takes him a moment to remember that Ellen always bought her outfits there. "I will take her to Laura Ashley and buy her one of everything."

"You should go to Mothercare first!" Woodward's mind turns immediately to practicalities as the two of them trudge back toward the Adviser's tent. "She'll need little shoes and knickers and things."

"A school! Where will she go to university?"

"Maybe we could work on a nursery school first, but when the time comes I'm told that Lady Margaret Hall at Oxford does a very nice job with young ladies. My Jenny went there."

"Lady Margaret Hall it is!" the Adviser decrees. "After all, Oxford is my alma mater." He is pleased. It seems to him that the practical difficulties are sorting themselves out quite nicely.

"What will you do for a living?"

"I hadn't thought of that. I'd need a profession where it doesn't matter if you're a little crazy."

"Teach history," Woodward suggests. "Listen, do you have a home somewhere?"

"I hadn't thought of that either. We'll need a house, won't we?"

"Look, why don't you bring her to York until you sort things out? Jenny and I have this large garden where she could play, and . . ."

"Is there room for a goat?"

"Our garden has always needed a goat." Woodward smiles. "You'd better let her pick it out because, well, I'm beginning to suspect that you're not really an agronomist from Manitoba."

"Okay." The Adviser is excited now. Back in the tent, Bint and Ali Rashidi are deep in conversation, but the moment the Adviser appears, Bint flies into his arms. There are tears on her cheeks, and she seems frightened.

Ali Rashidi is upset. "I am saying the wrong things," he apologizes in English. "I was thinking that she knew about her family."

Oh. All the dead people in Bait al Muktar. She also will need to say good-bye. This time, the Adviser resolves to say clearly what needs to be said, although he suspects that Bint must have suspected all along that her father and brothers and sisters were all now with Suleiman in Paradise.

"There was much fighting at Bait al Muktar, daughter. I do not know who is left alive there. Perhaps no one."

Maktub. What is written is written.

She looks up at him, crying noiselessly, nodding very slightly. There is a smudge of Cadbury's chocolate on her cheek. The Adviser moistens his handkerchief with his lips and tidies her. The child has delicate skin, he observes. I have to buy her a soft flannel washcloth. Maybe Jenny Woodward could make me a list of everything I need. There must be a book I can read. Something by Dr. Benjamin Spock. How to be a father. Without a wife. Six Easy Lessons. Six Hard Lessons.

"What do I do?"

"You can come and live with me. You will be my daughter, and I will take care of you."

"Will you hit me when I am bad?" Pragmatically, Bint begins to negotiate.

What will it be like, the Adviser wonders, when she's an adolescent? She will be beautiful and want to go out with boys. Young thugs with motorcycles and pimples. I'm going to hate that.

"You will never be bad. I will love you too much ever to hit you."

"I could bring you your tea. And watch your goats."

The Adviser begins to explain that he has been thinking of acquiring a few good goats, but Ali Rashidi is shaking his head.

"You cannot adopt her, sir," he voices his objection in English. "It is against the law of this country. I think you are being a very good father, but you are not a Moslem, and the government is not liking."

"Christ, I hadn't thought of that!" Woodward frowns. "Last year, a British officer and his wife tried to adopt a kid. There was a great hue and cry from Muscat, and in the end they were told it was impossible."

The Adviser feels decisive. "I'm not worried. Except for the three of us, nobody even knows she exists. I'll just take her out of the country, bypassing the customs and immigration controls. There's a lot of desert out there."

"My dear chap, how are you going to take her anywhere? The nearest coach station is in Portsmouth. There is no commercial transport in Dhofar Province!"

"I can do it!" vows the Adviser. "Look, being a father is going to be hard for me, I recognize that, but sneaking across international boundaries is something I've been doing all my life!"

"But how are you going to get out of Oman?"

"A piece of cake!" The Adviser is on his feet, pacing. Bint is looking up at him confidently. "Look, who inherits Napalm's Morris Minor?"

"His widow, I suppose. She lives in Norwich."

"Fine! Give me the address, and I'll deliver it to her door."

Dazed, John Woodward produces the packet of documents that he took from Napalm's tent. He is looking for the Reverend Geoffrey Wentworth's home address when the Adviser claims Napalm's passport.

"You're going to travel as him? My friend, you don't look much like the mad Rev," Woodward objects. "He had that huge beard . . ."

"Mind your manners when you address a man of the cloth. I have shaved off my huge beard, which is why I no longer resemble my passport photograph. And all Europeans look alike to Arabs. At least until I get out of the Middle East, I am—what's my name again?—I am the Reverend Geoffrey Wentworth. What's my rank?"

"He was a captain."

"Then I am suitably attired." The Adviser points to the silver pips on the shoulders of Dick Barnet's uniform.

"You'll never get away with it!"

"I will, you know," the Adviser says seriously. "I was a senior field officer for the Long Range Reconnaissance Group. And I was the best they ever had. Can you give me some gasoline?"

"We've got three jerrycans of petrol in the back of the Land-

Rover and a box of British Army field rations. But how the hell are you going to do it?"

"I've got ten hours of darkness!" The Adviser is studying his map. "If I leave now and shoot right up the Midway Road, I can be out of *adoo* country before sunrise. Once I reach the Empty Quarter, I'll swing East and run—let's see—it looks like about six hundred miles of desert track to Nizwa. Can you give me about thirty gallons of gasoline?"

Woodward nods. "There's enough here to get you to that Texaco station in the Buraimi Oasis. It's the last resupply point this side of Abu Dhabi."

"Got it. Then what do you reckon? Straight up the west coast of the Persian Gulf to Ras Tanura, and then West along the Tapline Road to Jordan? I'll rest up for a couple of days at the Philadelphia Hotel in Amman. Can I get through Syria on an English passport? Or do I need to bribe the border guards?"

"Twenty Syrian pounds for enlisted men, and two times twenty for the officers," Ali Rashidi explains. "Do not pay more for a transit visa."

"And if you're pretending to be English, remember to haggle," Woodward tells him. "You bloody Americans always pay full price for everything."

"John, you should be home from the hospital by the time we get to England." The Adviser leads the way, holding Bint's hand, and they file out of the Um al Gwarif Hilton. "Did you say something about Christmas in Yorkshire?"

"It'll be bloody marvelous," Woodward promises. "We'll have a Christmas tree and mulled wine and Yorkshire pud and real brown ale. If my leg is better and your shoulder is okay, we could even walk the moors. Jenny and I will find the girl some mittens."

"I want her to have those little red boots kids in England always wear," says the Adviser, but it is time to stop fantasizing and get the Morris Minor ready. The night has only so many hours and he wants to get over the top of the *jebel* before the sun rises.

Staggering under the weight, Ali Rashidi drags three ten-gallon jerrycans of petrol out of the Land-Rover and stows them in the back of the little estate car, piling in boxes and boxes of

British Army field rations so there will be enough to eat along the way. The Adviser throws his duffel bag in the back while John arranges an army blanket on the front seat to make a little nest for Bint. The Adviser checks the oil and water in the Morris, but poor Napalm's maintenance has been impeccable. The engine is humming confidently and the spare tire is inflated.

Suddenly, there is nothing left to do. The Adviser gets behind the wheel.

"Well, good-bye it is then," says Sergeant Major Woodward awkwardly. "I've put a slip of paper in Geoff's passport with our York address and phone number on it. I'll be there in a few days. Ah, and call me, lad. Whenever you get to a phone. I'll be worried."

Bint looks dubiously at the Morris Minor, but Ali Rashidi explains and helps her gently into the passenger seat. It is late, and the child is exhausted. She waves good-bye to Ali Rashidi and accepts a kiss on the cheek from her Uncle John and then puts her head on the Adviser's lap.

"Good-bye, Ali," says the Adviser. "God bless. I forget exactly how many times you saved my life today, but I appreciated it each time. And I hope . . . well, I hope you've actually won the war this time."

"In God's hands," Ali Rashidi murmurs. "The little girl will be growing up far from here and that is good. But you must tell her about us. One day, perhaps she will come home for a visit."

"One day." The Adviser shakes hands out the window with the little sergeant.

"Off you go then!" Woodward produces one of those goofy British Army salutes, palm out, forefinger to right eyebrow, thumb pointing at Adam's apple.

"Good-bye, John. Look, I'll be in Yorkshire before Christmas. You're sure Jenny won't mind?"

"You and the nipper are invited. Remember to stop for petrol at the Buraimi Oasis. And listen, it could still be ticklish up on the *jebel*. Take my Sterling and I'll say I lost it in the bean field."

"No, I have my automatic." The Adviser takes out his lady pistol.

"Are you okay?"

"I'm okay. I think I'm okay."

"You should be okay," says Woodward. "This is your last run, lad."

"Good-bye, John."

The sky is clearing, and the moon is hanging bright over the Indian Ocean. I'm happy, he thinks, putting the Morris Minor into gear and pulling away from the Um al Gwarif Hilton.

At the main gate, the Omanese guards wave him out onto to the darkened dirt road. Brandishing the lady pistol against the terrors of the night, the former Technical Intelligence Adviser from the Long Range Reconnaissance Group heads north for the *jebel,* his daughter's sleepy head upon his knee.

Maktub